THE AN[illegible]
THE APPRENTICE
VOLUME A

THE APPROACH –
BEN

HENRY MILLS

THE ANGEL AND THE APPRENTICE, VOLUME A

ISBN: 9781520760575 (e-book)

CHAPTER ONE

THE FIRST TIME BEN SAW MARCO was across the lawn at the LSE. It was the freshers' drinks, the party to welcome the new undergraduates. Ben's parents had wanted him to go to Oxford or Cambridge like most of his friends. But Ben had refused, drawn to the lure of the big city. Now, as he stood on the lush, springy grass, still green as August became September, with the sun setting and the warm autumn evening drawing in, he knew why: freedom – no conventions, the chance to reinvent himself, endless cosmopolitan possibilities.

It was 2000, the start of a new millennium, Robbie Williams' Rock DJ and Madonna's Music were in the charts while a new Kylie Minogue song was due any day. Things were looking good, even if Internet stocks were starting to fall. He would be nineteen in less than two months and had informed his parents that henceforward they would no longer be referred to as 'Mummy' and 'Daddy'.

Moreover, he was out, at least in theory. His parents were still blanking it and he hadn't really discussed it with his schoolfriends even if they knew he'd done some things. He was no virgin although his tally of six felt low. He was more confident of his looks, reasonably tall at six feet and definitely fit and strong from all his swimming. Now he was looking for his first real adventure in love, something different and exciting.

As he looked at this alluring foreign object, he saw a more perfect echo of Simon Greaves, the third and hunkiest of Ben's schooltime lovers. Simon had been nice, a Rugby player who was willing to roll over after a pint of gin. But he was also very dim, at agricultural college now as he prepared to manage a small farm arranged by his stockbroker father. A bit like Ben's older brother Tony who had scraped a 2:1 in PPE at Keeble a few months before after Ben helped him with his microeconomics and was now starting the graduate training programme at Unilever.

But this man across the lawn surely was both different and exciting. He must be smart; after all, he was at the LSE. He was the same height as Simon, five foot eight or nine, and much more muscular, incredibly strong, in fact. His skin was enticingly dusky whilst still being European, his black hair thick and lustrous, his body tight against his clothes. Ben stared over the shoulder of the girl talking to him and drank in the sight of this Latin stranger, laughing and leaning on an urn as he took swigs from his bottle of beer and listened to two other freshmen.

Then he glanced aside and noticed Ben staring. His eyes lingered and he smiled and returned to his companions. The smile made Ben rock on his feet. He felt he'd been undressed and never been happier about it. He smiled back, but too late for anyone but the girl talking to him, Daisy, here to study finance and to get as far from her parents in Yorkshire as possible, to notice. She twisted her head to see, sighed and said, "My mistake. You like them short and stocky. I prefer tall and slim."

Ben saw her disappointment and laughed out of embarrassment. He hadn't even guessed, just thought she was nice and interesting.

"I don't know what I like," he said. "That's what I'm here to find out. Do you know who he is?"
"Marco Salazar. He's from Uruguay. Very rich. He's studying international relations – should be right up your alley."
With that, she walked away. Ben turned back to Marco and just stared. Uruguay! Even the name sounded sexy, definitely the reason Ben was in London. At this angle, Ben could see how Marco's red T-shirt clung to his frame, all muscles, more muscles than he had seen on a man. Marco's biceps rippled as he lifted his arm to drink. His ripped Levi's emphasised both his crotch and tight arse. Short and stocky? No, he was of average height and far from average physique. And that smile! It kept coming, although no longer directed at Ben. Its radiance matched the glint of the slowly-setting sun in his dark eyes.
Ben crushed his half-full plastic beer glass and dropped it, walking, hurrying, then striding over to introduce himself. He didn't know what he would say, but he'd think of something. But as he finally drew near, one of Marco's companions put his arm round Marco's shoulder and all three of them walked down the gravel towards the stone gate to the street. Ben put up his hand and Marco noticed and smiled that confident assured smile, even as he continued walking.

Ben stepped onto the gravel. "I'm Ben," he said. But the sound came out hoarse and Marco was several feet in front and walking away. Marco inclined his head and then he was gone. Ben grimaced and wondered whether to try again. But it was Freshers' Night and he needed to meet people. He picked up another plastic cup of beer and circulated, thinking constantly of Marco as he tried to remember people's names and courses. He had three years; he'd find this Mr Salazar again.

But for two months, he didn't. The LSE was big and dispersed, while London was even bigger. It was a disappointment, but perhaps not a surprise. Two days after he arrived, Ben joined the Pink Club, a statement of intent. Over the next nine weeks, he slept with five men, three from the Pink Club and two from saunas, where he'd picked up his previous two scores in London. Pink Club or sauna, they all fitted a pattern: white, middle-class, English. Safe. On balance, he preferred the saunas with their clinical anonymity to the clinginess of the Pink Club, whose members had even less sexual experience than he did. Two of them were virgins, and all of them he would have to see at lectures over the next three years. And the Pink Club was just too earnest, too political as it agitated for full gay marriage, not just civil partnerships, and LGBT committees in every employer. The dykes were aggressive and intrusive and often sensationally ugly and the undergraduates he'd noticed so far and hoped might be gay, including Marco, were never there. By the start of November, he was settling into a new life, on the swimming team and starting to do well. At the coach's suggestion, he'd shaved his chest and armpits. He'd also shaved his balls. Both were big decisions, but it was the armpits that felt like the gayest thing he'd done so far. As for Marco, Ben now wondered if he was gay at all, although that linger and then the first blinding smile suggested reason for hope.

So, in the changing room of the leisure centre early one evening after a delayed session of the swimming team, he looked up as he pulled on his jacket and there, in front of him, was Marco. Just out of the shower, he had a towel round his waist, and was rolling his thick black hair in wet lines as he ran his fingers through them. Ben gazed over his body, the thick shoulders and raised upper arms, the heavy pecs and tapering chest to his solid and pronounced six-pack. Then he looked at Marco's face to find him smiling that astonishing smile.
"Hi! Ben, right? I heard your name that night. And I saw you in the pool just now from the weights machine. Nice butterfly stroke. Beautiful back, amazing shoulders."
Ben felt weak. Simon Greave had been the conquest of a very hunky but fundamentally straight man, but now Ben wanted to be conquered. This was the man he'd picked from the first moment and now here he was, presented to Ben in a towel that was steadily loosening from his waist. And the accent? A lilting lullaby, even if surprisingly high-pitched, just the right mix of Spanish and American, exotic, new, entrancing.
"Yeah. Marco, isn't it?" he said, his voice also annoyingly squeaky. "International relations?"
"Dead on. I see you've been checking."
Ben was abashed, but that smile was still there. "You're so perfectly English. Where have you been? I haven't seen you anywhere."
"At the Pink Club."

"Aah! Then, not surprising. I leave the politics to my father. I'm here to have fun, not make speeches." With that, he pulled away his towel and began to dry his back, still standing face-on to Ben. It was a blatant prick-tease, but Ben didn't mind. He liked the view he was being shown because of the muscles in his own upper back and he was happy that his still-rudimentary gaydar was indeed functioning. Ben was careful to take in what was being revealed to him, a fine creamy-dark cock, short and fat, hanging over loose balls, all in a nest of neatly-cropped dark pubic hair. When he looked up, Marco's smile was teasing. "Like what you see, Mr Subtle?"
Ben laughed in embarrassment. He was fighting back his excitement.
"Ever had a Latino before?"
Ben shook his head.
"I've been looking for a real Englishman but couldn't find one. Real Wimbledon strawberries and cream. Everyone in London seems to be a foreigner." He started to sing the Jimmy Buffett song, "Do you like pina colada?", shaking his hips so that his cock swung. The line was wrong, but Ben didn't mind. He'd like to get caught in the rain with this man and make love at midnight on the dunes of the cape. And surely they both had half a brain. He laughed.
"Hey, nice smile, man. And dig the blue eyes and that mousey English hair." He leant in and ruffled it and Ben gave in to his body's urge. "And the fresh skin, never sun-burnt." He ran his finger down Ben's cheek. Ben was getting harder by the second and put his hand forward to touch one of those taut chocolate nipples in those rock-hard pecs.

"Whoa!" said Marco, stepping back, although still smiling. "You want some Hershey's kisses, you gonna have to pay me. Take me to a real English pub."
Ben stepped back and Marco turned to dress, deliberately raising his tight dimpled arse to Ben as he pulled on a yellow posing pouch and then his ripped Levi's. Ben just wanted to tear them both off, push Marco onto the bench and sink his tongue into that crack. Marco stared at Ben's erection as he pulled on a white T-shirt and then a dirty brown leather jacket. He looked like James Dean.
"Looking good, my friend," he said as he ran his hand over Ben's crotch. "Maybe it's not just your back and shoulders that'll be nice."
"Can I fuck you?" Ben asked.
"Get me drunk first," said Marco and gave a high-pitched giggle.
Ben took him to Ye Olde Cheshire Cheese in Fleet Street and drank bitter. Marco loved it, asking all about its history and the history of Fleet Street, revelling in a pub that was 350 years old and had been featured in A Tale of Two Cities. And to his equal relief, Marco did have more than half a brain.
"A pub here since 1538? That's cool. Montevideo wasn't founded until 1724."

Ben let him talk about the differences between Uruguay, Argentina and Brazil, their contrasting histories and political systems, content to take in his dreamy lilting mixed-accented English. Marco was rich and had attended private school in the US. His father was in Congress, a junior minister looking for promotion, and he had two sisters and a younger brother. Ben heard the names Buenos Aires, Montevideo and Rio de Janiero and wished he was there, marvelling that Marco could be so enthralled by rainy old London.

"Eight million people in the city alone," replied Marco. "Uruguay has less than four. But I'm disappointed; I wanted to see the fog."

"Not since the 1956 Clean Air Act banned the use of coal. Now there are even salmon in the Thames. But you could have gone to New York; there are eight million people there too."

"Yeah, New York's cool. But London's more international. And I'm Hispanic. I don't want to be in a place where I'm only half a step from being a Puerto Rican or a Dominican."

The conversation fell away. Ben hadn't been to New York any more than Rio, let alone Montevideo. But he knew how he wanted this evening to end. Marco was opposite him, slouched over a wooden bench, arms draped wide along the top, expanding his chest, tightening the T-shirt that Ben just wanted to rip off. And all the while that mesmerising smile. Marco's face was alive, his cheek as dimpled as the one down below.

"Shall we go?" he said.

They walked back together, Marco talking about some of the guys he'd met since coming to London, how few English people there seemed to be at LSE. And then they were at Ben's room. "You want to come in?"
"It's only 9.30. Take me to another pub."
So, Ben walked him to the Garrick Arms close to Leicester Square. But after a pint and a half, Marco intrigued by the concept of a half-pint, Marco said, "We're close to Leicester Square, right? Let's go to a movie. You've seen me naked, we've had a drink, now we should have a movie, maybe dinner afterwards. An etad – a date backwards."
"You've used that line before."
"No, Ben. You're a first in many ways."
And Ben, for all the eleven men, more boys than men, that he had slept with, had never been on a date. The line was new and he liked the idea of being a first, even if Marco hadn't been a virgin for a long time. But that was good too. Two virgins at school and two at the LSE was more than enough.
In Leicester Square, Marco stopped and clapped his hands. "Oh! Oh! Let's see this one! Ewan McGregor! He's so sexy, so English!"
Ben didn't explain that Ewan McGregor was Scottish, but it was clear Marco was warming to the idea of getting Ben out of his clothes. It was Eye of the Beholder, which Ben was quite keen to see as well. He bought two seats in the front of the circle.
"Circle? In a cinema?"

As the lights went down, Marco took his hand. That made Ben hard again and they shared glances until Marco slid his hand onto Ben's thigh. Ben reciprocated. He was now enjoying the film, but it was clear Marco was getting restless. About half-way through, Marco leant over and ran the tip of his nose from the edge of his eye to the side of his mouth and then to bottom of his ear. At the same time, he slid his hand into Ben's crotch and began slowly running his palm up and down the ridge of Ben's erection.
"You look like perfection," he whispered. "A true English rose. Dinner can wait. Now it's my turn to see you naked."
It was only a fifteen-minute walk back to Ben's room, but they still took a taxi. As Ben slammed the door of his room, Marco said, "Strip."
Ben did; he wanted Marco to see and was rewarded by the best smile yet. And then, the first part of Ben's anatomy that touched Marco's lips was his glans. On his knees and still fully clothed, Marco blew him with force, eagerness and experience. He'd swallowed too as Ben fell to his own knees with a groaning, "Oh, God!"
Marco smiled a grin of victory as he stood and stripped in turn. The creamy-dark cock was still fat but now far from short. "Your turn, rosy-cheeks, and then we really begin."
Ben had most of the force, all of the eagerness but less of the experience and Marco drew him further in for the explosion. Ben swallowed for the first time, he could hardly not, and found it was all right, better than all right. Marco laughed, a high-pitched twitter of excitement and glee, as he crouched on Ben's narrow pine bed and offered that tight dimpled arse, his head turned in anticipation.

But for all he'd never swallowed come, Ben had fucked all of the previous eleven men, boys, except the first. Ultimately, it was what he liked doing most in a bed and Marco, even though that tight incredibly powerful body could have hurled Ben through a wall, was submitting without even a question.
And Marco had some moves there too, he'd worked out the muscles inside his body as well as those closer to the surface. It was the most shattering orgasm of Ben's life. Ben flopped onto Marco's hard, arched back as Marco finished himself off underneath. But Marco seemed pleased and nuzzled him and then turned round so Ben could hold him.
"Yes, perfection," he said as they both fell asleep.
And for the first time, there was someone next to him in his bed when Ben woke at ten the next morning. Definitely not at school, definitely not in the saunas, and frankly not at the LSE where the clinginess made him flee at the end of each session, even if one was slightly before six. Marco came into Ben's small bathroom to watch him piss and Ben did the same in turn. It was odd, but London was about growing up, including losing silly inhibitions, and Marco was proving perfect for that. Marco pulled him into the shower, they washed each other, pulled each other, and then washed each other again. Marco dressed and, with a pat to Ben's still naked chest, said, "My place, tonight."
He gave Ben a card and another sensational smile and then was gone. It was only an hour later as Ben finished his Special K that Ben realised he'd fucked the man before he'd kissed him on the lips.

That was corrected over the next six and a half weeks, although it was obvious Marco preferred it when their lips were elsewhere. They saw each other every night and Marco altered his gym schedule to watch Ben in the pool from the weights room window although he always worked out for another hour afterwards and only watching Marco soap himself down afterwards could really compensate Ben for the lost time.
During the day, they explored London. They went to the Tower of London, which Marco loved, the mix of the old of the fortress next to the new of the City's towering buildings, the violence of the executions complemented by the violence of HMS Belfast moored opposite it, the grandeur of the Crown Jewels. They went to Moorgate to see the ruin of the brick-laced Roman city wall at London Wall. They went to see the Changing of the Guard at Buckingham Palace and Ben recited the AA Milne poem, something that earned a kiss as well as that smile he lived for. It was time for tea and they went to The Savoy and Marco loved that too. They went to the hidden intimacy of Shepherd Market and had dinner.
"Let's come here every month," said Marco.
Yes. Ben knew now, if there had ever been any doubt. He was in love, in love with chocolate eyes and a blinding smile, in love with darker but still European skin, skin that exemplified its wearer's encyclopaedic knowledge of Latin American politics and history, for all Marco said he had no interest in politics, and the softly-lilting Spanish-American accent that expounded it. He was not even put off by the twittering laugh or the camp swagger, two things that explained the nightly parting of those dimpled cheeks for Ben's delectation.

A week before Christmas, his mother called. "You've been silent. Enjoying yourself in the big city? Are we to expect you for Christmas?"
He asked for a couple of days and called his brother Tony, three years older.
"I want you to meet someone. His name's Marco. I need to know if I can bring him to Dorset."
Tony said nothing on the phone, but let rip at the Lamb & Flag in Covent Garden, both drinking London Pride. "You've known him six weeks. You've just turned nineteen. Yes, he's been the first one who was still there in the morning, but you're just a boy Ben. Sure, do him as long as you like, but spare the parents your puppy love. I know who you are, but they are still processing your bombshell about that Tommy person four years ago. I'll defer final judgement until I've met him, but now you have to wait."
"You're not much older and you're taking Estelle to Dorset for the second year running!"
"Yes, I have. But I'd been seeing Estelle for nearly two years before that and only now am I forcing the parents to acknowledge it. And we've always been in separate bedrooms, or so they think. Wait until you're twenty-one as well."
Marco joined them when he'd finished at the gym, and came over with that smile and those swaggering hips, again in ripped jeans, brown leather jacket, another tight T-shirt. He nuzzled Ben who sought a kiss but didn't get one, perhaps out of deference to Tony, and said twittering, perhaps he was nervous, "Hi Tony; I'm Marco. But what's that? Beer? I'll get you something better," and disappeared back to the bar.
Ben looked at Tony but his brother's teeth were gritted. "What's wrong?"

"He's a faggot, Ben. And a hustler."
"I'm a faggot, Tony. And he's not a hustler; he's clever, rich and going to be very successful. And I'm in love with him."
But Tony's hostility didn't let up as Marco handed round three Pina Coladas. They managed a stilted conversation about the LSE, Marco was getting disappointed by it, only Ben really bringing to life the dreams he'd had about England.
"No fucking way," said Tony as Marco went to the bar to get another round of cocktails. "Even Uncle Henry wouldn't get this guy."
Uncle Henry was their flamboyant, sexually-ambiguous maternal uncle, for all he was married with three children. Ben's heart sank, but he'd invited Tony to meet Marco for a reason, and now he had the reply he'd sought. But not even Uncle Henry? That was harsh. The man was more of a faggot than even Ben.
"Give him a break, Tony. He knows more about South American politics than…Simon Bolivar!"
"Twenty-one," said Tony. "If you're still together when you're twenty-one, then I'll help you introduce him to the parents. Until then, keep him away from them and, frankly, from me too."
"What are you two nattering about?" asked Marco as he returned with the drinks. 'Nattering' was a new word Ben had taught him.
"What should happen at Christmas," said Tony.
"Let's go to Spain," said Marco. "For all there's no fog, I hate the weather. Let's go to the sun, lie on the beach, drink sangria and fuck in the swimming pool at midnight."

Ben saw Tony grimace, but was surprised when he turned brightly and said, "Spain sounds brilliant. You kids go and enjoy yourselves."
They did. Marco hired a small villa on Ibiza with a swimming pool at its centre, white painted walls, burnt terracotta roofs, blue painted windows and the largest double bed Ben had ever seen. Marco insisted they go clubbing every night, house and techno with Marco in a tank-top, hands in the air and dousing himself with water as he laughed and flicked his hair, giggling when groped. And they did fuck in the swimming pool, or on its edge, at two in the morning under a moonlit sky studded with stars, but also in front of all those other windows many of whose lights were on, more as Marco shouted in Spanish as he approached orgasm.
Ben told himself he was just repressed. Marco was the most liberating person he'd ever met, his joie de vivre finally released in the sweat-filled intoxication of the clubs. He was both sorry and relieved by the cold shower of clammy grey London. It was his chance to catch up on the other half of his reading list from the previous term.
"Forget it," said Marco. "You're nailing it, my English rose – a hot Latin in your bed and a gold and two silvers from your swimming."
That was true; the gold hung from a nail on his wall.

The next six months were different from the previous two. Marco had all the same force, eagerness and experience in the privacy of their rooms, but he also wanted to go out more. Ben took him to Windsor Castle, and then to Stonehenge, Bath, Blenheim Palace and Oxford. As summer approached, he took him punting on the Cam. Marco loved all these places, and showed it in his submission, calling him 'perfection' each time, but he really came alive in early March when Ben took him to Brighton to see the Royal Pavilion and they raved all night. Ben was groped, took poppers and dropped acid for the first time and both of them thought it was perfection.
"Are you two mates, mate, or just mates?" said a taxi driver as he drove a finally satisfied and dressed-up Marco to their memorial dinner in Shepherd Market in April for the first time since November.
"Mates," said Ben.
But Marco was intrigued. For the rest of the journey, the taxi driver happily explained the dual meaning of the word. At the end, Marco smiled and nuzzled Ben. "You're my mate," he said.
It became their word, their bond to each other and the city they had met in and where they had fallen in love. In that third term, Ben's grades, already down from straight As to A-s sank into the high Bs, but he didn't mind. Marco's were far lower, but still a solid 2B, and he never did any work. They raved at least twice a week and Ben reminded himself he was nineteen and in London.

As their first year came to an end in June, Marco said, "Gay Pride on Saturday. March with me, tall and proud. You've got it; now flaunt it. I'm off to urine-guay two days later and I want something to remember while I'm away. I've found us our costumes."
He yanked open a cupboard and pulled out two pairs of skimpy Speedos. One was emblazoned with the Union Jack, the other with the flag of Uruguay. In spite of himself, Ben laughed and Marco bent down and pulled out two whips and cowboy boots.
"Couldn't you find a bigger cliché?" Ben asked.
Marco just gave his high-pitched twitter and clapped his hands. "I'm gay, you're gay – now everyone will know!"

The day of the march was bright and clear. Marco had at least booked a taxi to take them to the start of the march, but the taxi driver kept staring at them through the rear-view mirror. For all that he regularly wore nothing more than swimming trunks, Ben felt very naked. He glanced at Marco, but Marco was slouched comfortably in his seat, his crotch prominently visible. Ben caught the taxi driver's eye, looked away and sighed. For all the exhilaration, keeping up with Marco was tiring. He eased slowly into the throng, many of the others dressed in as little as they were, sometimes less, just the posing pouches that Ben now loved ripping off Marco, thongs and sandals. The music blared, the marchers and crowd cheered, shouted and danced, waved flags, shouted slogans. The sun blazed down, the dykes no longer seemed ugly, drinks were handed round as marchers darted in and out of pubs along the way. A group of Japanese tourists took photos of him and Marco next to the statue of Eros in Piccadilly Circus. Ben felt naked again and wished for a well that he could dive into, that would swallow him up and where he could be at home. But Marco turned to the tourists and lashed his whip, making them jump back even as they laughed.

But for Ben being part of the swaying, shouting, singing, pulsating mass of the march was unlike anything he had experienced before. Instead of a hundred gay men at a Brighton rave, now there were thousands, maybe tens of thousands, all happy, hugging, kissing, laughing, even fondling one another. Music blared from the floats, Britney Spears, Jennifer Lopez and Destiny's Child. When *Bootylicious* came on and the six men on the nearest float bent over and waved their thong—encircled backsides, Ben frowned even as Marco let out a manic laugh. It was almost hypnotic, but also unnatural. Increasingly, he felt like a performing monkey to the gawking crowds. He told himself it was no different to the Notting Hill Carnival, good natured, innocent, fun, but then he saw the TV cameras and began to worry that he might appear on the nine o'clock news. The relationship was approaching nine months old, but was he ready to give birth to it in the court of public opinion, outside the rarefied cloisters of the LSE and the anonymity of big city life?

Marco was lapping it up, cracking his whip, kissing the other marchers, groping and being groped. Ben knew it was just fun, but he didn't like it. When Marco kissed the fifth man, Ben couldn't take it any longer. He pulled them apart. "Push off. He's mine."

The stranger, dressed in gold spandex, gave a cat whine and flounced off. Ben looked at Marco, at that smile. "Are you jealous, my best and only mate, my perfect English rose?"

Ben tried to be angry, but he just said, "Yes. And I'm going to rumba your arse tonight."

Marco pulled him in and nuzzled him, tickled his hard nipple. They had arrived in Trafalgar Square and the speeches had started.
"Do you want to listen?" asked Marco.
The sky had clouded over and Ben shivered, although that might have been Marco's finger running down his chest. He shook his head.
"How about we go to the pub?"
"Okay."
But when they pushed open the door, there were catcalls and whistles. Marco grinned and made to walk to the bar, but Ben put his hand firmly on Marco's arm. They caught a taxi and sat together in silence, not touching. Ben felt relieved as he closed the door of their room.
"Rumba me," said Marco, stripping off his boots and Speedos.
And it was almost like those first few weeks.
Afterwards, Marco lifted his face from Ben's chest and said, "I don't like the stubble. Let it grow out. When you fuck me next term I wanted it to be by a real man, hairy and capable".
So, smooth-skinned Marco went back to Montevideo, to help his smooth-tongued father successfully become a senior minister after elections there. Marco might say he wasn't into politics, but he looked the part of an eager son in the online videos, and he knew how to lick arse to get what he wanted.

CHAPTER TWO

Ben caught up with his reading over the next few months, even as he waited for Marco to come back. Marco hardly ever called and Ben had to keep restraining his desire to call or email himself, but it was all worthwhile when Marco emailed that he wanted to share a flat with his mate. Ben put down his reading list and made a list of possible flat instead. Marco chose one in Clerkenwell that Ben also liked, even if much more expensive than Ben had in mind.

"Hey, mate. You want me in the mood for love or not?" said Marco, punching Ben quite hard on the upper arm. "And if you're feeling poor, I'll cover two thirds of the rent."

Ben did want Marco in the mood for love, it had been a long summer. Marco soon filled the flat with his stuff, a poster of Enrique Iglesias, a two-seater white leather sofa from the Conran Shop, the biggest stereo and TV Ben had ever seen.

"Hit me, then we'll hit the town," Marco said.

They hit the town a lot more than Ben hit Marco, but Ben was happy to be living with someone. They went raving three nights a week all term, yet more groping of Marco, who had started to grope back, prick-teasing Ben, turned on by his frustration. He did consent to go back to the restaurant in Shepherd Market for their first anniversary, although not for Ben's birthday.

"You rave with me; I rave for you."

They got back at seven the next morning and the sex was sensational, Marco pulling him into him, throwing back his arms and squealing, then demanding Ben do it again. Marco still took poppers, but had stopped the acid, and he reluctantly agreed that Ben's swimming was more important than a complete loss of control between the sheets.
"Gotta protect those swimmers," he chuckled, tapping Ben's balls too hard and then got down and blew him.
Ben's grades were falling again, but they'd started the term as straight As after his summer of reading and were still borderline A-. And his swimming was still going well, something Marco encouraged as he worked out watching Ben and the movement of the muscles in his back. Ben won several more medals, including three golds, and they hung on the wall on nails, an island amid the flotsam of Marco's clutter. Graeme, his coach, wanted Ben to start shaving his body again, but Ben's resisted.
"I'm doing well enough," he said.
"You could be better. You're letting yourself down."
Ben knew it was true, but Marco made the pressure all worthwhile one night in early December. "Really digging the chest," he said. "Those hairs on that physique, loving it. Visible, but not too much, nice and springy. Perfection. Just like my first time."
Ben rolled on his side in bed and cupped his hands in front of him. "Tell me."

"I was fourteen, turning fifteen, aware of my body and the stares I got and starting to work out. It was on a beach outside Montevideo. I stared myself by then and had been checking out this one guy all afternoon as he surfed. Then he saw me looking, came up and stood over me. That was when I saw what a guy looks like in his trunks, me underneath, him so large and looming. I got hard and he saw and stripped off which just made me totally hard. He yanked away my trunks, blew me and then fucked me bare-back, using my come for lube. We were behind some rocks, my parents lying on the sand just the other side, and he put his hand over my mouth to stop me shouting. I totally loved it, licking the come on his palm as he did me. When he'd shot his load all over me, he watched me jerk myself off and then left. I don't know how old he was, probably about twenty. He never said a word, but that was when I knew I liked a fit young guy to fuck me. Just like you do, my twenty-year-old mate."
Ben smiled and accepted the kiss. "I was fifteen," he replied. "It happened at one in the morning in some cloisters at school. But it was far more than just an afternoon of horniness that got me out of my clothes. I'd been fantasising about the guy for months."
Marco leapt onto his knees and clapped his hands. The bed bounced. "Ooh, tell me, tell me! Cloisters at a school? Who was he, the school prefect? The headmaster?"
Ben chuckled. "Yes, a prefect. His name was Tommy Rutledge." He explained how old his school was and its religious origins.
"Is it like Eton?"
"Yes. Not Eton, but like it."

"Show me," said Marco, straddling Ben. "I want to see it. Take me there." He bounced Ben beneath his thick thighs until Ben felt seasick.
A couple of weeks later, they took the train and checked into a hotel in the small town that nestled intimately, if not always comfortably, with the school. The next morning, Ben walked Marco through the school grounds, showing him the red brick classroom blocks set around a courtyard, the old stone library converted from a granary, the medieval chapel, the lush green cricket fields, the modern sports centre with its swimming pool, squash and fives courts, his non-descript nineteenth century boarding house with its byzantine staircases. It was the first time he'd been back since he'd left and he found himself walking down backstairs, as he had as a pupil, something that made Marco laugh. It had only been two years since he'd left, too soon to feel nostalgic, but he felt a familiarity, a warmness towards the place, that surprised him.
"Show me where it happened," said Marco, pulling Ben by the hand.
It was the school holidays, but Ben didn't want to be spotted by someone he knew, an old teacher, perhaps his house master, didn't want to explain Marco; this wasn't London. Marco had teased him about Tommy as they sat at the graffiti-chiselled wooden desks of his old Latin classroom, where his teacher had swayed as he slurred and tried to hold on to his tin mess cup of 'coffee'.
"Is this where you turned, stole a surreptitious glace of his handsome form, sitting so studiously behind you?" Ben had laughed at that. Tommy had been three years older so they hadn't shared any classes together.

But the thought, the memory, of Tommy Rutledge loomed large as they walked to the cloisters, Ben striding ahead, to the old chantry chapel sitting at the centre, surrounded by neatly mown grass with the listing stone walls and their marble plaques around it. He smiled. Yes, this was where it had happened, a late night, cold warm and lovely. He pointed at the spot with his foot.

"So, this Tommy? Was he big?" asked Marco. He was leering but Ben found it endearing. He hadn't shared Tommy with anyone for a long time.

"No bigger than average, I know now, but he felt wonderful."

Marco chucked.

"Flowers and chocolates?"

"Hardly. But so desirable. I can't even remember when I started obsessing. I would ogle him – check him out – but it must have been a year before anything happened; I was just content to dream. He was so hot, seventeen but a real man: broad shoulders, flat stomach. I would gaze at him as he read the lesson in chapel at night and as we sat in hall for dinner, hoping he'd look my way, acknowledge me. He always seemed so poised. He stood so straight, his shoulders back, laughing, and I imagined myself sitting on his knees laughing with him as we held each other. He would go for runs in the morning before breakfast and shower downstairs, so I started to go down to the toilets there, so I could walk by and see him washing. I got so obsessed. I was too scared to talk to him. If he came near, I'd just walk away, even though I wanted to do the opposite, would have loved him to talk to me. One summer evening, he found me on a bench y the cricket field, but I didn't know what to say and nor did he. It seems so silly now, but I kept a journal of it all, everything he did and every time he looked at me."

"So how did you ever get it together, consummate this passion of yours?"

Ben sighed. For all the romance of the imaginings, the longing, it had not been the dreamed-for romantic seduction, at least not at first. Tommy wold soon turn eighteen, it was his last year at school, striker for the school football team. One Saturday night in late March, he came back drunk from an away game and woke Ben up, lying down beside him on the bed, stinking of Bailey's, shaking him and slurring, "Come downstairs and let me bugger you."

For a moment, Ben had hesitated. But then Tommy put his arm under the thin sheet and tore the blankets away. As Ben turned round, Tommy pulled him up by his crossed arms, found his hand and led him down the winding stairs to the gardens. It was after midnight and Ben felt the chill air around his waist under his flapping pyjama top as Tommy unlocked the door of the house, but Ben was warm, hot even, feeling himself become aroused and sweating in his anticipation. Tommy said nothing as he guided Ben into the cloisters, onto the grass damp beneath Ben's bare feet, and pulled off his shoes and socks and ripped his T-shirt over his head. Ben was mesmerised, he knew what was coming but couldn't believe it. He just stared at Tommy's naked torso, not hard but defined.

"Strip," Tommy said as he yanked down his jeans.

Ben pulled off his pyjamas. He was already hard, but any embarrassment about showing it openly disappeared in the relieved thrill he felt at seeing Tommy's own emerge from his underpants. For a moment, they both faced one another. Then Tommy pushed Ben to the ground, lay down beside him in sixty-nine and seized Ben's cock with far more confidence than Ben had expected as Ben struggled to copy him. The fumes of the Bailey's down below were as bad as from Tommy's mouth, but Ben didn't mind; it smelt sweet and warm and he quickly came as Tommy, sweet and warm, did too. Ben loved the feel of the cock in his mouth, its pliability, the reality of ejaculation. Tommy sat up, spat onto the grass and Ben copied.

"And that was it?"

"No. He had a hipflask of Bailey's in the pocket of his jeans. He pulled it out, took two swigs, gave one to me, Frenched me until I was hard again which was pretty soon afterwards, rolled me onto my back, pushed up my legs and fingered me as he played with me."
"He'd done it before!"
"He had, as I discovered the second time, when we actually talked a little. That time, he told me he'd been fourteen and underneath and the other guy had been eighteen. He said he'd looked up how to do it after the incident at the cricket field because he didn't want me to go through what he'd gone through. But believe me, when he thought I was ready, he was just focused on what he wanted. Luckily, I was ready and, while it was pretty weird, it could have been a lot worse."
"Did you get off?"
"I did."
"He was good and you were lucky. He must have liked you, even if he was drunk. Was he gay?"

"No; not really. He told me the second time that all the prefects knew I had a crush on him; it was a dare. But he liked me enough to do it a second time, as I said, and warned me to stop making a fool of myself, following me around like a mooncalf. In fact, it was three times altogether, although he'd been drinking each time. I didn't mind; I wanted it. I wanted the sex, I wanted the attention and I wanted him. He brought lube the second time and kissed me the third and held me a little after both. It was the last time that he told me it was obviously not a phase with me. I knew that, but I also needed to be told. He gave me good advice, to wait at least another year before doing anything again, to pick someone older than fifteen and to be discreet. He kissed me once and then stood up, said he hoped he'd helped and not hurt me, wished me luck and left for university to study Classics. I never saw him again, although I hear he's got a girlfriend now. But it's that first time I'll always remember, the feel of him entering me. the look on his face as he did it, the concentration, the excitement, the straining of his young muscles, the weight on me and pressure in me, the noises he made and his exhilaration when he came. He let me beat myself off and watched and I came before he did."

"And no latent straightness since?"

Ben shook his head.

"None at all. Tommy was spot on. Not then, not since."

"Did you love him?"

"Of course I did. But I knew he was straight, or would be once he left school behind him, and to get him three times and to have him kiss me and give me advice like I was a senior boy was more than enough. But that summer, during the holidays, with Tommy gone but still large in my mind, I steeled myself and came out to my parents."
"And?"
"Have you told your parents you're gay?"
"Hey! Uruguay may be a conservative, Catholic little backwater, but we have gays and Rio's just round the corner. They asked me, if you'd really like to know. My father sat me down on the sofa when I was sixteen and asked me point-blank: are you a homosexual? I wondered if he'd heard about me and Brynn from high school, but apparently not. He just said he'd guessed and wanted to know in case any journalist asked."
"That must have been difficult."
"You bet it was. No kid likes to talk about sex with his dad, especially if the result is an order not to discuss it ever again or ever do anything to embarrass him. What did yours say?"
"They blanked it even as the words came out of my mouth. I looked at my brother Tony for support, but he just shrugged so I carried on. I got angry and then even angrier until I was shouting. I told them I'd done it with Tommy three times, three times! I held up my hands, two fingers in one, one in the other. My mother slapped me and stormed out of the kitchen, shouting that she would sue the school, I was all their fault. My father just looked away and told the grey stone wall not to do to others what Tommy had done to me."
Marco laughed and kissed Ben.

"He probably did it himself when he was that age. That's how I consoled myself as my dad read me the homily. Catholics are the worst hypocrites and Catholic politicians the worst of those. You really should come with me to my sister's wedding."

But Ben knew he couldn't. Marco had asked him to go before and Ben wanted to, but what Marco periodically chose to forget was that his sister had already said she didn't want Marco there with his boyfriend, hogging the limelight on her special day, Nor did his father, who said he didn't need the media distraction so early in his new position. To make the unholy trinity, Ben's father had threatened to cut off his allowance if he missed a second Christmas in a row.

"Don't you know how hurt your mother was?" he rasped down the line when Ben called him. "You just going off partying with your smart London friends, all grown up in the big city like we don't matter anymore. You're a big disappointment to us sometimes, Ben."

Tony was more consoling. "It's only another ten months until you turn twenty-one. Frankly, congratulations on making it this far, I didn't think you two would make it to Christmas." But he once more declined the opportunity to see Marco again.

"You I can't come to your sister's wedding," Ben said. "And you know why."

Marco pouted. 'Don't drink, don't smoke, what do you do? And who did you do when it was your turn to be on top on this pristine English lawn?"

Ben grinned. "I took Tommy's advice and waited until I turned seventeen. Then I took his advice again and chose Jeremy de Gurney on the night of his sixteenth birthday and every week thereafter for several months until someone in his year found out, told everyone else and they teased him. He walked off and wouldn't speak to me again. Then, in our final year, there was Simon Greaves twice."

"And who was on top?" asked Marco, running his arms over Ben's shoulders.

"Me. Jeremy was very camp, the first genuinely gay person I slept with or even knew, much gayer than me. He let me have my way, wanted to be told what to do. He couldn't really handle it and the term after the bullying started, he dropped out and ran away to Brighton and became a bartender at a gay bar. I heard he's very happy now. But with him, I learned what I liked and just worked on Simon until he succumbed, the alcohol helped as well. He was easily the best-looking of the three of them, a big guy, a rugby player, muscled like you."

"I bet he liked your muscles as well," said Marco, running his fingers down Ben's front and then up the inside of the cashmere sweater he was wearing next to his skin. "Did you have that nice strong swimmer's body then as well?"

"Yes, and I was a big lad, even at fifteen. By then, I'd been swimming for a year and a half already and the exercise was good training for my muscles as I matured."

"And that nice hairy chest of yours?" asked Marco, extending his fingers up the light curls extending his crotch past his belly-button, up his chest and across his pecs.

Ben laughed.
"No, that came later, although Simon liked it too, said it made him feel like he was just messing around with another straight guy. I only started shaving it after he turned me down when I tried for a third go."
"Wanna fuck a gay guy?" chuckled Marco. "Right here, right now?"
They were in the cloisters of a school, under a weak winter sun at three o'clock in the afternoon. Ben shook his head.
"Coward!" Marco taunted as he leaned forward and pulled the sweater over Ben's unsuspecting head. He tossed it aside and tore off his own jacket and T-shirt. For a moment, Ben thought Marco was going to insist, but his face must have given away his alarm and distaste because Marco screwed up his own, surprised and disappointment. "Race you back to the hotel," he said. "And if I beat you, then I'm going to plough that virgin arse of yours for the first time since Tommy."
But Marco was no match for Ben. He might work out in the gym two hours a day and have a rock-hard body to show for it, but for him, it was all the weights. He did no cardio and Ben had to stop three times so he could catch up. Back in their room, Marco bent double to catch his breath, panting. Ben saw that hard, broad back and pushed Marco forward to plough his own far-from-virgin arse. But today, he thought of Tommy, Jeremy and Simon as he did so, for the first time in years.

And then in January, after Ben had spent another lonely month trying to catch up with a lengthening list of unread books, they had their first real fight. Marco wanted to rave for the third night in a row, the night after he'd stripped another clubber of his T-shirt in the middle of the club and then sprayed his chest with beer, laughing manically until the other guy stripped off to his thong and tipped beer over himself, looking between Marco and Ben as he did so. Marco nudged him. "Threesome, why not?" Ben shook his head and left.

He shook his head again the next night as well. He had an essay due in the morning and it was nowhere near finished. "Come; it'll be fun." Ben refused. "You're such a loser," Marco jeered. "More boring than the Channel Tunnel." Ben gritted his teeth. "If you don't come with me, I'll find someone else who will. And I mean…" Ben knew what he meant. Marco left and Ben cried all night. The essay was terrible; he scraped a flat B?+, the lowest grade he could remember. Marco didn't come back until nearly ten in the morning and declined to discuss the evening.

But they patched it up. A few days later, Marco said the other guys had just been nettles compared to his perfect English rose. "You know you're the one I really love, don't you?"

Ben believed him. He couldn't be angry with those chocolate eyes melting in remorse and a desire to be held. He tried harder. Over the next two terms, they saw Constable Country, Bronte Country, Ilkley Moor and Whitby where Dracula landed. They saw HMS Victory and the Mary Rose, the white cliffs at Dover and the white horse at Uffington. Ben even allowed them to stray dangerously close to his parents' house for the Giant at Cerne Abbas.
These all worked, affection and excitement lavished on him, especially at the sight of the naked man with an erection even if Ben's own would not materialise in Dorset. They also compromised on the raves. Ben only had to go out twice a week, once until at least two and once until at least one. He used his free nights to arrest the decline in his grades, although they still gradually slipped, never as low as a B?+ but still not good. Even in the pool, he started to get a lot more bronzes.
And the sex was slipping to just two or three times a week as well, only really working after one of their trips, but Ben was running out of ideas for places to go. And when he needed Marco to do something, he wouldn't. Ben's schoolfriend Tom lost his parents in a car crash that Easter. Marco declined to go to the funeral. "I don't know him," he said. "I don't know any of your schoolfriends. I'll go to Amsterdam for a few days and see you then."

It was true – he didn't know Ben's friends, and didn't have many of his own. Indeed, they seldom saw other people at all, just going to a few socials at the Pink Club and the occasional birthday party of some of Ben's straight friends. But Marco always got restless after an hour or so and Ben could hardly blame him; they weren't raves, just talking about assignments and drinking bad wine to the sound of bad music. And people talked to Ben much more than they did to Marco and that just seemed wrong, so Ben began to shun them as well. The only person Ben saw regularly was Daisy, the girl from the first night, when they took a coffee break in the library together most afternoons. So Ben went to the funeral alone and spent four days in Somerset with Tom and his other friends. Marco spent ten in Amsterdam and then Hamburg, 'to see where The Beatles started out'.

But he seemed pleased to see Ben when he got back and once more blew him without undressing him as soon as they were alone. In May, half-way through the remaining ten months until he turned twenty-one, Ben's father answered the phone for once instead of his mother and it gave Ben an idea. "Can I have my party at your club? You hardly use it and it might actually be cheaper than having everyone ship themselves all the way to Dorset."

"You'd have to dress up."

And that was an even better idea – black tie at his father's gentleman's club in Pall Mall; he could even wear his wing-collar for the first time since school. Marco would love it. It would be Ben's coming-out party, in all senses.

Marco laughed as Ben explained. "I'll be the belle of the ball!" The novelty carried them through to the end of term, when Ben's results were just-about all right, and then came a crisis: their second Gay Pride march. Marco wanted them to both wear thongs. "Will there, or won't there, be hundreds of others dressed the same way? And besides, don't you want everyone to see how perfect you are?"
But that was exactly the problem: Ben didn't. Speedos and boots were his limit, the whip technically beyond it. A thong was many steps too far. "Why do you have to keep raising the bar?" he said. "Why does it always have to be some new thrill for you?"
"Why do you have to keep lowering it? We're young; we should be seeking thrills!"
"Please. I just don't want to."
"I'll go alone if I have to."
"No!" Ben cried. A year that had finally started to work was falling apart. He bit back the tears that came with his fears on those empty nights with Marco raving. "I couldn't bear that! You'll meet someone else!"
"Maybe I will – and maybe I should," said Marco. Ben heart hollowed. Perhaps Marco saw it as he added, "At least wear the Speedos."

Ben took the concession, but he felt how fragile his world was. He had almost conceded himself, and knew he would have hated himself for it forever. But even as he leant over and kissed Marco in gratitude, he knew now what he hadn't known before the first march – this relationship had limits. He had no problem being seen on TV at a Gay Pride march or in Speedos in a swimming pool, but both together were unacceptable, even for Marco. He put on a white T-shirt over the Speedos; it was uncomfortably tight but made Marco sighed and nodded even as he said, "Oh, Jack. Jack, Jack, Jack. All work and no play is making you very dull. Maybe I'll jack off myself tonight."
But Jack the dog jumped over Ben's candlestick in the end, the adulation of the crowd as they responded to his frank gaze and blinding smile the aphrodisiac he needed and he rode Ben face-on and came messily into Ben's fist, leaning over afterwards to give Ben a deep but increasingly-rare kiss. Ben did feel like a Jack as well – good in the pool, at his books and somehow holding onto Marco, but decreasingly a master of any of those things.

And then Marco finally did some work, although exactly how much wasn't clear. He went to Barcelona for six weeks to intern at a management consultancy arranged by his father. Afterwards, he stayed with the Uruguayan ambassador at his summer retreat near Cadiz before going to Gibraltar 'to see the bobbies and the pillar boxes', Casablanca and an exiled Argentinian politician who lived in Tangier. Ben wanted to go as well, at least to Gibraltar, but he was also interning. He had a three-month position at Braithwaites, Europe's largest and most prestigious public relations firm. He had to stay: it was exactly the job at exactly the company he wanted. They usually only hired from Oxbridge and simply getting the internship was Ben's biggest success of the year so far. He didn't need his brother to tell him not to fuck it up, but Tony did anyway. Ben tried to catch up on his final year reading list in the evenings, but after working until at least eight every day, he was exhausted and just swam a little when he got home and then slept.
After his return from Spain and Africa for their final year, Marco had become distant. It rankled with Ben that, back in London, whatever work habit Marco had developed in Barcelona did not survive the start of their final year. And in Barcelona, the two times they spoke by phone, each time Ben calling Marco, Marco wanted to play at phone sex, 'I'm jacking off to Jack', he would say. 'Ooh, presentations! Ooh, client meetings!' Ben smiled, but he was in an open-plan office and had to hang up.

Only the first two days were good, three months of studious seclusion brushed aside by Latin warmth and immanent summer, but in days he said, "God, I hate the rain. Almost as cold as your spunk sometimes, Jack."
That put Ben off for days. "Did you score?" he asked after they finally tried it again two days later.
"Moroccans are meant to be hot. I heard even the king is gay."
"Now why would I go for someone dusky when I can do that at home? I prefer roses and pansies."
Ben had told Marco what 'pansy' meant and was content. But something had happened, a few shared lips, a fumble or two of hands, another man stripped of more than his outer layer at some rave or other, probably Marco too; he was always threatening to. But at least he was back. He went out a lot, told Jack to stay in and read his dusty old gardening books or whatever they were, but also told him he wanted to see more gold medals on the wall and he was always beside him when Ben woke at seven each morning. Ben had heard about married life, and this seemed like married life to him.
In early October, two weeks before Ben's twenty-first birthday, Marco returned to their flat one evening after exercising. Not for the first time in the last few weeks, he ignored Ben as he passed, even as Ben looked up for a kiss. "Is everything okay?" he asked.
"Okay?" said Marco, half turning as he walked on. "Everything's fine."

Ben was losing his nerve. A party he had waited two years for was almost here. His excitement revealed itself only as stress, awake at three or four in the morning, gazing across the bed at it either empty or full. That space was reserved for the man he had chosen, the one he would exhibit to the world. Marco's dinner jacket had arrived, hand-made at one of the most expensive tailors in Jermyn Street, but he still hadn't modelled it for Ben yet.

"Are you in tonight? We could go to a movie. We haven't done that for a while. You like movies. We could see Signs. It's still on and it's got Mel Gibson and Joaquin Phoenix in it."

Marco spun round. Ben waited for some kind of slap, but none came. "No, I'm just going to the pub for fish & chips. I haven't done that for a while either."

He headed for the bathroom and Ben heard him shave. He rarely had to do that and certainly not at this time of day. He came back to the living room in his usual James Dean look of T-shirt, dirty brown leather jacket and ripped Levis, but something was not the same and, when he left at seven, Ben followed him. He'd like some fish & chips too and he'd also like to know what was on Marco's mind.

Marco was hurrying. He usually walked so slowly, drinking in the sights and atmosphere, the hum, of the big city. Ben weaved through the crowds and, after half an hour of restless haste, he realised Marco was heading not for the Garrick Arms but for Leicester Square. He was queasy as he pushed the confused, ambling tourists aside, losing sight of Marco and then spotting him again. The sickness of fear spasmed. He bent over and leaned back against the wall of one of the many cinemas to rest.

He looked up. Marco was standing not just in front of a cinema, but in front of the one that was advertising Signs, the same one where they had watched Euan McGregor almost exactly two years before.
Ben retched, a thin stream of bile stretched and then tumbled onto the pavement. So, who was he waiting for? Marco gazed intently up the square and smiled that earth-shattering smile. Ben followed the gaze to Rio Takehashi. He was in Daisy's finance class, and possibly now in Marco. He was also smiling and hurried as he spotted Marco. Roses and pansies. But not a white pansy, a fucking yellow one – and a right one to boot. They were leaning into each other and kissing hard, deep and not for the first time.
How long had this been going on? Ben's stomach constricted with indignation, righteous anger. Marco had sucked him off just that morning? Violated, he glared at the couple, willing them to see him. He clenched his fists and marched towards them, his stride lengthening and accelerating as he approached. When he was five feet away, their mouths disengaged and they saw Ben. Marco still had his hands clasped to Rio's arse. He had enough decency to blush, although his face hardened immediately afterwards.
Rio let his arms slip from Marco's neck and stepped back, astonished but not blushing. "I…" he said.
Ben wasn't listening. "You bastard!" he shouted at Marco. "You cunt! You cheating little fucking whore! Two weeks before my birthday!"

He smashed his fist into Marco's face. For a moment, Marco didn't react, too shocked. Ben might be strong, but he was never violent. Now, Ben didn't wait. He attacked again; he was going to split some of that polished skin, maybe break that stupid nose that nuzzled him instead of the lips he craved.

The nose didn't break, but it bled. Blood dribbled over Marco's bared teeth. "Fuck off, Ben," he said. He shoved him hard, out of those powerful shoulders, all his gym-work coming through.

Ben struggled to retain his balance. "You want that up your arse," he shouted, steadying himself and coming at Marco again.

Marco squared his shoulders and put up his fists. "I said, fuck off, Ben! I don't want you anymore. We're through. Fuck off and leave us alone."

All the beauty of Marco's Spanish-American accent was there, the cadences that Ben had loved for two years; they made the words incomprehensible. There was no gorgeous smile, no dimpled cheek, just that snarled dismissal. There was not even hate; only poorly veiled contempt, as if Ben should have known long ago.

Ben's eyes clouded and a sob bubbled up from within. "But I loved you," he said. "Loved you from the start. You said you loved me too."

Marco's lip curled. "Not for a long time, mate."

Ben reeled.

"You were fun for a while, but you've got very boring. I don't need a tour guide to England anymore and I don't need your over-eager prick doing the same thing again and again. So, just fuck off and leave us alone, will you? Rio's what I need. No battered fish & chips; smooth, lean sushi instead with lots of hot spicy wasabi inside; everything I like."

He leant forward and groped Rio's crotch and the man squirmed and giggled. Ben saw it was over, but the hurt, the jealousy and the resentment overpowered him. Two weeks before his birthday. Marco had even bought his dinner-jacket. If Ben hadn't come out tonight, Marco would have worn it at the club too, even as he wore Rio at the same time.
"You two-faced two-timing little shit!" he screamed. He hurled himself against Marco, but this time Marco was ready. He raised his arm and simply smashed Ben in the face.
"Look," said a voice. "The fags are having a cat fight."
Ben ignored it. He stumbled and fell messily to the ground, banged his head against the black iron railings of the park. Tears blurred his eyes. He put his hand to his jaw, felt the pain, the blood on his tongue – he had bitten it. A crowd was forming. "You'll do the fucking off, you cheating little turd," he said, blood spitting from his mouth. "I'm changing the locks. Don't come back tonight – don't ever come back!"
Marco's eyes showed no sorrow or regret, no guilt at all. He shrugged his massive shoulders, pulled Rio into him and now gave him that beautiful smile, tainted by blood. "Come on. Let's go in. We're done here. It's spoiling our evening." He turned one last time, hawked a bloody snotball onto the pavement in front of Ben and led Rio into the cinema.
Ben watched them go and then glanced at the staring crowd. "What?" he shouted.

Most turned away and walked off. A few lingered and then turned away too. Ben was left on his own with his bruised jaw and bitten tongue. He drew his legs up in front of him, put his hands over his eyes. His body heaved. He retched until another thin string of yellow bile fell from slowly onto his trouser leg. He stared at it, it would stain, and then the convulsions began, racking great dry tears only later turning to wet. He wiped his eye with the back of his sleeve, his favourite sweater, blue, thin and worn next to the skin to show off his chest, but warm to keep away the winter. Also ruined. "Great fucking birthday present," he muttered to no one in particular.

CHAPTER THREE

Eventually, the crying had to stop. Ben crouched on the cracked concrete of the square, his back against the hard iron railings of the little park in its centre. His mind draining of thought he flicked at a few chips of concrete between his legs. A jagged edge caught the side of his finger, three drops of blood added to the bile and tear stains on the sweater, a final condemnation of it to the fire.

"Fuck!"

He looked up and noticed the cinema in front of him. It wasn't the one Marco and Rio were in, but it was one he'd been too often enough with Marco before, up in the balcony, Marco leaning in and nuzzling his cheek, whispering those magic words 'You look like perfection' as his hand slid into Ben's crotch, seeking – always successfully – to arouse him, just as he had that first night. Another thing ruined, the cinema and the memories. No one would ever be able to slide their hand into his crotch again.

And no one cared. No even glanced at him, just another bum in Leicester Square, another hard-luck story better avoided. He rocked himself, clasping his knees tight to his chest. The old iron railing rejected his back, pushed back. Fantastic, now he would have flecked paint and rust on the sweater as well. He sniffed, swallowed a great ball of goo, and ran his sleeve again across his damp, smeared eyes. Then he put his hands behind him, grabbed hold of two of the railings and hauled himself up, crab-like. On his feet, he tottered as his mind slowed its spinning. Then the thought: what if Marco was now nuzzling Rio's cheek, sliding his hand into his crotch and telling him he looked like perfection? The vortex opened again inside Ben, threatening to suck him down, consume him. He shut the thought down; anger would shut out the pain tonight.

"Bastards." And then louder, "Heartless fucking bastards!"

He meant Marco and Rio, but he also meant the hundreds passing him and taking no notice, not helping, not reaching forward to comfort someone crying out for a kind word and a gentle hand. One couple, all long Burberry mackintoshes and matching scarves, did hear. Probably tourists; who else wore Burberry? But they swerved and gave him a wider berth as they hurried away. Ben staggered after them, brushing his eyes again as he snarled before he fled, "Yeah, run cunts! Run!"

He began the slow, long trek back to his flat, their flat, alone. "Cunts! Fucking cunts!" Tonight, he walked even more slowly than Marco, jostled constantly by fast-walking impatient locals, barged by gaggles of Eurotrash teenagers, none apparently with any idea how pavements worked or what was like in a major world city. He put his head down, a wounded bull, and stared at the cigarette butts and spilt coffee beneath him as he ploughed through the crowd. A man banged his shoulder so hard he spun round. "Sorry." Then the man was gone. A Londoner at least; too polite to be a tourist.

Marco and Rio? What the fuck! And for how long? Ben searched his mind for clues, signs he had missed. And they were there, little things. Could they be real? Marco never called, he was always out, he seldom kissed, always preferred to nuzzle and whisper. And those recent pauses before Marco went down on him? Ben had thought they were a chance to savour the sight first, Marco always was a prick-tease, revelling in his power to arouse. And the pause did arouse. But perhaps Ben should have seen the hesitation, the comparison and dislike. And Rio did what in the bed, assuming they made it that far? Ben honestly couldn't tell. Marco had sometimes liked to be rewarded for his teasing with roughness in return; unlikely that Rio did that for him. Was it as simple as a different shape, the unfamiliar texture of Rio's smooth yellow body? Would he be underneath, made aroused and denied release until Marco had had his? That was the only likely scenario, although never in two years had he made any attempt to get inside Ben, never rimmed him, barely even fingered him.

Now Ben wished he had. Perhaps then, it would have been different. And 'boring' resonated, although Ben reckoned he'd tried as much as any human could expect of another. Maybe his prick had started to plough the same path, but he thought that was what Marco liked, and Ben always let Marco get off on his power to excite, to tantalise and delight, what ultimately made him so breathless to be around. Flipping the positions and the continents together made some kind of sense. But why not just flip Ben over? He would have. What else was wrong that meant only spicy wasabi was good enough when Ben would have smeared mustard on himself if that's what Marco had asked to lick out of him? He'd only had to say. But he never did, just asked to be ridden roughshod, one of those words he liked.

Ben opened his front door and saw the problem. He'd ridden Marco roughshod in that bed, on that sofa, on that rug, on that table, against that wall and that door and Marco had lapped it up. But the rest was different. Ben had chosen the area, together they had selected the unit, Ben had signed the lease, but inside this was Marco's flat. In everything about it, he had ridden roughshod over Ben and Ben had lapped it up. Their nuzzling sofa was hideous. The TV was better suited to the home cinema of a drug lord's hacienda than. He constantly walked into the stereo's speakers. The shade of the table lamp that he turned on as usual when he came in, the one with naked classical Greek runners on it, was barely half a step up from a Hawaiian hula bobble doll. He wanted to turn it all upside down, smash everything, and he did crash a Priapus paperweight onto the floor. But the dick didn't gratify him by snapping and so he just sank onto the sofa, over-priced and tasteless and sticky on the thighs in hot weather. He clasped his hands over the top of his head and stared at the sheepskin rug, which stared back. He'd never really liked that either, showy. Shag. A shag rug for shagging. Another stupid little word game.
He thought of Marco and Rio shagging. Naked, fucking, laughing, fucking laughing at him. "No! Oh God, no."
He opened his eyes. And they had been happy here once, naked, fucking, laughing, then lying on the sofa, Marco nuzzling him as they occasionally watched Merchant Ivory films on that ridiculous flatscreen plasma TV. Honestly, who needed a TV fifty inches wide?

Marco was everywhere. His stupid camel-hair overcoat with the velvet lapels, which he thought made him look more English. It was where he always left it until Ben hung it up, draped over the back of the kitchen chair. He never tidied up, too many servants back home. His dumbbells filled one corner of the room and his kettle bells another. Not only were the quadriphonic speakers in the way, Marco couldn't work them either and, truth be told, Ben detested the Latin singers that filled those stacks and stacks of CDs. He didn't even really like the one of Pomp and Circumstance on the top that he had bought after a long evening when Ben had spent half his monthly allowance on scabbed tickets to the Last Night of the Proms. True, Marco had loved that night and had showed how much when they got home, but the price for a couple of nights of affection was high. And next to the DVD player lay a stack of porn DVDs that Ben said they no longer needed, but which Marco said had sentimental value. Perhaps he got sentimental alone after coming back from the clubs when Ben was asleep. And then there were the clothes; two wardrobes and a six-foot chest of drawers full of the stuff. Storage space was one of the reasons Marco had wanted the flat. Ben had liked it because of its light, its openness and high ceilings. Once the second wardrobe came in, the light found it harder to do the same.

Bile poisoned his throat. What not just take one of those fucking kettle bells and fling it against that stereo, rip the sofa to shreds, cover the sheepskin rug in paint, burn those Greek runners, toss it all out the window. But then, what if Marco wanted to come back? What if he too wanted to undress them both and leave the clothes on the floor as they always did? Ben sighed; it came out so long, so slow. Pushing at his knees to straighten himself, he stood up. Methodically, he carted everything onto the landing. Some things he even put into boxes, but he soon stopped doing that, just left it in a heap outside the door. He rolled the dumbbells, but could barely lift most of the kettle bells and had to drag two across the floor, scraping it.
The poster of Enrique Iglesias tore in his hand; he had ripped it in half. He rested for a minute, curled in a chair at the kitchen table, his fist in his mouth to stifle his screams. It was the one impulse purchase Ben had been able to identify with: bought for 50p from a junk shop in Camden Lock.

Four of Marco's porn DVDs involved Asian actors, another clue. And then there were the photos. Of them together, Marco draped over Ben's willing shoulder. In Ibiza, in front of the Tower of London, at that restaurant Ben loved in Shepherd Market, the picture taken by the owner on their first anniversary, at Cerne Abbas, the giant's giant cock clearly visible. He took them down, but put them face-down in the top drawer of his bed-side table, along with his condoms, lube, handcuffs and blindfold, as well as the poppers Marco still used. But there would be no more need for any of those, so he scooped them up, tossed them into the bin and then, unwilling to see them in the morning, closed up the bag and took it out to the wheelie bin. Then he went back to the drawer, took the photos out of the frames and left them on the landing on top of the DVDs.

It was three-thirty in the morning. He closed the door and sank onto a kitchen chair. The denuded flat was barely functional. No TV, DVD or stereo, no sofa, no rug, just a few clothes that he didn't really like but which Marco had said looked good on him, a few books Marco had never given him the time to read, the iPod Marco had given him for his twentieth birthday, such a new invention and still loaded only with the Robbie Williams, Madonna, Kylie Minogue and The Cure that had been Ben's sole contribution to the house music collection. He'd left the bed, it was too big to move, and there were his swimming medals, ten golds altogether, more silvers, on their nails on the wall. There was the kettle and a microwave, his instant coffee and box of Special K, milk in the fridge. Marco had tea and toast with marmalade for breakfast, he said it made him feel English, but the white china teapot was on the landing now and the loose-leaf Orange Pekoe Tea, the wholemeal bread and the thick-cut marmalade were also in the wheelie bin. He sighed, lay forward on the table, closed his eyes and fell asleep.

He woke up at six with a crick in his back and slid into bed, still fully-dressed. At seven-thirty, he smelt Marco's musk and ran his hand across the sheet instinctively. In two weeks, it was his coming-out party, his chance at last to show off Marco to his parents, his friends, the world, to show how he loved and was loved in return. The two-year ban imposed by Tony that first Christmas was finally almost over and Ben was going to be so proud, proud of Marco who somehow always passed his exams, about to be truly out loud and proud himself in a way he hadn't even been at the first Gay Pride march. Tony's tune had changed completely over the last six weeks. Ben had made it; Tony had been wrong and now admitted it. After steadfastly declining to meet Marco again, his brother was now promising to act as best man at what Ben hoped would be little less than their wedding reception, all their family there, all their family's friends and children, uncles, aunts, grandparents, everyone that mattered from school, the LSE, the swim team. Marco had been so excited, black tie in a London gentlemen's club. He had promptly taken Ben to another kind of gentlemen's club that Ben hadn't known Marco knew about, the waiters also in black ties but little else as they served champagne. Marco had groped them too as he tipped them, another sign Ben had missed. Yes, as they circuited the ornate reception room of the club, arm in arm, maybe hand in hand, Ben would have shown off not just that fine body in its tailored dinner jacket, that overpowering smile, that lilting Spanish-American accent that would reveal his knowledge of Latin American politics and history and his love for London and English culture, but also the grace and easiness of a Senator's son just happy to be here, so successful that everything came easily to him, with job offers pouring in from consulting firms even as Ben struggled through his internship. Ben had snared a swan who glided effortlessly through his life, his work, finals and relationships. They were made to be together. For Ben's birthday, he would make it all about Marco, but in turn Marco would make it all about Ben, as he pulled him into a corner and nuzzled him and told him how he looked like perfection and was his mate.

His hand couldn't find Marco. The bed was empty, just the musk remained. He would have to wash the sheets. So, no fucking chance of his dream now. He hadn't just been cheated on physically; he'd been cheated of his future happiness. Why now, of all times, just before his birthday, his twenty-first birthday? All the sacrifices, keeping his lives separate, losing touch with so many friends. All for nothing? His student years, the chance to have some real fun, were almost over and all he was to have left was an empty flat of souring memories, its lease too expensive to break?

But he had cried last night, more tears would solve nothing. Gloria Gaynor came to him, very gay. The lyrics were inappropriate. He no longer knew how to love and doubted he had all his love to give. Marco had already walked out the door and not come back. No one would get in now, get through the door, see the spacious sunlit brightness of this room in a May morning and of his true heart. Broken, it was flayed and flinching now. He had been so naïve, convinced it was forever, but the naivety had been beautiful.

He pulled away the duvet. At least his core muscles were still tight as he pulled himself up. He stripped off last night's ruined clothes, clothes he had been so vain and proud to wear as Marco admired them and egged him to buy more of. He showered and shaved, dressed again, looked in the mirror. He still looked good. On any other day, he would have walked naked round the flat, showing himself off, eliciting a wolf-whistle and a playful slap, maybe a tussle on the floor, but not today. He put water in the kettle, tipped coffee into a mug and added the boiling water and milk, ate his Special K and yoghurt. He needed to go to the supermarket.
What else had he missed from the clear-out? He found the whips and the flag-speedos from the gay pride march. He shook his head; he hadn't enjoyed that, the public exposure in all senses. Like everything, he had done it for Marco. He was happy to walk naked around the flat, tussle with Marco, make love on the kitchen table, but only in private. Marco was intoxicating, reckless, yes freeing as they marched near-naked through Central London, doused both of them in water and soused Marco in E at a rave in Ibiza, made love by a Spanish swimming pool under the stars, but it was pure hedonism. Marco never worked, nothing was ever a struggle. It was part of his allure, but it was also why Ben was failing, kept from the work that needed to be done sooner or later.
He added the whips and Speedos to one of the boxes outside the front door. So much stuff, had he really moved all that the previous night? Then, without drinking any of the coffee, he picked up his own Speedos and a towel, checked he had his keys as there would be no Marco to let him in if he didn't, and walked to the swimming pool.

He managed his usual fifty lengths. The water absorbed him, temporarily stilled his beating jangling heart, but pushing himself out onto the side, he keeled over and lay on his back on the pool edge, faint, dizzy, lethargic. After the water, the air was cold and he shivered and hugged himself, the way he'd always wanted Marco to hug him, but seldom did. Another clue. He knew what low blood sugar was and this wasn't it. It was low soul energy. He wanted Marco come and wrap a large, soft towel around him, rub his arms and sides to warm him, knead his shoulders, the way he had in those first few weeks only, another clue. Ben had never managed more than a few of Marco's endless gym sessions either, it was true, but Marco hadn't even come to watch Ben at the university championships their second December, even though they were in London and Ben had won two golds. But, just like Leicester Square, no one came as he lay by the pool and panted. Again, he pulled himself up by his abdomen and ran to change. He decided the muscles would survive some minor abuse and went to a greasy spoon he had passed many times and ordered a fry-up of bacon, sausages, fried eggs, fried bread, mushrooms and baked beans. Perhaps some cholesterol might put him to sleep. He just felt violently sick.

He passed a branch of Boots and bought a beard trimmer, a bag of disposable razors and some shaving cream. As he trudged home, a gust of wind caught him and he caught a glance of black clouds promising rain. He hoped the heavens would open and soak him. But he was home before the storm began and, as he climbed the stairs to his front door, a different hope coursed through him, pulled him up two at a time. But there was no Marco. All the things had gone as well.

There was a post-it note on the front door. 'Sorry. This had been coming for a while. I didn't know how to tell you. Sorry about your party.'

Ben punched the door. "Fuck you too!" He tore away the note and hurled it aside, but it was too light and floated gently down the stairwell. He couldn't even do that right. He doubled over as his stomach convulsed, dropped his keys, stretched out an arm to keep himself from falling.

In the bathroom, he stripped to the waist in front of the mirror, first trimmed and then lathered up his chest. No teasing fingers to run, glide, laughing through the thicket of hair, twisting a clump playfully around a nail until Ben squealed. Marco, beautifully bare-chested himself, was hated even more by Graeme, Ben's swimming coach than he was by Tony. Graeme hated the hair, how it slowed him down, created drag. And as Ben scraped it all away, he scraped away some of Marco. He would arise free, clean, unblemished. His chest clean and smooth, he raised his arms and shaved his armpits as well, something half the squad did. He would heed Graeme now in all things. Men, all men, would be forgotten and discarded; he would focus on his swimming. Yes, swimming was his first love, even before mud-caked and slightly drunk Tommy had opened him up to life one late night at school. Swimming had never let him down and it would save him now, save him from drowning any other way, as its cool waters welcomed him in and applied balm to his feverish heart.

For five days, he swam twice a day, an hour at a time, morning and evening. The sixth day, he woke up dizzy and disoriented and threw up a mostly empty stomach, retching at the bitter taste and the memory of the last time he coughed up bile.

"You've got an infection, your inner ear," the doctor said. Ben had barely been able to walk to the office, but the doctor was clinically dismissive. "It's quite common at this time of year, when people are tired and alternate between warm and cold. Take some pills, rest and no swimming for a week."

No swimming for a week. Now, finally, Ben gave way to the tears in him.

Too ill to move, he lay on his bed, his head spinning, unable to keep anything down beyond vegetable soup and dry bread, and not always those. When he finally improved, it was only three days until the party. He had missed a week of classes and been deselected from the next competition. When he heard that, Graeme calling apologetic and sympathetic, he just laughed. The only benefit was that he hadn't seen either Marco or Rio, the latter according to Daisy having apparently skipped their mutual politics classes for some reason.

Daisy was the only person he saw as she brought him vegetable soup and dry bread every day, a baguette that he tore at with his teeth and then wanted to throw up. She was looking to sympathise and he was grateful for her attention. Even when Ben returned to class for the last two days of the week, Rio wasn't there. Perhaps he was tied to a bed somewhere, drowning in his own ecstatic ejaculate. Of Marco, there was no sign at all.

On Thursday, Ben asked a few people he knew as he confirmed that they would be coming to his party, hesitantly dropping the question into conversation, but they gave him odd looks and just nodded and said they were looking forward to seeing everyone and they hoped the booze would be good and he stopped asking. The next day, he walked the linoleum corridor, past noticeboards and posters, wondering if people were staring at him but not having the courage to look them in the face and find out. Daisy's hand dropped lightly but insistently on his shoulder. "I'm glad you're finally back," she said. "It's tough, but you're a survivor." Daisy did make an effort, did cross the street to help. She came to him every day, so assiduous. Pretty much the first person he'd met at the LSE, that night at the freshers' drinks, she deserved his real gratitude. On the lawn, she had seen his interest in Marco, told him his name, been the first to say that he would be 'right up his alley'. How right she had been that evening, and how so obviously wrong now. Cut off by Marco from so many others, she was one of the few real friends he had. She might have been hitting on him at the freshers' drinks, but now she was his confidante, always willing to listen, and to feed him. The relationship had been much easier after she finally found her first boyfriend; she was single again now but in that respect her sights were firmly focused elsewhere.
"I spoke to a few people yesterday," he said, "but they were so distant. Everybody knows, don't they?" He kicked at a curling edge of dirty blue linoleum peeling towards his shoe.

"Oh, don't be so glum. Yes, people know, but you're not the topic of salacious gossip. On the contrary. No one likes Marco much, he's too shallow and entitled, too loud and frivolous. Don't beat yourself up. I'm sure you'll be with someone much better before we know it."

Ben sagged and kissed her on the cheek. She leant into it.

"You'll be there tomorrow?" he asked.

"Of course, dummy. Wouldn't miss it." She looked genuinely excited. "A grand London club; it'll be a change from plastic beer glasses down the brew cellar. I want champagne and smoked salmon canapes and lots of both. And I'll scout the guests for someone suitable. You know the adage, the best way to get over a man is to get under another, or vice versa or…whatever."

Her remark faded away into embarrassment; she might be his confidante, but she wasn't usually this candid and he'd spared her the gory details. And there were gory details other than who was on top as he fought to use sex to keep the fire alive. He refocused his attention from his crowded thoughts back to Daisy, her questioning eyes, her heightened colour. He smiled, squeezed her hand and kissed her cheek again.

CHAPTER FOUR

The room Ben's parents had hired for his party was the size of a swimming pool. It was on the first floor of his father's club in Pall Mall. Ben had actually requested membership for his twenty-first birthday, knowing how excited Marco would be to wear a jacket and tie, sit and dine, sip port, gin or whisky, flick through back issues of Country Life and The Spectator in a real London gentleman's club. Then Ben would pull down bound nineteenth century anthologies of Punch and explain the cartoons to him. He had bought facsimiles of the two issues with the 'Bedside Manner' and 'Curate's Egg' cartoons for Marco's twentieth birthday and Marco had loved them, posting them straight to his father in Montevideo with a long covering letter, something he never did.

Now, Ben saw that the club membership was a stupid mistake, that he would almost certainly let the subscription lapse; even his father rarely used it. He ran his finger under his collar to free his neck. Wing collars on black tie was an affectation, something he had picked up at school when it was all the rage, but it also seemed stupid now. Why had he even specified black tie for a drinks party? Just a good idea at the time, pleasing his parents and making Marco jump for joy and clap his hands before pulling him onto the bed.

A glance around the room showed him that Daisy would not be disappointed: there was plenty of champagne and smoked salmon canapes, as well as white and red wine, sparkling water and orange juice, goats cheese on rye bread, chateaubriand on white and a dozen other snacks for impecunious students and maiden aunts to gorge on, two dozen waiters dressed the same as him apart from their lack of jackets to pounce on dry and hungry guests. Twenty feet of rich burgundy damask hid the four long windows that looked down on the street, but the three chandeliers reflected in the mottled mirrors on the inside wall made the room appear twice its size.

He was late, or what his parents considered to be late. They had arrived at five-thirty and Ben was there an hour later for a party scheduled to begin at seven. His mother tutted and fussed, fiddled with his tie and smoothed the front of his dinner jacket. His father shook his hand and nodded, Ben's formal admission into adulthood. His elderly grandmother sat on a stiff-backed gilt chair against the mirrors, talking to his aged spinster cousin Meriol. He gave them both a perfunctory kiss and then Tony arrived with his South-African girlfriend Estelle. Tony frowned, dumped Estelle with his mother, and pulled Ben aside. "Where's Marco? Isn't this really his party? I thought he'd be here now, shocking the parents, that you have him arrive while it's quiet. Or did you ask him to come later, steal the show like a real diva?"

Ben winced even as saw his brother's love, his concern. He knew he had to tell him, but he didn't want to say it, make it real.

"He's not coming."

"Huh? But this is the whole point of the last two years, your coming-out party."
Ben shrugged. "He dumped me. Cheated on me so I dumped him. Some Japanese he'd probably been fucking for a while."
Tony hugged him. Ben swallowed the sob, so grateful for human touch, Tony shielding him from their parents until he had pulled himself together.
"I know you didn't like him," Ben sniffed. "But I did. I really, really liked him."
"I know, but what I think doesn't matter, certainly not now. And there'll be others. Who knows, you might even meet someone tonight."
"What, like Uncle Henry?" said Ben, blowing damp snot from his nose.
Tony wiped it away as he grinned. Uncle Henry was married with three children, but he was flamboyant, bouffant white hair and a handkerchief in his jacket pocket that always matched his cravat. He worked in the silver department of one of the large auction houses. Even since Ben had told Tony he was gay, it was their joke that he had inherited it from Uncle Henry.
But they had no time to talk further. A delegation of family members arrived, aunts, uncles, cousins old and young, near and distant. Ben greeted them all, kissed them, and then spent ten minutes back with his grandmother. She had always been good to him as a child, taking him to the safari park and for picnics, even if these often ended up on her drawing room floor because it was raining so hard outside.

A vast number of friends of his parents soon followed, the price of having them pay for the party. They came with a few of their visibly-reluctant children, children turned to young adults that in many cases Ben had not seen for half a dozen years or more, longing to get away to the pub and their real friends, also scratching at their collars. Ben's LSE friends arrived in three batches. The straight ones, about fifteen, were mostly in dinner jackets even if several had obviously been borrowed from somewhere. They were mainly people on his courses and only Daisy was a true pleasure to see, an actual friend. He promised to catch up with her later as she squeezed his hand. The gay ones, six of them led by Sebastian Fuller-Smith, the chairman of the Pink Club whom Ben had slept with in their first term before he met Marco, were all immaculately if flamboyantly turned out. Finally, the university swim team came and swiftly took position as a clump on the far side of the room, drinking water and orange juice and trying to stay as far away from the smokers as they could.

His parents required him to stand by the door with them, greeting them all formally. It was the worst possible travesty of a wedding reception line-up, the bridegroom missing. This was his party but what was the point? Designed around Marco, but already too much a chance for his parents to settle their social debts, he suffered their friends' hearty congratulations with polite thank-yous and handshakes and swapped emails with their bored children and agreed they should indeed meet up again, always scanning the door, hoping against hope that Marco would appear at the top of those stairs and smile at him. The room was getting hot. His collar was starting to wilt. He wanted to sit but went to talk to the swim team, even though he didn't really want to hear how well they were doing without him.

Daisy beamed at him. "Great do, Ben," she said. "You look smashing in that collar, straight out of the Roaring Twenties. But not enough free gays, I think. Quite a few who might work for me, though."

With a sigh of relief, he stopped and explained who some of the men were that Daisy had spotted.

"And who's that? The smoker? A bit of a smoker too in a nice, quiet way."

Ben turned and saw that his schoolfriends had finally arrived. With them here, this party was finally starting to make some kind of sense. "His name's Chris. We were at school together. Don't get your hopes up too much; I'm not sure he knows what a girl is – or a boy. Sorry, but I need to go over. I've hardly seen them in two years."

Because of Marco. Daisy released him with a squeeze to his hand and Ben hurried over. The conversations with his straight LSE friends had been stilted; he just didn't know them very well. Two excruciating minutes with Sebastian, who intercepted him with a wave of his wineglass, was more than enough, his hauteur, his satisfaction at Ben's abasement after Ben had pushed him away that first term. "Of course, I saw it coming, even if others didn't, a slow-motion car crash. And you had the nerve to call me clingy!"
"Well you just enjoy the party too, Sebastian."
Ben walked off. Sebastian was an annoying, affected man with an annoying, affected name and he was glad he had pushed him away, and glad that it had so obviously stung. The man might aspire to *Brideshead Revisited* and have some of the money for it, certainly much more than Ben, but a fuller's job was to bang pieces of cloth with a club while a smith banged pieces of metal with a hammer.

So, with relief he reached his schoolfriends. Chris had come down from Edinburgh where he was studying to be an actuary. Paul, who was at the Sorbonne, had taken the train over from Paris with his French girlfriend Cecile. Tom had come up from his farm near Taunton. He has dropped out of Cambridge six months before after his parents were run off the road in Portugal and he inherited a grey stone house built by Robert Adam in the 1760s along with seven thousand acres of land. He was living in four rooms of one of the wings of the house, on the site of and partially including the previous Jacobean house, the rest under dust covers while he pulled both into shape. Ben should have understood when Marco refused to go to the funeral. Alex, Nigel, Derek and the others had come down from Oxford and Cambridge, with their girlfriends in tow. But they all ditched their other halves as Ben came over to greet them. These people were all from a happier time, before Marco, simpler and more innocent. Ben was safe, no longer the only one in a wing collar, although he knew tonight would be the last night he would wear one.
Chris hugged him, a cloud of cigarette smoke making Ben choke. "What?" said Ben. Chris was not known for any displays of emotion at all apart from nervousness and discomfort. Chris was looking over his shoulder so he turned and saw Derek and Nigel shifting on their feet, twisting at their wine glasses. Derek made a face. "Word's getting around," he said. "The LSE crowd are talking, especially that Sebastian bloke – is he really your friend? Word is you've just been through a bad break-up that left you flat on your back with a bug for a week. You never get sick."

Ben looked at them all. He had never discussed his sexuality with any of them, although Nigel had asked him once about Tommy and then not spoken to him for months and Tom definitely knew about Simon Greaves. Marco's refusal to attend the funeral had denied him a perfect opportunity to show them who he really was.
"Well, the word is right," he said. "His name was Marco and he was a…tosser, a tosser on whom I wasted two years of my life. Who robbed me of my real friends. Thank you all for being here tonight. I don't deserve it after ignoring you for so long."
A wave of emotion came over him, nausea, and he bit it down. Nigel punched him playfully on the arm. "Must have been a good one, though, for you to spend two years with him."
Ben chuckled. These people were easy, an extended family. He had seen them every day for five years, eaten with them, got drunk with them, smoked those first cigarettes with them, talked about girls – and boys – with them, who was doing who. No, there were many things Marco had not been good at, even as he glided effortlessly through his life, provoking resentment, robbing Ben of his peace of mind.
"That's better," said Alex. "You do look like shit, though. That bug must have flattened you; you've lost all that usual sickeningly-healthy glow you have."
"Thanks, Alex. Just what I needed. Two knock-out blows in a week. I'm just standing here waiting for the next meteor to strike."

The others laughed. "Want to talk about it?" asked Chris. His caring concerned solicitude was completely out of character and almost made Ben laugh. Not for the first time, Ben wondered if, under the fog of fags and booze, Chris might secretly be gay.
"Not really. Nothing to tell. I was traded in for a better model, a Japanese guy named Rio. I wish I knew why. I wish someone would tell me what I did wrong. Did he just get bored of me? Am…I mean, am I boring?"
"Hard to tell," said Derek. "We've hardly seen you these two years. No more boring than the rest of us, I imagine. But, yes – you have a bookish streak. With those exam results, nobody really understood why you chose the LSE."
Ben had five A Levels, as dumbing-down made that the new maximum, all top grade As, and even one S Level, a Distinction, taken just before they were abolished, even though only Oxbridge required S Levels. Derek looked to the others for support and they all nodded.
"The course suited me better, and I wanted an adventure."
Nigel laughed. "And it sounds like you found one. Now, get back out there and into the game. Put some swimmers back into those swimmers of yours."

Ben laughed, but he wasn't ready yet and he didn't like the direction the conversation was taking; he didn't want Marco to infect his relationship with these people too. He turned it to work placements and upcoming exams and the difficulties of job-hunting. A while later, he noticed his uncle Henry waving at him from across the room. He ignored the man, too annoying and stressful on an evening like this, and turned back to hear Chris expounding on the importance of actuarial science. After graduating, he wanted to be an insurance analyst at an investment bank. When Ben finally clocked back into the conversation, he said, "Christ, and I thought I was boring!"

It got a laugh.

"You should go and say hello to whoever it is waving at you," said Derek. "Any more and I think he might take off."

"It's my uncle. I'm sorry. Just give me a few minutes."

"Come for New Year," said Tom, looking round at the others and seeing them nod. "All the gang will be there. I can't promise any hot guy-on-guy action, but I'm opening up the house for the occasion, I need some company too, and I can promise log fires, mulled wine, maybe a bit of gin and lots of roast lamb, long walks in the country and overall a bit of peace and quiet."

Yes, that was what he needed. Tom was too modest, of course, he always was, but a chance to get away was what he needed, to forget the LSE and remember school. Marco would have loved Tom's place, lapped it up, come at the very thought of a quintessential English country house, but Ben knew it would be better without him. For the first time, he was glad Marco hadn't been at the funeral.

"Thanks, Tom. I'd like that. Very much. Please count me in. Chris, go and talk to that girl over there in the paisley dress. Her name's Daisy and she's a friend of mine from the LSE. Very nice. She's reading finance."
With that, he excused himself and wound his way between the chatting guests towards his uncle, a look of relief in the man's red face as he approached. After pausing only occasionally to shake a hand or smile as someone patted his shoulder, he arrived at Uncle Henry, who put his arm round Ben's shoulder and clasped him to his side tightly. Ben smelt a lot of alcohol, gin, on his breath. He was also wearing a cravat and a smoking jacket; it made Sebastian look straight. "I heard and I'm sorry," he said.
Ben was surprised. "Thank you, but it's nothing, Uncle Henry. These things happen."
"Oh, pish. No more 'Uncle Henry' either. Your mother's clucking like a startled hen at finding out, but she's a silly old fool, even if she is my dear sister. Too long mouldering away in the country with that dry old stick of a husband. Your brother's doing a sterling job on your behalf – met him, loathed him, but sticking up for the pair of you like Horatius at the Bridge. But we know better, eh? You're finally a true adult, at long last. You need to get your heart broken at least once before you can say that. This is your coming-out party, so call me Henry."
"OK. Henry. Thank you."
But Ben wanted to squirm out of Henry's embrace, get away. Uncle Henry usually ignored him, or just watched him quizzically and silently, before launching into some rendition about his latest appearance on The Antiques Roadshow. This hearty intimacy was unsettling. He was also getting drunk on the man's fumes.

"Now, what are you doing about picking yourself up? The only thing to do when you take a fall is to get straight back on that horse again."
Daisy, Nigel and now him, all with the same message.
"Should we really be talking about this?" Ben said with asperity. When this evening wasn't being hijacked by his parents, it was being hijacked by a Marco who wasn't even here. All the damage and none of the glory. He missed him. With a pang, he scanned the room. No sign of him.
"Of course we should. Now, your mother told me at the time about you and that footballing prefect Tommy, how you thought you were gay, and how she hoped you'd grow out of it. I never saw the need to mention any of it until tonight, none of my business, but I've been looking out for you. You meet all sorts in an auction house, including more than a few 'creative' types. I have just the one for you. His name is Patrick McLeod. He's twenty-four and works in the East Asian ceramics department. He's very smart and very presentable; his father is a High Court Judge. Very quiet, straight-acting. I suspect even your mother might like him. I've mentioned you to him before; I'm sure he'd love to meet you."

Ben pulled himself away and looked his uncle in the eyes. 'Presentable'? That must have been Tony's word. Marco was presentable, his father was a fucking Senator and a cabinet minister, and Ben had wanted, intended, to present him tonight. Tony would have been shocked into silence to see Marco in a dinner jacket. But a part of him was also grimly amused. People cared, they were trying, even if they made fatuous suggestions, didn't understand he wasn't ready. So far only Tom had got it right, a bit of quiet recuperation. Everyone else seemed determined to jump in, feet first, trample on his miserable bleeding heart, making it disappear under their busy footprints.

"Please, Uncle Henry – Henry – no. Don't do it. Really. I'm happy just to be by myself for a while, get over it all at my own speed. After all, I've got exams to prepare for and job applications to send out."

"Nonsense," said Henry. "I'm sure your parents would be happy to see you cloistered away over your books like some ghastly old monk, but I know what you need, even if you profess not to: cock. Twenty-one year-olds should not be celibate." He pulled out his phone and typed something. "There! Message sent. Your new boyfriend is on his way, and by the accounts of your university friends, a much better and more suitable one."

Ben lost his temper. "Henry, you're an…Ach!" He stormed off. But then he saw two senior executives from Braithwaites, the firm where he had interned over the summer, and had to calm himself. He had invited them, never thinking they would actually turn up, and he needed their good opinion. They saw him, smiled and walked towards him. He quickened his step and put on a smile that he even half believed in. "Thank you both so much for coming. I really appreciate you taking the time."

But they said they were delighted to have been asked. They talked shop for fifteen minutes, even managing a little light office gossip, and some of Henry's intrusiveness faded.

"Now, you'd better go, Ben,' said one of them. "There are too many other people who need your attention tonight. But please make sure you apply this winter."

"Thank you. I will, of course. You're my first choice. I really enjoyed this summer, learnt so much."

They seemed gratified and he walked over to the swim team, as different an environment as he could hope to find in what was now a hellishly hot room. They made space for him naturally and then carried on talking about the last competition and the upcoming Christmas meet of the European universities championship.

"Get back on form and you can get back on the team," said Graeme, the coach, with a nod. "You're still the best butterfly stroke we have."

It was what he wanted to hear, but they had done well at the competition without him and, even as he wanted back in, he felt left out and was indeed being almost ignored in the conversation. He stayed for ten minutes, listening, smiling, and then excused himself. He wanted a real drink. It might be his birthday, but the party was in full swing around him, two hundred and fifty people happily talking to each other. He accosted a waitress, retrieved a glass and turned, wondering who he should talk to next. He saw Daisy with Chris and decided to leave her alone. Then he noticed a stranger, the first person he didn't recognise at all.

The man started and then collected himself, shaking himself straighter before walking forward. Ben realised how hard he must have been staring and stood as he worked out who this could be. The man was sort-of handsome in a faded, modest way. He was only a few years older than Ben, but his parted mousey hair was thinning, almost wispy, and his face had that absent, vacant look of someone who habitually wore glasses and had temporarily taken them off. He wore a tweed jacket over an open-necked blue cotton shirt, which revealed a mass of mousey hair, and light cotton chinos, which looked odd since this was a man who would wear black tie comfortably and naturally. There could be no greater contrast to Marco, this man's chest and shoulders narrow, his long body thin. If this man worked out, it was Pilates not weight-training, but Ben doubted he worked out and doubted even more that he would find him attractive. He was thin, not slim, and had an air of weakness, defeatedness, to him, a lack of colour in his cheeks. Other than a long time on the shelf, why else would this man seek out Ben in his own reduced condition at the press of a text message? For this was obviously the Patrick Henry had raved about so recently.
"Hi," he said. "I'm…"
"Patrick McLeod. Twenty-four and works in the East Asian ceramics department. Son of a High Court judge."
The man looked mortified and cautiously hopeful at the same time. "Sorry. I know this is your birthday. But your uncle said…"
"What? That I needed a place to put it tonight?"

Patrick reddened. Ben knew he was being unnecessarily offensive, but felt disinclined to apologise. After seeing Daisy and his schoolfriends, maybe setting Daisy up with Chris although he doubted it, getting Tom's invitation to New Year, meeting the two PR executives, allowing Sebastian to patronise him, chatting up his grandmother and extracting a semi-invitation to start swimming again, he was tired and ready to leave. How dared Henry impose in such a way? What was he, twelve and fighting shy of his first disco?
"That you might need a friend, someone to talk to. London's a big, lonely city. At least I think so sometimes and I've lived here most of my life."
Ben examined Patrick closely. His skin was pale and freckled, not dark; his eyes blue, not brown; pronounced stubble on his cheeks and chin led Ben's eyes down to that incredibly thick, unruly mat of hair spilling out from his collar, none of Marco's smoothness. And then there was the difference in builds: Ben wondered if he fucked this man, whether Patrick might actually snap. The thought brought him a cold smile.
"Look," said Patrick. "If you want me to go, that's fine. I see it was wrong of Henry to invite me and wrong of me to impose."
Yes, it was and Ben noticed he'd crossed his arms even before Patrick reached him. But it was perhaps unnecessary to be quite so rude. Twenty years of parental training in manners eventually won through and, with some effort he uncrossed his arms and relaxed his stance. "No, make yourself at home. Everyone else is. Half the LSE Pink Club's here. You might find yourself a way to be less lonely."

He heard the bitterness in his voice and saw that he was looking anywhere but into Patrick's face. He made another conscious effort and looked him in the eyes. He saw the hurt and offence there and said, "Sorry, it's not your fault, but Henry was completely out of order. I don't know what he was thinking."
Patrick nodded. "I understand. If it helps, I was dumped a while back. It can take a while to find your feet again."
"And how long has it been?"
"A year."
"And have you found your feet yet?"
"I'm finding them."
"I recommend a sauna." What was it about this man that drove the devil in him? A little righteous revenge on Sebastian Fuller-Smith perhaps, who might be affected but unfortunately wasn't stupid.
"That's not really my thing…"
"More of a dinner and the theatre type, are you?"
"Actually, yes, but I see it's the wrong time to talk about it. Look," he said, pulling out his slim, gilt-edged black leather wallet. "Here's my card. If you'd like to have a chat – or even see a play – just call me."
Ben took the card and even managed a 'thank-you'. Patrick nodded and then he was gone, quickly absorbed into the crowds around them.
"Get his phone number, did you?" said Tom, striding up with Derek and Chris beside him.
Ben summoned a tired smile; he wanted to go home. "In a manner of speaking. He doesn't give out phone numbers; he gives out business cards."
"Is he your type? He looked a bit of a dweeb."

Ben sighed. "I'm not sure what my type is anymore. I thought I knew, but I have been repeatedly informed that I was mistaken. But he's apparently very presentable. His father's a High Court judge and my uncle tells me that even my mother might like him, so he must be all right."
The others laughed. "As I said, we'll expect you for New Year," said Tom. "Three or four days, whatever you like. There'll be ten of us, plus you. And if you want to bring Mr Fish-faced Dweeb, or anyone else for that matter, feel free. There are enough bedrooms for everyone."
"Thanks."
Tom grasped his hand and shook it hard, then leant in and hugged him. "We're going now, but we'll see you after Christmas."
"I'll be there."
"Great party, by the way," said Derek as he hugged Ben. "Queers and Grandmas, a potent mix, but somehow no explosion. Well done."
Ben laughed out loud and the others waved and were gone. As he looked round the room again, he saw there was no one he wanted to talk to, queers or grandmas. Then it struck him how white it all was, a Nigerian and a Korean among his straight friends from the LSE, a Singaporean-Chinese from the Pink Club while his schoolfriend Nigel de Souza was Indian, but that was all. He wondered if Patrick was still there and whether he should go and apologise, but then he saw him talking to Henry and the thought vanished. He faded into the throng and was accosted by Iona, the daughter of his parents' oldest friends and, he discovered, the first woman Tony had slept with.

We were both thirteen. On that camping trip in the Lake District."
It was far more information than he needed and he nodded and he was pleased to see the room slowly but steadily empty behind her. A stream of people said good-bye to him and he smiled, shook their hands, accepted their pecks on his cheek, tried to ignore their half-hidden looks of pity, but he was happy that most simply left. Somehow, that felt appropriate. Designed for Marco, hijacked by his parents and even more so by Marco's ghost, it was a blessed relief to see it ending. He heard the lines of the Lesley Gore song, *It's my party and I'll cry if I want to.* He did want to. Judy and Johnny, Marco and Rio, oh what a birthday surprise, although who was wearing whose ring was unclear. You would cry too if it happened to you.
His parents looked over as he approached the door. "We'll take all your presents home with us and you can get them at Christmas," said his mother. "What a different lot of friends you have. I really didn't know what to make of some of them."
He had to get away. He saw Graeme leaving and quickly kissed his mother and shook his father's hand, thanked them both for the party, and ran after him, finally extracting what he wanted: a firm invitation back to the training sessions and a promise to be on the team for the December meet if he could recover his form.
It was enough. There had been victories tonight, even if his main army had been routed in the pass and destroyed: he had goals for the rest of the year. Henry was a meddling interfering old bore, but Patrick presumably had had a far more humiliating than Ben; what was he thinking offering Ben his card after Ben's behaviour?

He walked home, oblivious to the damp and cold. As he pushed open his front door, he saw the emptiness inside. It was his twenty-first birthday, but he was alone, sober and home before midnight. He stripped off and flopped into bed. He'd washed the sheets and the cleanness, the absence of Marco's musk, just left another hole. He did want cock, but what it would or should look like, he had no idea He thought of Marco and hardened, he hadn't masturbated in two weeks, but then Marco faded and Patrick came into view. Repulsed, he turned on his side, pulled the pillow into his chest and fell asleep.

CHAPTER FIVE

The rhythm of university life wasn't much fun, just eating, working, swimming and sleeping, but Ben got compliments from his tutors and was readmitted to the swimming team. He accepted a few party invitations, but found he really didn't know these people and would leave quietly when no one was watching. Such a waste what Marco had made him miss, but it was Ben's final year, time to think of his future, his degree and his career. He wasn't even really masturbating, something he was reminded of with a jolt one night as he had his first wet dream for years, if ever. It was Simon Greaves, the rugby player from school, implausibly dressed in a tweed jacket and Levi's, the worst of Marco and Patrick. Ben felt the mess and groaned with dismay.

He had filled in the application forms for all the PR agencies he was interested in with scrupulous care, paying particular attention to the one where he had interned that summer. At the end of term in early December, they sat in a pile for double-checking before he sent them off. He had bought some simple furniture from Ikea that he didn't really like but which at least filled the flat up, as well as a small LCD flatscreen TV. For the first time in two years, he had read his entire reading list for the term and even begun to work through some of the back reading lists from previous terms. He was getting regular As for his essays He was swimming faster and further than ever, and feeling less tired afterwards. He shaved his chest regularly, as well as his armpits, and enjoyed the sight of the muscles there as well as the feel of the water, sliding off his smooth skin. But he was lonely and tried not to think about it, burying his head in another book or dunking himself in the swimming pool.

He still had Patrick's card and even thought about calling him once, but then put the card away as soon as he looked at it. Patrick just didn't interest him. No one did. The only consolation was that Daisy said Marco and Rio had broken up, Marco cheated on him with a Nigerian called Arthur. But even that only lasted a couple of weeks and Marco moved on to a Turk, then a Swede and then a Malaysian-Chinese. What was it with that man? Yes, apparently London was indeed a very international city, but did he really want to sleep with the whole fucking United Nations! Clearly his fetish with all things English was long over. That thought did not console – was that all Ben had been, a fetish, an exemplar, not a real living, breathing, thinking, loving being? And if Ben now knew how shallow Marco was, why could he still not shake him from his heart? Being called perfection, an English rose, as his cheek was nuzzled by a man with a smile that overwhelmed. Sometimes, it was just nice to be loved.

The party invitations dried up as others also turned to job applications. He finished his last essay, re-checked his applications and posted them, closed the final page of the last of the spring term's reading list and packed his bags for the final challenge of the year: the European university swimming championship in Dusseldorf. After that, and a presumably excruciating Christmas at home, it would be time for New Year at Tom's.

He was hardly off the plane when his phone trilled. The text said, "Sorry for the short notice, but I scored four tickets to Othello at the National Theatre on Friday. Best production since Olivier. One spare. Interested? Patrick."

Christ, no. Was the man mad? A doomed inter-racial love affair, people dying in every direction? *She Stoops to Conquer* possibly, *Rosencrantz and Guildenstern are Dead* at a push; he liked Stoppard. Hell, if he wanted to see everybody die, then *Iphigenia at Aulis*. In the school production, Tommy had played Achilles. They had started sleeping together by then and at one point Tommy slipped accidentally into Greek; Ben had thought it was for him and floated on air for a week. But not Othello.

And it was all beside the point. Patrick was intruding, imposing where he wasn't wanted and hadn't been invited. Ben's irritation was marginally lessened by being many hundreds of miles away and with the beauty of a genuine excuse, but he still boiled at the intrusion. He had thought he'd made it clear that first contact would be made, if it would ever be made, by him, not Patrick. And how had Patrick got his phone number anyway? Fucking Uncle Henry – he'd probably provided the tickets, making sure there were more than two so it all looked neutral. Doubtless, he thought he was helping, but he really wasn't. Ben was enjoying his peace and quiet, even if he was also remembering the feel of Marco's nose on his cheek, the bristles of his chin on his chest, the soft touch of his fingers on the small of Ben's back. Then he would remember the sight of Marco kissing Rio, holding him, and Ben knew why it made him so angry, so hurt – all that belonged to him, it was his and his alone for two years, a long time that should have gone on forever. That he still wanted, yearned for in his troubled dreams. Patrick was in the way and Henry had no right to throw him there.

"Can't. Sorry. In Germany. Swimming competition." Then, in a moment of weakness, "Thanks anyway."

He sent the message and instantly regretted the ending. Fuck his parents for making him so polite. He hoped that would be the end of it, but it wasn't. As they sat in the bus for the ride to the campus, another message.
"No prob. When are you back? Time for a glass before Christmas?"
Ben gritted and then ground his teeth. He didn't need this. "Next week."
His phone went blessedly quiet and he focused on the competition. He made it through the heats and into the finals of the relay, the butterfly and the freestyle.
"Looking good," said Graeme, patting him on the shoulder. "Keep it up and the Krauts will just have to settle for winning the football."
He nodded and turned in early. He felt good the next morning and it showed in the pool. He won his leg of the relay, although the team had to settle for silver, and he won the butterfly. As he looked up at the scoreboard and saw his name, he felt aroused; it was the most fun he'd had since the wet dream – and with none of the unpleasant after-effects. He punched the water.

He was the only one racing the next day and he others went out that night without him. They were leaving the next day so it made sense, but Ben felt all his loneliness return. His room was Germanically neat, modern and comfortable, but it was also bare, a mirror to the abandoned flat he was inhabiting. Apart from the survival Ikea furniture, he had mainly filled the floor with larger and more precarious piles of books. He stared at the white polyester ceiling tiles, even these were clean, and thought of Patrick. How easy, he presumed, it would be to get that man out of his clothes and onto his back. Although Patrick visibly lacked the muscles Ben liked, Ben found himself masturbating to the thought of doing him, the sense of power, of dominance and control, a consolation, an aphrodisiac. He fell into a troubled sleep, with confusing dreams of standing on the winners' podium receiving his medal and then doing some sort of Patrick on the bare boards of Ben's flat.

He was listless in the morning, even though he'd been awake since five, unable to stay sleep. He did his warm-up, but Graeme could tell something was wrong. It didn't help that Graeme was hung-over.

Everyone seemed to have fun except him. But then he remembered. Patrick was offering and he'd been to parties and Daisy still made a real effort. Anger swept over him – at himself and at everyone else. He breathed deep, closed his eyes, and calmed.

"That's right. Focus, Ben," said Graeme. "You did it yesterday and you can do it today. Freestyle. Your butterfly will make mincemeat of the competition."

Ben nodded, but his heart wasn't in it. He didn't know exactly what he wanted, but he was tired. Not from a bad night's sleep, but from life. It had been a long year and he was tired of it. He wanted to be somewhere else, away not just from the swimming team, but also from the LSE, from London, from prying eyes and the demands of others. He wanted to be in Tom's house outside Taunton, in the bosom of his schoolfriends, where there would be no questions.

He slid into the pool and took his position. He closed his mind to everything but the lane, the water and the starting gun. He raced. He turned. He finished. He came up for air, swishing water from his eyes as he turned his head to see the board.

A photo finish. For a moment, he struggled to see who it was. Then the board came up – Connelly and Martens, times identical to two decimal places. He looked down the lanes to Jan Martens, the Dutchman paired against him. Ben was better – had beaten the man just the day before. Ben saw the anticipation and dread on Martens' face as he stared at the board, but no longer cared. Whether he was first or second, he had let himself down; his time was way more than a second slower than it had been the day before for the same distance and the same stroke.

The judges gave up. Joint first was announced, Ben's second gold of the games, but when Martens raised his arms and cheered, Ben slid out of the pool and sat on the edge, dejected. Not a defeat, like Marco had been a defeat, but not a victory either. This year was turning into one better forgotten.

Graeme put a towel round his shoulders. "It's good enough," he said. "I'm sure it was just fatigue. And you still got two golds, more than anyone else on the team. Take a rest over Christmas and you'll be fighting fit again next year."

Ben nodded, received his medal and applause, raised his arm dutifully, even if Martens was grinning and waving wildly beside him, and then went to change. As he put his phone in his tracksuit pocket, he noticed another text message. "Did you win?" it said. "I googled your competition and saw it ended today. Hope all went well. Patrick."

Ben growled and raised his arm to throw the phone at the wall, but then restrained himself. He didn't want to get a new phone and, anyway, at least Patrick was showing an interest. It was more than his parents or even Tony had done and certainly much more than Marco; none of them ever asked him about his competitions, even if Marco liked to see the medals. On the bus, he texted back, "Second, first and joint first."

The response was almost immediate. "Congratulations! Do you like pantomimes?"

So unexpected that Ben just stared at it until he was in the bus and it had set off for the airport. In truth, he did, or had when he'd last seen one aged twelve, so long ago now, almost a decade. But he also knew he was being asked out – again. Jeez, that man must be desperate. No dignity at all when Ben had basically spat in his face at his birthday party? He waited until he had checked in and they were all waiting for the call to board. Fuck it. I just don't care anymore. And anyway, the way things were going, Patrick and Uncle Henry would doubtless only try something else in a few weeks.

"Thanks. And yes."
He looked at what he'd written, shrugged and slumped in his seat. For better or for worse, he was committed. But it was the path of least resistance, and who knew, perhaps Patrick might turn out to be more than just a dweeb. But he switched off his phone as the inevitable call came. Rather than deal with an over-excited antiques dealer, he fell asleep and didn't turn his phone on again until he was on the train back into London.
"Aladdin," trilled the voice message. "Saturday 20th. 3pm. Barbican. Matinees are better; more children."
So, he had a date. It was still almost a week away, but he would get to see Widow Twankey hoist up her fake boobs and the lesbian love-action between Aladdin and the Leading Lady. He called his parents and said he would come down to Dorset on the 22nd. Then he spent the next few days buying Christmas presents and wrapping them, wondering if he should cancel on Patrick. Never had he less wanted to go out.
He stood in the theatre foyer. He'd had a shower in the morning as well as the night before and even wondered for a while what to wear. In the end, he'd gone for a plain pink shirt under a blue jacket and over clean jeans. The jacket had been an odd choice, but what he wanted, he realised, was to show off his chest, to frighten Patrick off with his masculinity, and that could only be done under a shirt.

Patrick came through the outside doors, scanned and raised his arm. He had done the opposite of Ben, dressed himself in a denim jacket that didn't suit him and a sweatshirt over faded, heavily worn jeans. He looked better dressed as a college professor from the fifties. He still wasn't wearing his glasses. His shoes, though, were immaculate suede brogues. "Hi," he said. "I hope I didn't keep you waiting."
He thrust his hand in his jacket pockets so that they protruded like two concealed pistols. Ben shook his head. "Shall we go in?"
The bell for five minutes had already rung and they took their seats at the front of the circle, always Ben's favourite place at the theatre and safely away from the stage and its cast for a pantomime. He gave ground. "Good choice of seats."
Gratification and relief, hesitation and then a decision to plunge ahead. "You look…much better. Much better."
Ben grunted. If he slept with this man, it would be the easiest lay outside a sauna he'd ever had. "I was ill, but now I've recovered."

The lights went down and the orchestra struck up, mercifully ending any further need for conversation. The curtains came up, the lewd jokes came out, the children screamed, Ben found himself laughing and then it was the interval. For the first time, Ben glanced across at Patrick, who was staring at him. How long had he been doing that? The gaze was wistful. Ben smiled and Patrick smiled back, showing off neat teeth. Ben's first impressions were correct, this man was faded, weak, almost wraith-like, but there was potential there. Perhaps he might be regarded by some as quite handsome, although whether he still would be when he was forty or naked was an open question. Patrick noticed the inspection, coloured and said, "Would you like an ice cream?"

Ice cream at the Christmas panto, that took Ben back a few years. "Thanks."

Ben sighed with relief as Patrick shuffled down the row. It was easier for both of them if went alone, rather than try to hold some stilted conversation. The queue was mercifully long, but Patrick turned back several times, brightening each time their eyes caught.

They ate their ice creams in silence and the lights went down. It was time for 'he's behind you', it was time for the sweets thrown to the audience, it was time for the audience to sing the dreadful song, and then it was over. Everyone clapped and cheered, Ben most of all. As they stood to leave, he felt almost in charity with the man, pleased and relieved he had kept his hands scrupulously on his side of the armrest.

"Thank you," he said. "This was exactly what I needed."

A little colour rose in those pallid cheek. "You looked like you were really getting into it."

"I was. It's been too long since I had some real fun."
Patrick positively glowed. Hesitant, he asked, "Would you like to do something else? It's a bit early, but we could have something to eat. Or, if you like, you…you could come to my place and we could have a drink. I live in the Barbican, so it's not far."
Ben saw the heightened excitement, any minute he would start licking his lips.
"I could murder a chicken salad."
Patrick swayed, but recovered. "There's a nice Italian place around the corner."
It did have chicken salad, which Ben ordered. Patrick chose the fettucine carbonara. After an awkward silence that Ben wasn't sure how to end, Patrick said, "So, what was he like, this Marco?"
It was Ben's turn to be shaken, jolted upright. "He was a muscle freak, but when I parted those tight globes of his, he gabbled like a mynah bird."
Patrick reddened at the slap; it emphasised his freckles. But Patrick had no right to mention Marco. No one did – with the possible exception of Daisy.
"So, tell me. Who was it that dumped you?"
Patrick was thrown, both hurt and offended. He stammered, "His name was Edwin, Teddy. We met through some jobs fair I was at. He was a few years older. He dumped me after I refused to have sex on a hillside one day, said I was too boring for him."

The bitterness was obvious and the pain raw. For the first time, Ben felt some sympathy. He had steered Marco of exactly the same request more than once. He still could hardly believe he'd agreed to do it that time by the swimming pool in Spain. Marco was a whirlwind and had blown Ben away, but Ben no longer wanted a whirlwind. He wanted…what? Not Marco, but definitely not Patrick either. Someone in the middle, someone masculine but loving that he could invest in. But he'd never met anyone even close. When, how, where would he ever meet him?
"Lose that jacket," he said. "It doesn't suit you. If you want to be a young fogie, be one. Don't try to guess what others might want to see."
"You…you don't like it?"
And Ben knew the jacket had been bought for him. "I don't. And do you wear glasses?"
"I…I'm trying contact lenses."
"Well, wear glasses if you have to. Be yourself!"
"You're really not into me at all, are you?" His anger almost overwhelmed his bitterness. But it was true, Ben wasn't, even if he felt the pull of the familiar, the knowledge that a comment would be understood and appreciated, that a joke could be shared, that Patrick was eminently presentable in both Somerset and Dorset. But Patrick was too much like giving in, going to Oxford; Marco notwithstanding, Ben was still pleased he'd chosen the LSE. "Sorry. I need someone with more self-respect."
"You're a real shit, you know that?"
And for the first time, Ben was attracted to the man. It was the colour in Patrick's cheeks, the pallor temporarily removed, the spark of life briefly visible. "That's better," he said.

But Patrick was on a roll. "You think everyone's as beautiful as you? You think it's easy for the rest of us?" The colour gave him an energy that Ben found titillating.
"I'm not so beautiful that I don't get dumped."
"I'm not surprised you get dumped; I'm surprised you find anyone at all!"
Ben deflated and Patrick calmed himself, his fingers still shaking as he placed them on the table. "I'm sorry," he said. "I didn't mean that."
"No, it's OK. I deserved it. And you're right. And I'm not really myself at the moment. Thank you for the panto; it was genuinely fun."
Scarlet, Patrick took a large forkful of pasta, stuffed his mouth full of it, and then said, without having swallowed all of it, "How's your salad?"
It was good and Ben said so. He finished it and Patrick paid the bill. As they stood in the street, Patrick turned to Ben. "Would you like to come back to my place? It's only round the corner."
In spite of all he already knew, Ben was still taken aback. It was a new experience to have someone keep throwing themselves at him. "Maybe some other time, but thank you for today."
Patrick kept coming. "I've been invited to a nice party for New Year. Would you like to join?"
Ben felt a loss. This was clearly some kind of hell that he would only escape by agreeing to see this man. He wondered if transporting him back to his natural environment in the country might somehow improve him, or at least allow Ben to put on his beer goggles.
"I'm going to some schoolfriends in Somerset. Actually, I was thinking of asking you…"

"I'd love to," said Patrick, childish with glee. "The others can look after themselves."
Ben frowned. "You really do like me, don't you?"
"I'd like to, if you'd just give me a chance. You're smoking hot and not above laughing at silly double-entrendres. And despite some of the things you say, there's at least some indication there's a decent person in there somewhere."
Ben gave Patrick a side-long glance and walked off.
"Email me the details," Patrick shouted and Ben raised his am. Now what had he done? A bit of temporary colour in a man's cheeks and Ben was going to wreck the most precious New Year he could remember. Patrick had better look good in green wellies.

CHAPTER SIX

Only the arrival of Uncle Henry with his family for lunch on Boxing Day reminded Ben that he hadn't emailed Patrick, or contacted him at all, since the Barbican. He sat at the little, ancient computer in his father's gloomy book-lined study, full of biographies and histories of the Second World War, and dialled up an internet connection. As he typed, he felt no frisson of excitement, none of the anticipation he always had before meeting Marco again, before Tommy or Simon or even Sebastian that first time. Bloody saunas were better than this. No, this was a cold, clinical, almost cynical decision to get laid for the first time in months. Wham, bam, good-bye man! He was due at Tom's on the 28th and invited Patrick for the 29th, enough time to warn everyone.
"If you send me your train details, I'll meet you at the station. Sorry again for not writing before."
He hadn't 'hoped you're still free' or 'looked forward to seeing you'. He was giving Patrick the run-around, literally obliging him to run across the country to him, but Ben was in no mood to compromise; Patrick would have to sell himself before Ben would engage.
"No problem," said Tom. "I said you could bring someone. Do you want one bedroom or two?"
Ben had bought condoms and lube on his way through Dorchester, but as he looked at his friend, he wondered. "Better make it two."

"If you say so, but I don't mind. Do you know this guy at all?"
"No, not really. Frankly, he's on sale or return. This trip's a test."
Alex, Nigel and Derek arrived shortly afterwards with their girlfriends, as did Chris, and they all ate lamb stew on the floor of Tom's magnificent drawing room in front of a television wheeled in from Tom's den for the occasion.
"We'll eat in the dining room the other nights," Tom said. "But tonight we'll just relax."
The dining room's mahogany table could seat forty, while the drawing room, with its fifteen-foot corniced ceiling and eighteenth and nineteenth century full-length ancestors looking down on them, had three full-length sofas and six armchairs, two card tables and half a dozen occasional tables. They drank a full case of Burgundy, followed by three bottles of Sauternes, careful with coasters not to spill anything on the two hundred year-old Persian carpet.
There was some surprise when Tom said Patrick would be joining them. Derek and Nigel said they would judge whether he was worthy, while Alex's girlfriend Harriet, offended, said she would judge whether Ben was worthy, informing him flatly that he was honoured Patrick would break his plans to come all the way to Somerset and that it was outrageous to only contact him three days before. Harriet was, of course, quite correct, even as Ben refused to admit it.

On the 29th, he took himself off to Taunton station, willing himself to be nice. And he was pleasantly surprised by the sight that got off the train. Patrick was wearing a large blue and white Guernsey sweater over clean jeans and brown half-boots. He was also wearing glasses, round wire-framed. He looked more like himself – or what Ben imagined the true Patrick to be – than Ben had yet seen. Ben nodded, a sign of approval intended for himself, but Patrick noticed and smiled.
"Hi," he said.
Ben wondered if they should kiss, or at least embrace. But he put out his hand and Patrick shook it, surprisingly firm and steady. "How was your Christmas?" he asked as he heaved Patrick's suitcase into the boot of the car.
"I'm the youngest of three. Both my brothers are married with children, so I'm the great disappointment. They all live in Suffolk, at least when my father's not working, close to each other, and can't or won't understand why I don't want to as well. But village barn dances really aren't that much fun when you're gay."
Ben nodded. The 'great disappointment' comment, even if a throw-away concession to English politeness and modesty, might be unfortunate, but resonated from his own Ben's father. He spent the journey briefing Patrick on who everyone was.

But Patrick's run of pleasant surprises continued. He quickly remembered everyone's name and even knew two of Derek's friends and one of Harriet's from his time at Oxford. They played Twister that night and Patrick threw himself into it, knocking back three tumblers of Glenmorangie with water and laughing openly when he collapsed in a heap. Rather, it was Ben who had to remind himself that it was not just Patrick who was auditioning. He had a second gin and tonic, saw Harriet glaring at him, and stopped sitting it out when it was Patrick's turn on the mat. They fell down together, along with Chris and Nigel's girlfriend Amelia. Patrick fell on Ben, their faces almost touching, and Ben saw an innocent, happy smile that he struggled, successfully in the end, to imitate.

Two hours later, they walked upstairs, slowly and in silence. On the landing outside Ben's door, Patrick took Ben's hand. As Ben turned, Patrick put his other hand to Ben's cheek, leant in and kissed him. It didn't last long, Ben stepped away although he didn't remove his hand, but it had been pleasant. It was months since anyone had kissed him and it was warm, tender and friendly. He missed the sensation and realised he'd missed it for a long time. For all the gentle nuzzling, Marco always preferred Ben's cock to his tongue in his mouth. That too should have been a warning. And for all his faults, Patrick kissed well. The intensity had been perfect, assured but not too enthusiastic, just right for a first time. Ben tingled and wondered whether to kiss him in return.

"Do you want me to come in?" Patrick asked.

No, not tonight. This was a man who didn't do one-night stands and, kiss Guernsey and Twister notwithstanding, Ben was still far from sure.

"I think that's enough for one night."
"OK," said Patrick, idly waving Ben's hand and then dropping it. "But if you change your mind, you know where I am. I'd rather it was you beating me off than me."
And there it was, Ben's image for the night. The dead leaves of his broken romantic heart had just begun gently to flutter in the light breeze of Patrick's restrained willingness and then a winter gale of earthy crudity swept them roughly away. He did not open his lips for Patrick's second kiss.
As he stripped and lay down under the covers, he stared at the ceiling. His room was beautiful, lined in silk, blue twisting flowers on white, a Regency chaise longue in front of the shuttered window and an oval horse glass next to the marble fireplace, Meissen figures on its mantelpiece. But it was all ruined for him now. In the next room was a naked man, ejaculating to the thought of them together. Ben fondled himself, wondering if he could or should do likewise, but then gave up and turned off the bed-side lamp. It was all too real for a country house romance and he cursed himself for his hesitancy and high standards; he had no right to them.
There were a few questioning glances in the morning, but no one asked, so Ben said nothing. Besides, he had slept badly, his dreams filled with confused images of Patrick and him in the cloisters at school. Patrick, however, was all smiles, on breakfast detail and doling out plate after plate of bacon, mushrooms, tomatoes and scrambled egg. In a red woollen checked shirt outside his jeans, he seemed perfectly at home, a comfortable farmer not a queer lumberjack.

Tom had arranged for them to go riding that afternoon and Patrick proved as adept at that as everything else so far. Ben could ride, but disliked anything over a gentle canter, but Patrick pranced around, alternately encouraging and then chiding Amelia and Harriet, the shyest and most nervous. He wanted Ben to chase him and then galloped away with Tom and Derek, eventually returning near the end of their session, his cheeks ruddy in the cold air.

"He's all right," said Tom. "I'm not sure why you're so hard on him."

Ben was beginning to wonder the same thing. It would be so simple, and everyone would approve, his schoolfriends, Uncle Henry, perhaps even his parents. He looked over at Patrick, who caught his eye and gave a proud happy smile, open and without any hidden agendas. He made a point of smiling back.

They were all tired after the ride in the biting, fresh wind, and drank too much that night, starting too early. By ten, it was time to go to bed and Ben, who, despite a gin and tonic and three glasses of wine for himself, found being sober around drunk people alienating, stood up to leave. He glanced at Patrick, but Patrick was talking to Harriet, so he went upstairs alone. He relieved himself, washed his face, grumbling that houses outside London never seemed to have mixer taps – didn't people understand there were no fun in being alternately scalded and frozen? – and brushed his teeth. He pushed open his bedroom door, not thinking of much but looking forward to a deep sleep, and came up with a start. Standing just in front of the chaise longue, face-on and stark naked, was Patrick. "Sorry," he said. "I couldn't wait for you to come to me. It was Harriet's idea, but I think it was the right one."

Ben's jaw dropped. He had noticed it before, seen it through the top of Patrick's red checked shirt just this morning, but now there was no hiding it: the man was almost impossibly hairy. It covered his throat and pecs, narrowed slightly as it descended his chest and then expanded into a sea around his navel, before tumbling into an untamed bush of a crotch. At least there were no hairs on his back, but it was a mat of untended wildness. Worse, it was attached to narrow shoulders, a pigeon chest, almost skeletally-shrunken stomach and a small button cock. Despite Patrick's height and the acre upon acre of hair, this was the body of an eleven year-old. It was as if a bearskin rug had been thrown over an old wire coat-hanger.

He must have been silent for a while, because Patrick shifted on his feet and swung his arms. "My cock's better when it's hard," he said. "Strip for me and you'll see. You won't be disappointed, I promise."

Ben had no reason to disbelieve him, but as he continued to stare, he saw Patrick just didn't turn him on and never would. The hairiness might have looked all right on a bigger man, or the narrow body on someone smooth and firm, but the combination was just horrific. 'Otter' didn't begin to describe it. And he had taken off his glasses as well, leaving only a moon-shaped absence.

Patrick was becoming more uncomfortable by the second, actually using his hands to cover his genitals a couple of times. "Come on, Ben. Get your clothes off and fuck me. I want it and I've waited long enough."

He stepped forward and that, finally, forced Ben to act. He put up his arm and extended his hand for Patrick to stop. "What's wrong with you?" stammered Patrick, anger shaking under his confusion. "Don't you know a sure thing when you see it?"
He stepped forward again, his thick, wiry, chest hair rasping against Ben's palm. Ben stepped back and crossed his arms in front of him. "Sorry, but this is never going to work. You need to leave. It was an honest mistake, but it was a mistake all the same. I like you, I really do, and my friends do too, possibly more than me, but," he sighed, gathered his thoughts and wondered how best to say it. "But, I'm sorry. It's just not there. There's no spark. I'm just not attracted to you and, honestly, I don't think I ever will be."
Patrick choked and colour came back to those pallid cheeks as he bent down and picked up the bundle of his clothes on the floor. In his haste, he forgot his boots. "Fine," he snapped. "You just talked yourself out of the best blow-job you'll ever get. I may not have a six-pack, but I know how to please someone. If you're too vain to see it, that's your loss. I'm off. You can drive me to the station tomorrow and I'll spend New Year the way I intended, with my friends, people who appreciate me."

Ben said nothing as Patrick slammed first Ben's door and then his own, jumping at the power of eighteenth century oak on oak. He reached out and lowered himself onto the bed and stared at his hands, amazed and aghast in equal measure, both at Patrick and himself. The boots stared at him. Unable to think clearly, he stripped to his underwear, an acknowledgement that no lust would pass through his mind tonight, and once more stared at the ceiling, noticing that the cornicing was painted yellow and blue in intricate swirls and ruminating on the mess his life had become. Marco had wrecked it, but settling, conforming, especially with an eleven year-old even if he could ride and cook breakfast, simply wasn't an option either. It was a long time before he got to sleep that night and he dreaded the morning.

CHAPTER SEVEN

Even unshod, Patrick was sprightly in the morning, cooking breakfast for everyone, chatting far too much. Ben wished he'd stop. But when he took his plate to the dishwasher, Patrick whispered, "There's a train at eleven-thirty. Take me to it, please."

"Your boots are in your room."

They left quietly and drove to the station in silence. Patrick was wearing the same Guernsey sweater he had arrived in and again looked the better for it. He was also wearing his glasses and, other than push them up the bridge of his nose a couple of times, made no movement during the drive, looking steadfastly forward.

Only as they stood facing each other at the entrance to the station, Patrick clutching his ticket in one hand and his bag in the other, did Ben finally say something. "I'm sorry," he said. 'It's all my fault. I led you on and I'm sorry. I suppose I knew at some level, but it wasn't until you pushed it that I truly realised. I like you, you're a genuinely good guy and will make someone very happy. But us? It's just never going to happen."

"That was the most humiliating five minutes I've ever experienced. You're right – it was your fault, all your fault, you did lead me on. You're a heartless shit who deserves to die alone. And I think Nigel and Amelia saw me as I went back to my room."

Ben couldn't help himself; he barked a laugh.

"It's not funny," snapped Patrick, his voice rising.

"No, but it is! This whole thing is funny, ridiculous." Patrick said nothing. "I mean, you came to my party looking for a boyfriend, while I – to the extent I wanted anything – was simply looking to get laid. Now, here we are, you looking to get laid while I'm thinking how nice it would be to have a boyfriend."
Patrick looked ruffled, but also as if he was calming. "You're not fit to be anyone's boyfriend right now. You were right first time. Go back to your saunas, find some muscle dude and get the rip you want. Then do it again, and again, until you're fit for human company."
It was probably the best advice Patrick had given so far and the effort of saying brought back that rare colour to his cheeks that made him attractive again. It made Ben smile to see the man being himself. "I like you so much better when you're not trying to get into my pants."
Patrick looked startled, unsure, perhaps wondering if Ben was giving him a second chance. "Oh, fuck you!" he said, but that just made Ben laugh again. Patrick bristled once more and then relaxed, trying to hide his smile.
"What are you going to do tonight?" asked Ben. It was, after all, New Year's Eve.
"My friend Harry said that if it didn't work out with you, I could come over to his place. He's having a singles' party, although I think it's really a cover for him to try to get his claws into someone called Bill that he's been banging on about for weeks."
As Ben opened his mouth to speak, Patrick raised a finger. "Restrain yourself. That quip would be as redundant as you are unfunny."
"Ow!" said Ben. "You may not have much meat on your bones, but you've got one big tongue in your head."

"Yes, and that tongue could have been wrapped round your cock, but you were too proud and too vain to give it a try."
Another zinger and this time, instead of laughing, Ben blushed. He saw Patrick's righteous justification and a thought hit him that shocked him, but felt somehow right. "Can I come too?"
"Are you fucking insane? Why would I want that?"
Ben shrugged. "Well, you can go alone with your tail between your legs, explaining to Harry that I rejected you even when you threw yourself at me while I sit around the fire with Tom and the others, all of us laughing about your scrawny chest and tiny cock. Or we can go together and tell Harry that we'd rather be friends and I can show you how I can behave in polite gay company."
"Learn how to behave in polite gay company," said Patrick, but with little anger in his tone.
Ben looked humble and it mostly wasn't an act. "As you say."
Patrick paused and then said, "Look and don't touch. Leave them all with a positive impression of you, and by implication me, but no screwing around. You need to work off your anger at Marco and, as I said, the place for you to do that is the sauna, where no one will get hurt, not Earl's Court."
"So I can come?"
"It starts at eight. I'll meet you at the Tube station, main road side, at eight-thirty. Dress up and bring a bottle of champagne."
"Thanks," said Ben. "I don't deserve this. Thank you."

"No you don't – and if you get a text telling you I've changed my mind, you're on your own." He walked through the ticket barrier without giving Ben another look.

Ben hurried back to Tom's house, strangely excited. A gay party was just what he needed. He and Marco so rarely went to parties because Marco hated them. Mouldering away in the country, drowning his sorrows mournfully in another glass of spectacular wine, would have to stop. He'd once told Patrick to be himself, now it was his turn. He bounded up that massive marble staircase.

As he descended again with his bags under his arms that Tom came out of the morning room. "Are you leaving? What happened? Did it work out with Patrick then? He seemed particularly chipper this morning, although Amelia said…"

"Sorry, Tom," said Ben. "I had a really good time and it was fantastic to see you all again, it's been much too long, but I need to do this. I have to go. Back to London."

"Well, I won't say it hasn't been nice, because it has. It has been too long. But, are you sure? I mean, Patrick was a good guy but even I could tell he was hardly Mr Universe. And he does talk too much sometimes."

Ben dropped his bags and hugged Tom, who looked confused and only tapped him tentatively on the shoulder blades. "You're quite right and Patrick and I will never be anything, but Patrick is also right – I can't, no offence intended – be here. I will see you all again, soon and often, but I'm sorry; tonight, I have to start turning my life around and, for that, I need to be in London."

Tom looked put out, then pulled himself up and nodded. "Yes, I can see that. You're messed up, Ben Connelly. You've hardly been with us these last few days. You go to your gay friends, or Patrick's gay friends – I presume that's where you're going – and then you come back to us. Don't worry; we'll be waiting. We've waited two years and we can wait a bit longer."
Ben hugged Tom even closer and kissed him on the cheek. "You're the best, Tom. More than I deserve."
Tom patted him on the arm. "Just be nice," he said, a neutral, almost meaningless, remark, but correct and close to what Patrick had said.
Ben smiled. "I've missed you all."
"We've missed you too."
Gallows laughter. "Marco really fucked me up."
"Could happen to anyone."
"Apologise to the others for me, would you?"
Tom nodded. Ben was back in London by five and stepped under the shower. As he looked at himself in bathroom mirror, he decided to shave again, his chest included. He dressed carefully, jeans, a blue shirt, blazer and brown shoes with socks, but he was still early. It was barely six-thirty and he wondered what Patrick was doing. Probably hovering his fingers over 'send' on the text message that would confine Ben to the dustbin he knew he so richly deserved.
He made himself beans on toast, unsure if there would be anything to eat at Harry's place, bending over not to get anything on his shirt. He might be gay, but he was also a student even if he did eat wholemeal bread. But this only took ten minutes and he sat down in front of a talent show until, relieved, it was finally time to go.

Patrick was waiting for him outside the Tube station. Ben was pleased, but Patrick looked serious. "What did they say, your friends I mean? About you leaving so suddenly?"

"They were good, better than I deserved, I suspect."

"Hmph," said Patrick.

Harry at the door was all smiles. It wasn't nine yet, but the man was both tipsy and in a very good mood. He threw open the door so hard it banged on the wall, stretched out his arms and clasped Patrick to him.

"Patrick, dahhling. So lovely to see you!"

Ben was surprised, although less so when Patrick stiffened and gently pushed Harry away. "You're drunk," he said.

"Only on my good humour and good fortune. Bill came, well not came, at least not yet. He's been making all the right noises and we've been drinking port since six. I hope you brought some champagne."

He pulled himself back and gazed Ben up and down. His eyebrows went up and his ears back.

"I see you did" he said. "A real corker. I presume this is the infamous Ben? So, are you nailing each other or not?"

Ben was pleased and relieved when Patrick snapped, "Not."

Harry seemed unfazed. "Just friends, eh? Well, the night is young and if you choose not to, there's a smorgasbord of opportunities inside for the both of you."

And with that, he bowed theatrically and ushered them inside. The front room was crowded, men sitting and standing. A few looked their way. Patrick preened and disappear into the morass.

"Are you friends with Harry or Bill?" asked a tall, slim stranger in a tight and expensive shirt that showed off good muscle definition.
Ben was interested; he liked muscles. Perhaps Marco was taking it too far, but he definitely liked some. But then he remembered Patrick's strictures and said with a smile, "Actually I'm here with Patrick, a friend of Harry's."
"I don't think I know him."
The man stepped into Ben's personal space. It was the first step before he was grabbed and Ben pushed him away. "You should meet him. Amazing blow-jobs. Best in London. Quite put me off anyone else."
The stranger looked disappointed but intrigued and disappeared. Another approached, all smiles. "How do you fit in? I haven't seen you around here before?"
Ben was starting to enjoy himself, to be the object of attention in the pulsing rhythm of a truly gay party, a singles party where all the men were both singularly polite and focused only on a single outcome, was enjoyable. He probably shouldn't have made the remark about the blow-job, but he didn't care. Who knew? It might help him – and it might even be true.
"No," he said with a broad smile. "I'm here with my ex over there. Patrick. He got bored with my tongue, not a patch on what he could do with his."

This second stranger disappeared and Ben went to find a drink. He passed the buffet table with its large tray of beef goulash and spooned some onto a plate. As he turned to find somewhere to sit, or at least stand, Patrick emerged from the throng. "What the fuck have you been saying?" he said, pushing Ben in the chest. But he didn't sound truly angry and Ben shrugged. "Only what you told me yourself. That you give good head."

"I've had more offers than ever before…"

"So, what's the problem? Pick one and take him home. Fuck him or date him, or whatever it is you want to do. Get a few other numbers for back-up."

"You're a shit!" But Patrick had relaxed and a part of him was amused.

"Twenty-four hours ago you were choking for a fuck and now you're beating them off with a stick," said Ben. "Come on, man. Buck up. Get laid. Have fun. I'm telling them it was me that couldn't keep up."

Quite unexpectedly, Patrick leant forward and kissed him, parting his lips, although not his teeth. God, it was nice. So moist, so soft. Ben was genuinely sorry when it was over.

"I'm going to get laid tonight," said Patrick, glaring at Ben.

"I hope you do," replied Ben. "You deserve it. And I hope you meet someone you'll be happy with for a long time."

"Hah!" said Patrick. "And I hope you learn how to make civil conversation. Remember what you promised – look, but don't touch."

Then he gave a flounce and was gone. Ben took several forkfuls of goulash before he noticed another man staring. It would be so easy, just douse the misery, loneliness and injustice by diving into this man, a man who would mean nothing to him, whom he would never see again. He smiled even as he remembered his promise to Patrick.

The other man walked over. He was white, late twenties, tallish, well-built, very fit in fact, a little effeminate round the eyes but not the mouth and wearing a designer floral patterned shirt wildly inappropriate for the season, even if the room was getting hotter by the minute. "You must be Patrick's ex," he said.

"Word's getting around," said Ben, sipping his drink, now unpleasantly warm. "Do you know him?"

"Not as well as I should, clearly," said the stranger. "I've seen him a few times, but he's usually very quiet and a bit shy. He's a friend of Harry's and I'm a friend of Harry's, rather than he and I being friends."

"Well, strike while the iron's hot. I don't think he'll be on the market long."

The stranger laughed, but seemed in no hurry to leave. "I can't believe you will be either," he said. "Patrick's not really my type."

"Perhaps you should consider Harry," said Ben. Whether it was the heat of the room or the wine, he was warming rapidly to this man and wasn't sure if he'd be able to keep his promise to Patrick much longer. And Harry was the polar opposite of Patrick. He was surprised when, startled, the stranger stood up straighter and narrowed his eyes. Ben wondered and then, increasingly sure, put out his arm and said, "Ben Connelly."

The stranger hesitated and shook it. "Bill. Bill Harton."
Ben was right. This Bill was that Bill. And clearly his presence at the party was not confirmation Harry had secured his prize while his behaviour over the past minutes spoke of the worst. "Patrick raves about Harry," said Ben. "But this is the first time I've met him Good party, though. What do you think?" He watched as he sipped his drink.
Bill drew back an inch. "Yes, Harry throws good parties, Harry's known for his parties, but I think he loves them a little too much. He's a gadfly, flitters from conversation to conversation, man to man. I don't think he's been with anyone longer than three months and more than once he's had two on the go together."
The bitterness and disappointment boded well. It was time for the Good Samaritan. If he could get Patrick laid tonight, maybe he could do the same for Harry.
"Well, it can't help that five minutes ago you were hitting on me," said Ben. "Story I heard is that Harry threw this entire party just to get you under his roof."
Bill coloured. "He hasn't spoken to me for over two hours…"
"He has a house full of guests. And you spent a comfortable hour or two with him over the port earlier."
Harry materialised, clasping both Ben and Bill by the shoulder and leaning forward into the gap between them. Bill's reply was cut off. "What are you two love-birds talking about?" he said. "My mark for a great party will be if everyone's gone before midnight. So, I need you all paired up and out the door. Time's running out."

Ben glanced at Bill's poorly-concealed dismay. This was stupid and it was starting to piss Ben off. "I was about to leave with Bill when you came over. He was hitting on me because you've been ignoring him all evening. I'm hot to trot, but I suggest that if there are two people who need to leave this party, it's you two."
Harry recoiled, while Bill, although shocked, had a twinkle in his eye. Harry let go of Ben's shoulder and turned to Bill. "Don't," he said. "Don't leave…with anyone else, I mean. I'm sorry. I've just been…"
"It's OK. You're busy."
"I'll get rid of everyone."
They all looked around. The room was full; it was a party in full-swing.
"No," said Ben, surprised at himself. "I'll get rid of everyone. You two go now."
He picked up a mostly-full bottle of champagne and thrust it into Harry's hands. Then, before either of the others could say anything, he pushed them towards the door. They hesitated at the door frame and Ben bodily thrust them both through and closed the door behind them. As he turned back into the room, he dusted his hands and looked for something to do. He saw Patrick deeply engrossed in conversation with a handsome Indian man, quite a lot older but with a head of thick black hair and a strong upper body under nice shoulders.
Patrick looked up. Ben winked and Patrick smiled. The Indian man turned, put out, and started to rise. Ben walked over to heal the breach.
"This is Mahesh," said Patrick. "He sells contemporary Indian art."
Mahesh was standing now. "You must be the ex. I'm in the way."

"Not at all. Art is much deal more interesting than public relations."
Mahesh frowned and looked at Patrick, whose eyes were shining. That colour had come back to his cheeks and, just for a moment, he looked startlingly handsome. Mahesh sat again. Ben leant down and said to both of them, "I've done my good deed for the night. Put Harry and Bill on the right path, at least I hope, so everyone has to leave."
"But it's ten to midnight!" said Patrick.
"OK, then. Half an hour. Spread the word, please."
"We could carry on at my place," said Mahesh.
"I'd like to see that Moghul revival style you've been talking about," said Patrick.
It was a bit clumsy, but Mahesh didn't seem to mind. Ben was fading away from Patrick's happy eyes. He spread the word that the party would close at twelve-thirty sharp.

The radio went on, the clock was counted down, everyone cheered, toasted and embraced or kissed. No one sang *Auld Lang Syne*, because no one knew the words. Mahesh and Patrick were together, their foreheads touching, and then, carefully, was their first kiss, tentative and gentle. Ben half-hoped Patrick would look at him, but Patrick had eyes for no one else. Ben's eyes widened as Mahesh leant in for the second kiss, much less tentative and not gentle at all. The two walked out hand in hand, their sides bumping one another. Others paired off and left. Ben felt bereft. He was jealous or at least envious not just of Patrick and Mahesh but of everyone. Patrick would wake up tomorrow morning to find Mahesh beside him, caressing him, leaning in to kiss him. And Mahesh would likely be there at lot longer than just one morning. Ben sighed. Would he ever have that? He looked around. It was twelve-thirty and there were only three other people in the room.

"Come on; party's over, out you go!" He kicked the sole of one sitting on the floor, propped up against the sofa, where another looked as if he was about to lie down and go to sleep.

"Let's play strip poker," said the third man, sitting forward in his delicate wooden armchair. "I want to see a naked man tonight. You can go first, handsome."

"In your dreams,' said Ben, as he hauled the man on the sofa upright. "Get out your porn collection."

"No, get your kit off," protested the third. "I wanna see your cock."

Ben looked at them. The three leftovers weren't bad looking, just very drunk. "I'll order you a cab and you can leave and have a threesome. Start with strip poker and take it from there."

"I wanna see your cock too," said the man on the floor.
"I'm ordering you a cab," said Ben. "Then, if it gets you out the flat, I'll take off my top."
There was a murmur of approval. Ben ordered the cab which, to his surprise, he was told would arrive in fifteen minutes, and took off his top.
"And the rest," said the guy on the floor.
Ben ignored him and began collecting glasses and plates. When the cab arrived, Ben pushed the stragglers out the door.
"Come too," said one of them, running his fingertips messily down Ben's front. "I want to fuck you."
"You go and fuck each other and have a good time," said Ben, pushing them once more and then slamming the door behind them.
He walked back into the living room, tidied up the chairs, cleared the last of the tables of food and drink, opened the top of the sash window to let in some air and shrugged his shirt back on. He felt a wave of exhaustion. His phone said two o'clock. He sank back onto the sofa and closed his eyes.
The living room door creaked. Harry stood on the threshold, completely naked. "Sorry," he said. "I thought the place was empty. I just came down to find some wine."
"No; my fault," said Ben, standing up. "I kicked everyone out and then just sat down for a few minutes. I'll be off now."
"Harry? Who are you talking to?" came Bill's voice from upstairs.
Ben looked at Harry who, after a half-hearted attempt to cover himself up had decided not to bother, and smiled. He looked good.
"I guess it worked out, then."

"It did. Thank you," Harry replied. "And thank you for clearing up; that was beyond the call of duty."
"It was that or strip poker."
Harry leant forward and hugged him. Ben smelt sweat, alcohol and an overpowering aroma of sex. He withdrew as gracefully as he could. "Sorry you and Patrick didn't work out," he said. "But you're welcome here anytime. I won't say your little bombshell was comfortable, but it achieved the desired result. Thank you."
Ben nodded and shook the proffered hand. Fully dressed, sober and far from post-coital, he buttoned his shirt, picked up his jacket and walked into the night. It was not the New Year's Eve he had been expecting or even wanted, but it was a night he was glad he'd been at and one he knew he would remember.

CHAPTER EIGHT

Back at the LSE for the Spring term, Ben focused on his work and job interviews. He accepted all party invitations and was charming while there, but it was tiring, increasingly stressful and yielded diminishing returns. The combination of the need to look fresh for his interviews and his continued swimming obligations meant he rarely drank and he felt left out at parties, detached from the heart of the revelry. He was increasingly 'Hail, fellow, well met', but no more and the evenings were difficult and tedious. The music was always loud and the laughter raucous and he found himself increasingly a wallflower, engaging only when engaged, and edging closer and closer to the drinks table.

Whether it was a straight party or a gay one, everyone seemed to fall into one of two camps – either they were long paired up or not looking to do anything more than just get laid. Marco was never there, the LSE's walls too narrow now for his ambitions, as he continued to indulge himself and work his way through the United Nations. Ben was simultaneously jealous and contemptuous while Patrick insisted on sending him regular bulletins on how well it was going with Mahesh, even though Ben had told him and then begged him to stop. Then, in early March and after Patrick had texted him to tell him he'd just had dinner with Mahesh's family for the first time, he knocked back three Tequilas in a row and beat his customary silent retreat as the party reached its climax.

A few weeks later and with his alcohol intake up to six large cans of beer on Fridays and the same on Saturdays, he got the offer he had been waiting for, a place at Braithwaites, the PR firm where he had interned the summer before, whose executives had been so friendly at his party. The offer was conditional only on him getting a 2:1 equivalent degree or better and his work was easily good enough for that. It was a relief. The lease on the flat was pushing him into debt, he'd taken out a student loan which he'd probably need to increase before the end of the summer, too proud and ashamed to ask his father for help. But the letter with his offer, the best thing to happen to him in as long as he could remember, came the same morning as a text from Patrick informing him that he was so in love with Mahesh he wanted to marry him and asking if it was too soon to tell him. This time, Ben did throw the phone at the wall, although mercifully it didn't break, he really did now lack the money to replace it. He sighed as he crouched and picked it up. "Too soon," he replied.

Two days later was the last big swimming competition of the year. Nothing would distract him. If he couldn't find a boyfriend, at least he could swim. He threw himself into the races with angry, furious, determination. He fucked the shit out of the water, the way he wanted to fuck the shit out of that smug, deliriously happy Patrick. But he only won silver in the 400m butterfly and bronze in the 400m freestyle.

The team went to the pub. Ben was tired and it wasn't just the racing. He had let himself down, he always seemed to lose what really mattered. It was time to stop being the nice guy, the one who always did everything everyone wanted, the smiling face at the parties. He had a job and Matt from the swim team had asked him to share a flat in the autumn and that felt good, but tonight Ben decided to get drunk, seriously stinking drunk. Gin, beer, Tequila, more beer, more gin, maybe some Bailey's. When the team said they wanted to go to a girlie bar, Ben even went along. But the sight of the girls, topless in their skimpy knickers, made him horny even as they turned him off. Maybe it was his horny team mates. He downed his double gin & tonic and ducked out while the others were absorbed with trying to get the girls out of their pants without buying two bottles of over-priced whisky.
He stumbled up the stairs to the street and stretched his arm to steady himself against the wall. His head stopped spinning and he pulled out the water bottle he always carried, sipped, spat and then drained it. Feeling a wave of nausea, he squatted and took twenty deep breaths. But he knew what he had to do. He hailed a cab and gave an address south of the river, somewhere he had heard of but never tried, a place where he knew there was little chance of meeting anyone he knew, least of all Marco.

At the sauna, he downed two more bottles of water before stripping and stepping into the plunge pool, a bottle of beer for comfort. He pissed into the warm water, tonight he didn't care. Then he ogled the men who passed him, not caring if they found him rude or that he was showing an erection that was becoming more painful the longer he sat and failed to act. Outside the swimming pool changing rooms, the last naked man he'd seen was Harry thanking him at New Year and – God help him – Patrick at Christmas, and neither of those really counted.

Two men stood next to the pool, obviously negotiating. They were about the same age, late twenties, both good looking with nice muscle definition, one white, the other chocolately-brown. Ben stared and the darker man, mixed-race white and black with short, tightly-curled African hair and a European nose and lips, glanced over. Ben smiled and then winked, before taking a swig of his beer. The man looked away and then back. Ben lifted his feet from the floor and floated on his back so that his erection poked above the water. The man laughed and the white man turned to see. He scowled. Ben turned, lifted himself effortlessly from the pool, and walked towards them, still very hard. The two men stared, but Ben focused on the black man.

"Hi," he said. "I'm Ben." He put his palm to the man's cheek and kissed him, pushing his lips and mouth open. "You ready?"

"Warren," said the man. "And always."

"Good," said Ben, taking his hand and pulling it down onto his dick. "You can play warren for this tonight. Let's go."

"Hey!" shouted the white man.

"Hey to you," Ben shouted back. "Too late."

It was more bravado than he had shown before and he was heartened to hear Warren laugh, but, still drunk and cresting a wave, he felt sure of himself. Warren was excitingly different, slim but muscular, tall and self-assured, a broad back and narrow waist, V-shaped chest. A real man. In fact, Ben realised, just like him. The thought made him smile. And that black skin and hint of African in his features, Warren was exotic and intoxicating, new, fresh, different. He ran his fingers over Warren's naked arse and Warren just slapped his own. In an empty room, Ben pushed Warren against a wall, clasped his hard dick, stroked it as he kissed him, ran his fingers over his balls and between Warren's legs.
"I go next," said Warren.
"We'll see," said Ben, unable to think as Warren picked up lube and condoms and splayed his legs. When he'd been stimulated enough, Warren unfurled the condom and put it on Ben, such a turn-on.
"Turn around," Ben said. Warren complied and took him easily, just a slight grunt. He had a dimple between his shoulder blades, the way Marco had had. The sight of it between the rippling shoulders of Warren's raised arms sent Ben wild. He leant in and kissed it before running his tongue across those taut shoulder blades, tasting the man's fresh sweat. He fucked harder, pulling his hip closer as he jerked him off.
"Jeez," wheezed Warren, his face pinned sideways against the wall. "If you want to fuck my throat, come in the other way."

Ben ignored him. He lost control, releasing Warren's dick to grasp his shoulder and thrust until he came. Warren tried to lower his arm and Ben put it back up; this was his moment and his alone. As Warren, frustrated at the lack of relief, said, 'I'm gonna fuck you for this," he released over six months' pent-up tension, lust, anger, aggression and resentment into Warren. When he'd finished, he sagged against Warren's back, panting as sweat dribbled down his cheek, and slid out.
"Been a while, has it?" said Warren, chuckling and then added angrily, "Did you come in me?"
"A mark of respect," said Ben, pleased with himself. He nearly always came inside Marco. Jerking off the final strokes over him always just seemed such a waste, and by then Marco had always come anyway and liked the post-orgasmic internal rub-down.
"Respect? My arse." Ben giggled and Warren shook his head and pushed him backwards. "What the fuck? Oh, just get on the bed."
Ben was exhausted, drained, relaxed, almost catatonic. Part of him wanted to pass out, but the rest was ready to drink in the sight of the man before him, over him, a little hairiness but so firm, the six-pack coming and going as he breathed. He lay back and Warren lubed him and prised him open. Ben saw determination as a stab of pain tore through Ben. He winced and gritted his teeth against the cry.
"You're tight," said Warren, growling at being denied entry. "Relax or it'll serve you right if you're hurt. You done this before?"
"Once," wheezed Ben.

"I suppose I should be honoured," replied Warren. "Though it helps you're completely plastered. Don't shit on my dick." He lent forward and Ben felt the circular pressure, the unnatural stretch, continuous pain, the strange fullness. And then, for the first time since Tommy Rutledge, a man was fucking him. It hurt, fuck it hurt, Ben had forgotten how much, but it also felt good, easy. And tonight it felt right too. Just surrender; let it happen. He deserved it, deserved to be fucked. A silver and a bronze, he was a loser. Come in him and toss him away, a receptacle to end up in the receptacle. He'd pulled a real man, so much hotter than he deserved, beautiful and powerful.
But he hadn't felt like a receptacle with Tommy. No, then he'd been valued, a winner, victorious, justified. He relaxed and opened his eyes. Warren's chest rippled, his nipples were small and dark like chocolate buttons. There were a few tight curls of hair on his pecs, with a line of sweat running down the centre of his chest. Ben bent his head up to see Warren's belly button, neat, with the hair descending into his crotch. This was the best-looking man he'd ever been with. He could fall in love with that chest, those nipples, the brush of stubble on his cheeks and abdomen. He caught Warren's eyes, felt something inside him, bucked and gasped. Warren grinned and his eyes misted over as he went faster. "You like it, Mummy's Boy?" he said. "Go on, take it then, take my thick black dick you filthy little white boy animal!"

The breaker picked Ben up, raising his back from the bed and then the wave crashed him down. He couldn't stop this guy if he wanted to. Tommy had never done that, never abused him. Tommy had been pure, their time together as innocent as it was sincere, a schoolboy crush, but love all the same. He had loved the sight of Tommy read grace before tea, the Latin slipping fluently from his perfect lips, and as he scored the winning goal, mud splattering his thick thighs and ruddy cheeks. Tommy, for all that he was straight, for all that he lived in Oxford now with his girlfriend, a junior Classics master at one of the prep schools there, had taken the time with him, had loved him gently and urgently, had kissed him so tenderly, made him feel so warm, so special, treasured. He wished Tommy was here again, now, in this place, his strong arms enveloping him. Not under a powerful black man who knew his power, revelled in his dominance as he rammed into him.
"I love you, Tommy!" he shouted and then bucked again. He sobbed and spittle bubbled on his lips. A tear ran down his face into the nape of his neck.
"Christ!" sneered Warren. "What the fuck's wrong with you? Thank fuck I'm nearly done." He withdrew, tore off the condom and in a few strokes came. He was a thrower and the sight of the ejaculation was as erotic as it was disgusting. Streaks hit Ben's cheek, chin, neck, pecs, chest. Come on his chin; it was dirty, sordid, new and unpleasant, like being pissed on from a great height. He lay back, his arms hanging off the table, his stomach heaving, crying at his humiliated and pleasure.
"Give me your number," he whispered.
"Are you fucking kidding me?"
"At least kiss me."

"Get Tommy to fucking kiss you."
And Warren was gone. Ben curled up into a ball, wishing so much that Tommy would indeed walk in and pull him into that backwards embrace, that spooning, that he had done that one time. He had done it for Marco so many times, but never Marco for him. He shuddered dry tears and realised he was hard. Warren! Magnificent, perfect, utterly degrading! As he thought of it, he pulled himself off and came again, pulsing like a star, hating that he loved it, the best and worst sexual experience of his life. Warren's body, his experience, his self-confidence. And Tommy's loving-kindness, his gentleness, his consideration. That was what he needed. Oh God, did he need it! He slunk home, no longer beloieving in himself.

CHAPTER NINE

After his drunken evening in the sauna with Warren, Ben was happy to spend a quiet Easter at Tom's. There were long crisp walks in a countryside still shaded with winter, bare trees, wet ground, the few late daffodils the only colour as young lambs sloshed in muddy fields. Tom had a girlfriend now, Caroline, whose father was almost as rich as Tom. Although it was a relationship dictated by thought for future generations, a sort-of self-arranged marriage, it worked. Caroline was lovely, funny and kind, an English graduate a year above Tom at Cambridge with a side-line in estate management. She had blue eyes and a fresh English face never tainted by make-up, dusted by a few freckles laid there by a designer. She wore her father's torn brown jerseys with the same panache she wore hand-made ball gowns. Tom was obviously smitten; he had lost weight and never looked better. Better still, Caroline seemed just as keen on him. Ben looked at them over the long wooden kitchen table – even their kitchen was a work of art, airy, warm, homely, and wondered if he'd ever felt so alone. He drank steadily, at least a bottle every night, although the quality of the vintages limited his hangovers to just a generalised tiredness. Tom and Caroline said nothing and he was glad of that.

But back in his lonely flat, for all he had his things around him, the bottles began to flow increasingly freely. They littered the floor until he cleared them away once a week on bin day. The number of bottles soon meant he deliberately stopped counting and the vintages were nothing on Tom's. It became normal to wake up dazed in his hangover, something a greasy full English only cured at the cost of near-catatonia until after lunch.

In late April, Patrick stopped texting and made it worse by actually calling. "I couldn't just leave it to a text! Mahesh told me he loved me last night! You were right telling me not to rush it! You should have seen him! So nervous! So unsure! So…incredibly, unbelievably romantic! I couldn't breathe! I've never felt like this before! Oh God, I get hard just thinking about it – and we made love three times last night. Made love! Oh Ben! I've never been this happy!"

Ben drank two bottles that night, one of them Campari. Something told him to keep his essays clean and he managed it by working in the afternoons and evenings until he had finished, but after that it was wine, sometimes vodka, something he'd never tried until recently. He let his laundry pile up until there were no more clean clothes and then washed the lot in one go, no longer ironing anything, just letting it drip dry. He wore T-shirts and sweatpants.

He had stopped shaving his armpits after the last swim meet and then stopped shaving his chest. Then he stopped shaving his face and woke one morning in May to find he had a full beard. He told himself that it was a student thing, bohemian, and decided to keep it. He had enough self-respect to shower every lunchtime when he woke up and even clipped his beard as it thickened, but it didn't stop some self-righteous old bat who was seventy if she was a day muttering under her breath "You stink" as he passed her in the supermarket. The last swim meet long over, he had also long since stopped exercising in the pool, using the free time to eat a large bag of crisps as he read his way through his book list.

Nevertheless, despite the abuse, despite the ending of the party invitations and the shrill criticisms of Daisy and the weekly love bulletins from Patrick – they had been to Venice for a long weekend. Mahesh had bought him a little gold cross on a chain which he wore round his neck and which Mahesh would kiss as he fucked him, making his throat tickle until he was giggling. Was there any place better than Venice? – he continued to study in the late afternoons and early evenings. As June and finals rolled round, he had to deal with headaches that he knew had nothing to do with alcohol. In fact, alcohol was the only thing that could disperse them. Sometimes they were so bad that he wanted to cry, but he pressed on; it was his way of saying 'fuck you' to the world.

Finals arrived and he somehow sobered up for a few days and remembered what he'd read and been taught. He half hoped he'd fail, but a week later he heard the result: a borderline 2A/First. It went to committee, who confirmed the First based on his past three years' coursework, another unsatisfying photo finish. He had let himself down, even if his place at Braithwaites' was assured. Daisy jumped up and down, hugged him and then recoiled in shock. Trying to recover, she asked him to share a flat with her when they both started work, but then looked as if she regretted it.

It was five days before he called his parents, who were predictably and irritatingly thrilled. On the second call-back from his father, he finally promised to come down to see them, for the first time since Christmas. Tony was dragged down too and swore at Ben for forcing him to suffer a celebration that should have been entirely unnecessary.

"You're all set now," said their father, shaking Ben's hand and seeming determined to ignore the beard and sweatpants. "I'll take you to my tailor and get you two new suits to start you on your way."

"And some shirts and new shoes," added his mother, pouring some tea.

"Maybe in August," said Tony.

Their parents looked surprised, but then Tony took Ben aside, grabbing his elbow firmly in his wrist. "What the fuck's happened to you? What's this crap you're wearing and what's that thing on your face? You shave your fucking armpits! This isn't you, only the first is you, although God knows how you got it. And how much do you weigh?"

Ben had no idea and Tony dragged him up the narrow wooden staircase to their parents' bathroom. There was a set of old scales, Imperial measures only.
"Stand on it!"
"I don't want to."
"Just fucking do it!"
Thirteen stone, twelve pounds. Ben did the calculation, eighty-eight kilos. Ben hadn't weighed more than seventy-five kilos in as long as he could remember and normally less. The sight of the numbers crushed him.
"What the fuck's wrong with you? And how much do you drink? It's three o'clock in the afternoon and you reek of the stuff!"
"It's Marco. And Tommy. And Patrick. And Warren; he was beautiful, perfect. Two bottles a night."
Tony slammed his hand against the wall. "I know you're still cut up about Marco," he said. "But this is beyond ridiculous. Who the fuck are Patrick and Warren? No, I don't want to know."
Ben shrugged. "What would you know? You've been with Estelle so long I think you were born attached to her teat. University sweethearts who never had to worry about being cheated on or punched or abused during sex! Don't mind me; you just toddle off and get married and spawn a dozen beautiful sprogs."
"Oh, fuck you, Ben! If you weren't my brother, I'd smash your face in, you self-righteous little fuck. You're going on holiday! What's that place gay people go to? That island in Greece?"
Ben actually laughed, surprised Tony even knew. "Mykonos."

"Right. Mykonos. You go there. Get laid. Sun, sand, sea and sex –and lots of feta salads and absolutely no retsina. I've never seen you so pasty-faced, so drawn. You go there, shed your load again and again and then come back sane! And for the love of God, lose that fucking beard!"
"It makes me look like a student."
"Well, you're not a student anymore. You're a PR consultant. And it makes you look like a twat." Spittle shot from his mouth and the harshness of it calmed them both. Ben even managed a tentative smile.
"Look," said Tony, putting his hand on Ben's shoulder. "I'm your brother, your older brother. That makes it my job, and my right, to tell you: you're completely off the rails. I don't know exactly what happened, but I suspect it doesn't matter. Go to Mykonos and recover your dignity and self-respect."
Ben sat down on the side of the bath. "I can't go to Mykonos. Not looking like this? They'd just laugh at me. And quite right. Fourteen stone, Tony, fourteen! I've never weighed more than eleven and a half! I can't look myself in the mirror. I'm turning into an alcoholic. I get these terrible headaches, really really bad so I can barely think. And Marco never really loved me, just wanted an English boyfriend."
Tony crouched down and hugged him. Ben sobbed into his shoulder. "I have an idea," said Tony eventually. "Positano. Estelle and I went there two years ago, in the off-season. It's beautiful, beyond beautiful, and so restful. I'll book you in for three weeks and pay for it myself if the parents won't."
Ben clutched Tony, digging long nails into his back, nails he hadn't cut in months. Even the cuticles had become long.

But the parents did pay and two days later he was in Positano, on a clifftop in a vast airy white room, white walls surrounding a white double bed, rich quilts over a cast-iron frame and billowing white curtains leading onto a small wrought-iron balcony. He stood for a moment against the railings, half wanting to topple over them, and saw the grey expanse of the beach and the turquoise of the Mediterranean. Only a few perfectly white clouds drifted between him and the sun-dappled heaven, but they were enough to cut him off from his happiness. It was four o'clock in the afternoon, but he turned, stripped to his underwear and slid under the covers of the bed.

He woke at ten the next morning. He had missed breakfast. He missed breakfast five days in a row, passing out at nine and waking at ten the next day. No alcohol involved. Just exhaustion, mental and physical. He did nothing but come down at twelve for a chicken salad and then again at seven for soup and bread. What he did for the rest of the time, he couldn't have said. Just sat on the balcony, watched the lapping of the sea and listened to the rustle of the insinuating breeze.

He had brought two things with him, an old copy of Pride and Prejudice, his favourite book, and the iPod Marco had given him their first Christmas together. When he woke the sixth morning and realised his headache had finally gone, he picked up the book and walked down to breakfast, only cereal and orange juice, but he felt much better. He went back to his room, picked up his towel and walked down the steep stone steps to the beach. He baked all day, reading a princely twenty pages of his book. He enjoyed the sensation of the sun caressing him and the sound of the breakers gently soothing the smooth pebbles of the beach. He missed lunch but didn't mind. He climbed the steps, feeling every one and panting as he reached the top, and located a dispensary with clippers, razors and shaving cream. For the rest of the afternoon, he carefully pruned and then scraped his face clean. It took a surprisingly long time.

And then the shakes began. After almost a week when he couldn't stay awake, suddenly he couldn't sleep. He tossed, turned, clutched the pillow, tossed himself off and dozed, dreaming of Marco, Patrick and Tommy, all of them so happy, so fulfilled, Warren even with his cocky self-assurance. And then he woke in the morning shivering despite the heat of the morning sun, his sheets sodden and not in a good way. Each day, he would sluice himself in the hottest shower he could bear before heading back to the beach to bake his brains again. The sheets were changed daily, blessedly clean and dry when he returned, crisp, fresh, smelling of morning dew, but the sweats lasted another week days. When he awoke one morning and the fever, whatever it was, had finally passed, he looked at himself in the mirror and saw a thinner man. There was a set of scales in the bathroom and, tentatively, fearfully, he stepped onto them. Eighty-five kilos. He took heart and scraped away two days of growth from his face.
He had another chicken salad in the large, empty, airy but gloomy, old, restaurant and then went back to his room and decided to start with some easy Pilates Fives exercises. He struggled through one set and then his stomach rebelled. He turned over and tried press-ups. A dozen and then his arms gave way. He could do four consecutive sets of Pilates Fives mixed with three sets of burpees followed by twelve chin-ups without even thinking about it six months ago, more if he had to. There was a ledge above the bathroom door and he tried to pull himself up. He couldn't even manage one and struggled to find a footing as his hands slipped. He sat crossed-legged and breathed heavily to regain his composure.

But it was getting easier to climb the steps from the beach. He found a skipping rope in a forlorn shop down a dirt-strewn backstreet and for the third week, he skipped and did his reps. He ran down the beach at dawn. He even read forty pages of Pride and Prejudice a day. Slowly, some of it was coming back. Only the sea was an admonition. He had been here three weeks, but he hadn't been into the sensuous, demanding, loving, forgiving, water. Its soft perfection beckoned but still he resisted. He ate almost nothing, he wasn't hungry, and the scales at the end of the third week said eighty-four kilos. He could do two and a half sets of Pilates Fives and one and a half series of press-ups, nearly three hundred skips, although he was exhausted afterwards and the pull-ups were still beyond him. Each night, he was asleep by nine, waking at seven and those nights were filled with dreams of Tommy, the classics scholar. Tommy would have loved it here, quoting Pliny on the eruption of Mount Vesuvius, reciting love poems by Ovid and Catullus. Yes, Catullus was the right poet for here, devoted to a lover defined by her infidelity.

As the third week ended, he used the last of his student loan credit limit to extend his stay for a fourth. Finally rested and ready at last to enjoy this place, he stole out that night and tottered down to the pebbly beach. The moon was setting and lit the shoreline, sparkling on the gentle breakers. He lay on his back, the stones still warm, and gazed up at the darkening night sky. The constellations emerged, the Great and Little Bears, Cassiopeia, Pegasus, the smear of the Milky Way. He wished he could see Orion, but that was a winter constellation. He had brought Marco's iPod and put in the earphones. It didn't have much on it, still only the Kylie Minogue, Madonna, Robbie Williams and The Cure he had originally bought for it, but he pressed play and looked up. It was Tommy that like The Cure and he listened to Kyoto Song twice, but it wasn't what he was looking for tonight.
He scrolled through to On a Night Like This. It was pretty gay, but then so was he and he listened to it twice as well. As his mood lightened, he sat up and hugged his knees, looked along the beach and then back at the village on the clifftop. It was a special place, such a pity three weeks had been wasted. He hadn't even been to Capri, put off by stories of the prices. But you could fall in love in a place like this. Maybe he could bring someone here one day, someone with the purity of Tommy and the physique of Warren. It seemed unlikely, but he had to have hope. No need to go to Mykonos, surely, pretty as it undoubtedly was.

He flipped back through the iPod and found Millennium. That was a song he'd always liked, its strong leisurely beat. Fallen from grace, it was time to rise like a phoenix. It was time to add to his iPod collection as well, another development arrested by Marco. He ran up the steps to his hotel and then his bedroom two at a time. Before he went to sleep, he texted Daisy. "Still want to share that flat?"
"Only if you lose the beard and stop drinking."
"Already done."
"Then, I'd love to."
The next morning, he went swimming. He also went out to a restaurant for the first time. He swam morning and evening and ate out for lunch and dinner. For six days, he was in post-coital bliss, his mistress the water caressing him, soothing him, welcoming him back into her wetness and pleasing him as he moved through her. The workout routine was mostly back, although very few of the pull-ups; he was still too heavy. He was eating more but the weight falling off. Just under eighty-two kilos; the last few months began to fade into one of those bad dreams, a nightmare certainly, but a phantasm that no longer had the power to terrify and destroy. In the evenings, he wandered the cobbled streets with its painted walls and then someone waved at him.

Who the hell was that? The friendly face, eager if not over-eager, grinning like a clown was between two raised hands waving like windmills. Put together with thick, floppy, dark hair, a billowing white cotton shirt, bare legs that looked too thin over docksiders, it was like a performer at an ice spectacular. It was a man, obviously local, standing beside the table of a bar. But Ben didn't know any locals. He didn't know anyone. And yet there came his name.
"Ben. Ben Connelly."
Ben stopped and squinted into the gloom as he walked over. The man's gesticulations faded but his grin broadened, a gleam of hope lightening the air around him. Ben saw what this man wanted and decided he didn't mind. Perhaps it too would be cleansing. Tony had told him to 'shed his load' and really masturbation wasn't as much fun as it was cracked up to be.
The man was squirming in his seat, it was embarrassing to see. Then he jumped up and clasped Ben's hand, squeaking like a finger on a tooth in his anticipation.
"Hi," he said. "Me Giovanni. Oh, I want to say that many days! You Ben, Ben Connelly. I see your name on credit card and remember. How they say in America? 'Hi. Me Giovanni and I your waiter today.' How I want to say that! But is not Italian way. They criticise. But you not American. You English. I see name of your bank."

Boy, this would be easy. Ben felt bad for the man. He had served Ben his lunch for almost a week and Ben hadn't even noticed. He wondered if he'd tipped properly. Clearly he was still in much more of a mess than he'd had any idea. He always noticed gay men, checked them out by himself or even more with Marco, commenting lasciviously or acidly, comparing notes. Their tastes never coincided, another sign.

"I buy you drink? Welcome you in Italy? Red wine very good, very cheap if you with Italian. Or beer? Peroni? Is only couples here, honeymooners. Now a single guy."

And Ben knew what he did want. Not a slow comfortable screw or sex on the beach. He wanted a kiss. A long, passionate, silent, deep kiss. A loving kiss that was reciprocated, even if actual love would have to wait. He wanted lips on his lips, a tongue on his tongue. Not on his neck, nipples, abdomen or cock. Just on his lips, in his mouth, all that he had missed for so long, everything that Patrick had hinted at and Marco denied. He looked at Giovanni, how a continuous ripple ran thorough him from his head, shoulders and chest to his waist and legs. This was no Warren, would there ever be another, but he also wasn't Patrick and he was more than adequate for the task at hand. And he might surprise Ben. He had, after all, taken a risk accosting a customer. Ben knew he had to act, he was yet to speak while Giovanni was about to combust.

He twisted his handshake to hold it like lovers do and yanked Giovanni, who yelped in surprise and then looked pleased, towards him. "No," he said. "Show me around, please. I'm sure you know a lot of interesting places to go."

Giovanni squeaked, but managed "You follow me", swinging Ben's hand in his in a way that Ben liked. It was a long time since someone had held his hand properly and he caressed the top of Giovanni's with his thumb, causing Giovanni to lose the thread of whatever it was he was saying before starting up again. Ben wasn't listening anyway; it was just the nervous patter of an exhilarated man, full of history and statistics, his thick Italian accent with an odd spattering of American. Luckily, he didn't sound like Marco or Ben would have had to leave and he knew he didn't want to.
"And…here…here I live."
Ben looked up at the building, a white smooth-faced long eighteenth century building with a large wooden double door.
"It built..."
"Giovanni? Stop talking, please." He stepped forward. Noses, electricity, a gasp from Giovanni. A touch on the lips, parted. Giovanni put his arms over Ben's shoulders. Ben moved in further, a hand to the head another to the buttock, just what he wanted. Their crotches met. Giovanni gasped at the friction and intensified and Ben pulled him in. Yes, this was what he'd been missing, what he really wanted. To kiss, just to kiss, to feel the other's excitement, to feel his own reciprocated. And Giovanni's head was falling under Ben's own, giving it up willingly and readily, the breaths from his nose ragged. Ben wanted to do this all night, for the rest of his life. Giovanni showed his willingness to continue, but then he shuddered and pulled away, locking his forehead to Ben's, a nice sensation, and panted, breathless. He slid his hand down onto Ben's buttock, clasped it. "Jesus! I come! You very good kisser!"

Catholics shouldn't swear, but the words sang in Ben's ears. Praise. He'd got to kiss a man, after such a long, long, long time. And now praise! He laughed and, through his laboured breaths, Giovanni laughed too and it felt good. Really good. Ben looked up to the stars and they were singing too. It was better than sex.
"I clean up; then you really touch my dick."
Mention of dicks damaged the romance, the moonlight, the cobbles of the narrow street, the stately confidence of the old houses, the warm whispering breeze, the quiet purity and innocence of it all. And, apparently, his ability to kiss. But he wasn't far from coming himself and knew he needed it too, kisses and caresses that would finally get him off properly. "Or I see you at the restaurant tomorrow?"
Ben saw those soft, lonely, brown eyes seeking, yearning, searching for confirmation that he would not be abandoned tonight in a town of straight honeymooners. A new Giovanni appeared before Ben, faded, worn, used, and old, at least thirty-five, but Ben shook his head. A willing man was a privilege, especially after what he'd done to himself over the past few months. "Maybe now."
The years fell off Giovanni. He opened the door and led Ben upstairs to a very small flat, almost a garret, just a single bed, a small wooden table, an open-fronted cupboard with shirts on hangers, a sink, a hob with an old kettle on it, a shelf above both with mugs and plates, a mini-fridge sitting on the floor, a small open-fronted cubby-hole with shower and toilet. Giovanni was naked by the time Ben had shut the door, retreating towards his narrow wooden bed, hard and expectant. Ben needed to kiss him, stripped and was soon and finally arched over Giovanni doing just that.

And then he wasn't sure if he wanted the effluent, the titillation was what he really craved, the power he had over those inviting, surrendered lips, wet and warm. The permission to kiss relentlessly, touch anywhere he chose for as long as he chose, brooking and receiving no obstacle or objection, was what he had sought for so long.
But Giovanni did want the effluent. He ground and guided Ben's hands and head. He was teetering as Ben came back up and resumed the kissing, his grip on Ben increasingly unsteady, his lips fighting and losing, erotic. And that was suddenly and finally enough for both of them.
Three and a half months since the most exhilarating and degrading sex of his life, a year since his last true intimacy with Marco, Ben got to have a real orgasm. He shouted and his head span and Giovanni's hand still stroking him was all the invitation he needed to return to those moist, parted lips. He was still not sated, it had been too long, too lonely, and Giovanni saw that too and continued until he was, until they both were, the best thing about the evening so far, some true intimacy. They were both a mess, but with a cursory wipe of the sheet, they lay there. It was rest, peace. It was a stopping. Finally. Ben closed his eyes and slept.
Then he was awake, Giovanni stroking him, restless, muttering, guiding Ben's hands again. When he was satisfied he had Ben's attention, Giovanni reached under his bed and sheathed Ben. "Fuck me."

But Ben didn't want this, not now. Giovanni wanted to be controlled and satisfied, to lie there and have it happen to him front and back, but Ben didn't want to perform, his own needs were met. And Giovanni no longer wanted to be kissed; in his surrender, he was trying to take control. It was a mistake and rage surged in Ben. As he found entry, he thrust and Giovanni bucked and shouted, struggled and then acquiesced as Ben took him hard and fast, Giovanni fighting one hand free to bring himself off after Ben failed to take the hint. "You not nice," he said as Ben rolled off the condom. "We two people, not one. We make love, not war."
Warren's criticism. And from someone less secure.
"I'm sorry."
"Someone hurt you?"
"Yes."
"You tell me?"
"No, thank you."
"Maybe you go now. I think you good man, but you not nice now. You go, come back, learn. Maybe you get better, good one day."
Patrick's criticism. "I'm sorry."
Giovanni smiled, more than friendly this time, those lonely brown eyes still yearning for more. "Maybe tomorrow you better. You sleep now, then go."

And when he let Ben kiss him again, Ben knew he had to stay, repay the permission granted. Ben lay back and watched as Giovanni washed himself down and then made space as he lay down against him, murmured contently and fell asleep. The light from the bare bulb in the ceiling was harsh as Ben stared up at it. He no longer felt superior, proud and vain as Patrick had called him. Giovanni had been good for him, and good to him. Eventually, he also fell asleep.

He woke at first light. Giovanni was still asleep on his side. He no longer looked attractive, old, faded and dirty, but Ben knew he had at least one favour to return. He stimulated him until Giovanni rolled onto his back with his legs parted and brought each of them off in turn with Giovanni watching. "You good man; you give me good memory. Tonight, you make love to me, give me beautiful memory."

But tonight Ben would be back in Britain and said so as he washed himself down and dressed. "But thank you, and sorry."

"Is OK. Is enough, thank you also," said Giovanni as he consented to one last kiss. Ben left with his shirt hanging loose from his shoulders, unbuttoned, the soft, warm breeze tickling his nipples and ruffling the hairs of his chest hair. He didn't mind who saw this particular 6am walk of shame. It was a long time since it had all felt this good.

As he checked out, there was a message, messy cursive on a waiter's notepad. 'Sorry you go. Last night you give beautiful memory, last a long time. You very good kisser, better fucker when not angry. Giovanni.'

Ben smiled, it was a nice note, very nice, and very flattering. He crumpled the coarse paper and threw it into the cavernous, empty stone fireplace. Then, he bent down, picked it up, unfurled it, read it again, and threw it in the waste paper basket, where no one would read it after he had left.
He returned to Britain and his father's tailor who fondled both his groin and his backside. It was raining steadily, cold and blustery for all that it was August, and that seemed appropriate, but he didn't mind. He weighed just over eighty-one kilos.

CHAPTER TEN

He was back. It was a new beginning. No more LSE, no more beard and drinking, no more Marco. He was chastened and hoped he was wiser. It would be different this time, slower. For all he had mostly recovered his weight, he felt older, aged. He knew he would never be as ridiculously fit, as heedlessly energetic, as he had been before March and besides he had more than £12,000 of student loans to pay off. Now he would focus on work and purge, exorcise his demons, his residual longing for Marco, from his system through sheer application of will. No more bath houses. Only two friends from the LSE, Matt from the swimming team and Daisy, who simply wouldn't leave him alone, the sister he had never had. The three of them moved into a large high-ceilinged flat conversion of a nineteenth century house in West Kensington, where Daisy did most of the cooking and Matt most of the sleeping around. Ben contented himself with the cleaning. For the first few weeks, he and Matt would train at the local pool, but then Matt began to go out more and more.

"Got to put these muscles to use," he said one Thursday evening in late October when Ben berated him for missing their session. "Got to get laid, man, while I'm still young and capable. So much pussy out there waiting to be filled. You should try it rather than moping about like a wet rag. Hey, I'll even help you out, play your wingman, if you'll help me."

But Ben didn't want to play wingman to an increasingly erratic Matt. He saw shades of himself and many more shades of Marco in Matt's bed-hopping and wanted to put some distance between them. He wasn't the recluse he'd been that last year, but he would be slower, more controlled, get it right for once.

"Hey, I'll be your wing-woman, if you like," said Daisy as they sat at the kitchen table, staring at each other, after Matt had rushed out of the flat.

Ben laughed but shook his head. He was content for now, settled, focused on a new job, which had a startlingly steep learning curve. He would gently keep fit in the pool and go to bed early, refreshed for the rigours of work. He swam four nights a week and made a point of being in bed by eleven, even at weekends. In November, he had lunch with Patrick in a trendy but uncomfortable café bar, all chrome and glass and tables that were too small. Ben had been looking forward to it and Patrick did look good, more relaxed, his shoulders straight and pushed back, colour in his animated cheeks, but Patrick was too much, doing his level best to destroy Ben's new-found peace of mind and partially succeeding.

"You've put on a lot of weight."

It went downhill from there as Patrick followed that up with a remark that Mahesh was, in his opinion, the perfect weight, just under seventy-five kilos. His enthusiasm for all things Mahesh was wearing, tedious. Beyond enquiring in the middle of lunch whether Ben was seeing anyone and looking pleased when Ben said no, he didn't ask Ben a single question about himself. Throughout, Patrick played with the little cross on its gold chain round his neck that Mahesh had bought him in Venice and which Ben knew he was wont to kiss on occasion. Ben decided to drop the relationship for a while. He'd got his weight down to seventy-four kilos and then it had got stuck, six kilos over his fighting sixty-eight in March. He gradually resigned himself to the realisation that it would never go, that the extra weight, the best part of a stone according to his parents' antique scales, would be his penance, his forced remembrance for the mistakes he had made. He'd largely given up the butterfly stroke in exchange for the crawl and the pull-ups had never really come back, half a dozen pretty much his limit. And despite the ministrations of Giovanni, Ben's heart was still not healed, a pain that made him wince as Patrick talked on and on and on about Mahesh, his good taste, their trips together, how well his business was doing, how Patrick had for the first time penetrated a man at Mahesh's insistence, how it had only deepened their love and respect for each other, how they'd both been tested and were now making love without condoms, secure in the knowledge of each other's fidelity. No, Ben didn't want Patrick, but he wasn't ready for a relationship yet either. It came as a relief to him, and he thought to Daisy, when Matt announced just after New Year that he had met a girl called Rachel through his family over

Christmas and would be moving in with her.
"Nailed her twice a day ever since, and thrice on Sundays," he said, grinning manically.
Ben looked at Daisy and saw her silent sigh as she relaxed. Neither of them were getting any and neither of them needed to be reminded daily of that fact. Ben had invited her to join him at Tom's for New Year and they'd gone together.
"Strange turnaround in events," said Derek as they sat on the floor of Tom's drawing room, on that thirty-foot Persian rug in green and yellow and red, eating chocolate biscuits and Gentlemen's Relish on oatcakes, drinking China tea from china cups. "Did Ben tell you who he brought last year?"
But Ben had and Daisy rose to the occasion. She wasn't the natural that Patrick had been on a horse or the Twister mat, but she fitted in. And she knew more of the story about last year than any of Ben's schoolfriends and wasn't shy about telling it.
"I'm glad to hear someone's shaken some sense into him," snapped Alex's girlfriend Harriet, who clearly still hated Ben. "Serves him right that Patrick ended up with this Mahesh. Sounds like the right result all round. People who like you are a privilege, not a right."
That stung even if Ben knew it was true, had thought it about Giovanni. But his ears still burnt as he looked at Daisy for comfort. She smiled and put her hand on his knee, before leaning over and kissing him on the cheek.
"I like you, Ben," she said. "And Harriet, you're too hard on him. It was very sweet the way he loved Marco and what Marco did to him at the end was horrible, after two years and just before his birthday. I'm not surprised he's not fully over it."

As Harriet heard the full history from Daisy for the first time, she finally dropped most, but not all, of her previously uncompromising hostility.
"Thanks," said Ben later as they stood in the kitchen, Daisy making Beef Wellington in the vast green Aga and Ben tossing a salad on the large wooden-topped workbench with equally large wooden tongs.
"No problem," she said and kissed him again.
"What are we going to do about finding you a boyfriend?" he asked.
Daisy turned and Ben saw a smile in her eyes.
"What?" he said.
"I don't think you need to worry about me on that score."
"Why? Who have you found?"
"Chris, of course. I had a great time with him at your birthday and was really upset when he never called me."
That was surprising. Chris was handsome in his own way, reasonably tall, neither fat nor thin, with a good head of hair but he smoked too much, drank too much and had a tendency to sit up late playing computer games. Chris hadn't had a girlfriend in as long as Ben could remember, at best shy and at worst a complete introvert. Ben knew that, if he hadn't lived side by side with Chris since they were both thirteen, it was highly unlikely that they would have been friends. Chris only ever shown any animation when he was around close friends or was talking about his job, preferably both. But what now? Seeing Ben's incomprehension, Daisy laughed.
"Haven't you noticed he's been making doe-eyes at me for the last two days? And I haven't been much better. He's not getting away a second time."

"How can you stand the smell? If it's not the stale fags, it's the stale booze."
"Those can be fixed and you, sir, are not one to criticise as you well know. And underneath, there's a funny guy with a beautiful smile and a brain the size of London. He holds down a high-pressure job in the City and already makes four times what you ever will."
That was true.
"Well, just get him to wash and brush his teeth before you snog him."
And so, when New Year's Eve finally came round, Ben walked out of the dining room to get another bottle of wine from the kitchen and found Chris and Daisy kissing beneath the bend in the stairs. He tried to pass by unnoticed, but his footsteps were too loud on the bare flagged floor and they stopped, turned and saw him.
"Don't mind me," he said, raising his arm as he hurried past.
But it was too much for Chris' natural diffidence and, on his return from the kitchen, Ben found them back at the dining table, where they stayed with the others until three o'clock when they went to bed separately.
"Sorry I spoilt your party," said Ben the next morning as Daisy came into the dining room with a bowl of cereal. She smiled.
"It started with a kiss…" she sang and then added, "We've agreed to meet up again when we're both back in London. And I've got his phone number if he tries to back out."
So, when Matt announced he was leaving to move in with Rachel, Daisy stretched her hand across the table to cover Ben's.

"Let's ask Chris to move in," she said. "Please. Please, please, please!"

Chris moved in, on condition he not smoke in the flat. Since the flat was on the ground floor and came with a small patio at the back, Chris agreed. Daisy waited until he had been there a month and then jumped him, bursting into his room and taking all the initiative, and no noes, until Chris submitted, as it happened yielding up the flower of his innocence at the same time. After that, the late-night computer games stopped, the drinking declined markedly and Ben had to wait even longer to get in the shower in the evening, although the smoking still continued on the patio. Ben got used to seeing the other two holding hands in the kitchen or in front of the television, but found he didn't mind. A boyfriend for Daisy was long-deserved, while to see Chris this happy was to discover a new and quite unfamiliar person. The three of them ate out together on Friday nights and watched films together on Saturday evenings and Ben felt content.

"You need a boyfriend," said Daisy one evening.

But Ben shook his head. He was happy for now with his quiet life. It was a boon, having ready-made friends, and Chris was a vast improvement on Matt in that regard. Ben enjoyed the homely atmosphere, somewhere he felt safe and warm, he was still paying off his debts, and it was all a refuge from a job he was finding much harder than he'd expected.

There was so much to learn. It wasn't that he had bad bosses, although there were a few of them in the office. On the contrary, Sophie, who had just turned thirty and who always wore a trouser suit, blue or brown, over a white silk shirt, her hair and demeanour relaxed and open even though Ben knew she didn't have a boyfriend, was in many ways perfect. Her knowledge of the market was impeccable and she always took him along to meetings, even if he wasn't allowed to say anything except answer direct questions from her. Through her, Ben met all her contacts across the news media and with investment banks, law firms and accountants, anyone who could refer business to the firm. She was a newly promoted Account Executive and she was eager to prove her worth in her new position by building up as many new clients for the firm as possible. This meant that, as the months passed, more and more of the less important tasks were delegated to Ben, arranging lunches which he was allowed to attend, creating presentations for dissemination on Bloomberg. And then, finally, in April, some seven months after he'd joined, she stood up at her desk, opposite his in their open-plan office, staring at her BlackBerry, and said, "I need to go and see Curtis about his results. I won't be back until after six. Call Fred Manson at Reuters and tell him we need an interview with BlueTop this afternoon. They've increased their dividend or something."
Ben had met Fred Manson once, at a routine lunch that Sophie maintained with all her contacts, and had only ever spoken to the secretary of Roger Christie, the chief executive of BlueTop, a new client of Sophie's that she had brought in herself. This was his break, he realised, and he nodded.

"Got it. I'll email you when it's done."
Sophie gave him a quizzical look, as if just then realising what she'd done. But then she nodded and hurried away.
It took Ben half an hour and three call to get through to Manson, the first two times the secretary picked up and Ben knew he had to speak to the man himself. In the meantime, Ben used the short breaks between calls to check news about BlueTop. There was none at all in the financial press. He checked the stock exchange announcements feed and saw the company had indeed raised its dividend, by a half. Finally, he got through.
"Fred, it's Ben Connelly, from Sophie Landton's office. We've got an interesting little story for you, but you'll need to catch it today if you want it to stay fresh."
Ben could hear Manson wondering who the hell Ben Connelly was, but the man knew well enough who Sophie Landton was.
"Yes, of course, Ben. Nice to hear from you again. What's the story?"
Ben wondered. He knew who BlueTop were, they were one of Europe's largest manufacturers of plastic tops for bottles of drinks. He also knew they were also a perennial takeover target, which was why Sophie had been so keen to hook them as a client – lots of PR required. And then Ben saw the connection between the dividend increase and the endless takeover rumours, the 'angle', he realised and felt light-headed.
"The chief executive of BlueTop, Robert Christie, would like to talk to…"
"The bottle cap maker!"

"Sealants," said Ben, pleased he remembered the technical term. "Anyway, Mr Christie would like to explain how he is positioning the company for a secure independent future."
There was silence down the line. Ben wondered if it was whirs of thought cranking their way through Manson's journalistic mind, a scoop perhaps, or whether it was just a lack of interest. He felt himself closing in on the receiver. He couldn't stand it any longer.
"I called you first, Fred. You know the history of this company as well as I do; this could be very important."
"Fine," came the reply finally. "I've got half an hour at four o'clock."
"Thank you," said Ben as neutrally as he could. "I'll set up a conference call."
Only when he put the receiver down did he punch his arms in the air. A few people looked around, but he knew he still needed to set up the other end of the call. To his surprise and relief Christie's secretary confirmed that four o'clock was fine and then, to his utter consternation, Christie himself came on the line.
"I want to be prepared, Ben," he said and Ben noticed the use of his first name. "What did you tell him?"
"Only that you are positioning the company for a secure, independent future. I know you want to talk about the dividend increase. Perhaps you could frame it as a reward to your shareholders for their continued loyalty and support?"
At this, Christie actually laughed.
"Spot on, Ben. If this call goes well, make sure Sophie invites you to our next lunch together."
"Yes, sir."
"And you'll be on the call? In case I get into trouble."

"Of course, Mr Christie."
Me? On the call to save the day? The remark was as incredible as it was exhilarating, sending a frisson from his ears to his ankles. But the call didn't go badly. In fact it went better than Ben could have dared hope. Manson asked his questions and came away convinced that BlueTop was a badly maligned battler, sturdily fighting its corner and doing so well that it could offer an industry-leading dividend and still have adequate funds to invest and expand.
The article came out barely an hour later: 'Beating the blues – sealant maker rings in the next twenty years with aggressive plans'.
He emailed it immediately to Christie, copied to Sophie.
"Thanks, Ben. Well done," came another immediate reply from Christie.
And then the phones started ringing. Two of them were from Sophie, but each time he was on the phone already, the first time with the Telegraph, the second with the Daily Mail. It was only when he'd finished calls with each of them that he realised how closely he'd been listening to Christie speak. He quoted Christie back to the Telegraph reporter and then engaged in an identical Manson/Christie exchange with the Mail as to whether this was the 'last gasp of a desperate management team'.
He eventually spoke to Sophie shortly before seven when she got back to the office.
"What's been going on?"
He told her. She immediately called up the reporters at the Telegraph and the Mail, but they said the stories had already gone to bed, although each confirmed the articles were not hostile.

"I hope you've done the right thing. I never expected it to go beyond a couple of lines on Reuters."
Nor had Ben and he didn't sleep well that night, not helped by the sounds of Chris and Daisy coming from down the hall. And the traffic at all hours – did London never sleep? He was up with the dawn, miraculously the sun was shining even if it was still cold. He bought himself a latte just as the shop opened and all the newspapers.
"Royal Blue tops all expectations," said the Telegraph.
"Tip Top," said the Mail. "Dividend ensures twenty more glorious years!"
There was even a short paragraph in the Times which quoted some of the Reuters article.
Ben felt giddy and was the first in the office, copying all the articles and sending them to Christie. When Sophie came in, it was obvious she had seen the articles too. She was smiling.
"Good job, Ben," she said. It was the first time she had praised him, even if also the first time he had earned it. He grinned and slid down in his chair, allowing it to swivel.
Shortly before nine o'clock, Sophie called Christie.
"I've got Ben on the speakerphone," she said.
"Very well done," said Christie. "I'm glad I signed up with your firm, Sophie. This is the most publicity we've had for our results in three years. And well done, Ben. You were clearly listening to what I said to Manson by what I see in the Mail."
Ben grinned and then remember Christie couldn't see him.
"Yes, sir," he said. "Thank you."
"Oh, call me Roger. And Sophie, bring Ben along next time we meet up."

"Will do, Roger," she replied. "If you're pleased, then I'm pleased."

CHAPTER ELEVEN

After the praise from Christie at BlueTop, work didn't seem so hard any more. Ben had got to know three journalists in one afternoon and he spent the next few months trying to repeat the trick, with more or less success. Sophie had confidence in him and he began to have confidence in himself. After all, he reasoned one day after a particularly difficult but ultimately successful call to get Bloomberg to cover one of his client's results, if he could wrest a man like Warren away with the quip that he would have to be bottom and bring another to orgasm with just a kiss, how much harder could it be to get someone to write five hundred words about a share buy-back?

He went scuba diving in the Red Sea for a week, but got no action despite his lingering glances at the bronzed bodies beside him on the beach, a copy of Maurice open on the sand beside him. There were occasional glances at his own, but nothing definitive. Yusuf, very dark, very tall, very slim, brought him room service one night and fussed and dawdled until Ben caught his eye, stripped off his shirt and advanced on him. But Yusuf, despite a brief hiatus of hope, panicked and fled, never to be seen again. It was a disappointing end to a disappointing holiday, reading a disappointing book and swimming in disappointing coral, mostly bleached and with few fish. The Egyptians were rude and the Germans offensive.

When he got back that September, a year of work behind him, he was lonely and restless. He missed Giovanni's lips, he regretted the monumental fuck-up that was Warren, by far the best-looking man he'd ever been with. He still wanted Marco's arms around him in the night, their legs carelessly intertwined. He would have consented willingly to the dreaming spire of Tommy inside him again on warm, damp grass somewhere and actually looked him up on the net one night after he'd had too much to drink. Daisy and Chris were making far too much noise in the other room. He wanted the infuriating happiness that Patrick had somehow found, his updates still arriving when least wanted. Ben had told himself that the first year and possibly even the second would be about his career, but it was building now. What should he do?
"You need a boyfriend," said Daisy. "But now I've seen more of you, I agree with Patrick. Don't eat me, please – but don't rush it either. I see how you're still sublimating Marco through your work and, yes you are still just in the foothills of a very large mountain range in your career. But that doesn't mean you shouldn't go out more. You should – and it shouldn't be with just with me and Chris either. Go out and get laid. Hit the clubs and chalk up a few random scores; isn't that what being gay in your twenties is supposed to be about? Or get over yourself, call Patrick and let him introduce you to someone. It's your turn, as you well know, and it's been months. Get yourself readmitted to gay polite society and play that field, if it makes you feel safer."

Ben laughed, but the comment hurt. Daisy agreed with Patrick: that Ben was too screwed up to be eligible for a boyfriend. He knew he should get out and hook-up, but with Warren and the sauna in his mind, he actually texted Patrick. 'How about a coffee? It would be good to hear how you are.'
His phone rang an hour later. "A blast from the past! I thought you hated me! How are you?"
Ben shook his head. Every time he spoke to Patrick, the man's voice seemed to get deeper, more secure, more assured. He bit down the urge to hang up. "I'm fine. Busy at work, lots to learn. And I swim regularly; I just got back from Egypt."
"But single?"
"So, how are you? How are East Asian ceramics at the moment?"
"They're fine, booming in fact, Chinese money. But I'm guessing that's not why you texted. So yes, I'm still with Mahesh and never been happier, and Harry's still with Bill and they're even happier, if that were possible."
Ben sighed, hardly caring that Patrick heard. Daisy and Chris, Patrick and Mahesh, Harry and Bill. Three improbable relationships, six doomed hearts, all in some way fostered by him. But nothing for the bridesmaid. "I'm glad. Bill deserved Harry, even if Harry may not have deserved Bill," he said and then fell into silence.
"That was unusually deep for you," said Patrick.

Well, fuck you too! Ben took the phone from his ear and stared at it before hearing Patrick say, "Look, if you're not doing anything, why not come to a gallery evening Mahesh is hosting next month. It's not his usual stuff, but some contemporary fusion Anglo-Indian work by an artist from Birmingham. Very avant-garde. Harry and Bill will be there and you can meet Mahesh properly. It would be nice to see you again; we can have a chin-wag."
It was a better offer than another evening in front of the television, watching Daisy and Chris neck, although only marginally so if it involved a 'chin-wag' with a Patrick oozing smug contentment from every over-sized pore.
"Can I bring some friends?"
"A date?" said Patrick, his tone quickening.
Ben resisted the urge to hang up. "No, just my flatmates."
"Sure, why not? I'll tell Mahesh. Have they got money?"
"Chris has."
"What? Chris the schoolfriend? The chimney?"
"The same. He and my LSE friend Daisy are pretty much joined at the hip now and I'm definitely green and hairy."
"And ready to face the world again?"
This was why he didn't call Patrick, the carping older brother he didn't need. Tony did it much better. But he took a deep breath and swallowed his pride. How the tables had been turned between him and Patrick over the last couple of years! "I think so. Look, I'm sorry about before."
"Forget it, and come. And thank you. It'll be nice to see the new you. Very nice."

So, four Fridays later, Ben, Daisy and Chris descended from a cab in the gloom of an early winter evening. A hooked Victorian wrought iron streetlamp illuminated a quiet and immaculate side street off New Bond Street. The bright glass-fronted gallery looked warm and inviting. Inside, around and between the three dozen murmuring guests stood or hung what even Ben could tell were exquisite pieces, statues, sculptures and paintings. Patrick saw Ben immediately. He must have been waiting for him, taut, waiting to pounce. He was wearing a black roll-top cashmere sweater and Ben wondered what he'd done with the beret and paintbrush. But he was tanned and had finally put on some weight, although not nearly enough. He hugged Ben, waved airily at Daisy and Chris before ignoring them and then, no 'how are you?' or 'lovely to see you', pressed his hand into Ben's back and propelled him into the room. "Mahesh, my love, I don't think you met Ben properly that time at New Year."
And Ben finally saw how handsome Mahesh was. He'd liked what he'd seen that first time, but the man was a prize. Clearly not a fitness freak, he still had just the right amount of meat on his bones. His skin was tight and smooth over his cheeks and contrasted well with the crisp yellow shirt under his black woollen jacket. There were no frown lines or crows-feet on his face, although he must be in his late-thirties and his thick, waving black hair only had flecks of grey. He had a straight nose and a strong chin. His dark brown eyes were intelligent, enquiring, noticing, and he carried himself lightly as he focused on Ben. This was a man who had arrived and knew it but who was far too well-bred to let it show.

"All this stuff is gorgeous," said Ben, meaning it but floundering. It was nearly as crass as Patrick calling this man 'my love' in his place of work.
Mahesh stepped aside and only then did Ben notice that he had been talking to a woman as Patrick, rudely as it turned out, interrupted. The woman was dressed in a beautiful red and green silk sari, rich auburn hair piled up above a face that was paler than Mahesh's but still Indian, long golden earrings emphasising her neck. She was perhaps a few years younger than Mahesh. "Thank you," she said.
"This is Gita Macaulay," said Mahesh.
Ben frowned and then couldn't stop himself. He had two left feet and he inserted one into his mouth.
"Macaulay?"
"Anglo-Indian by name; Anglo-Indian by nature," she said.
"Well, I think your work is magnificent. Beautiful. I'm sorry I'm no connoisseur, but it seems a real fusion of East and West."
"The compliment of an amateur is often the most valuable of all," said Macaulay, her lips slightly parted, revealing very white teeth. "Have you heard of Gadara art?"
Ben frowned, trying not to cap 'amateur' with 'ignoramus'. His cheeks warmed and he noticed she was smiling. Was she flirting?
And then he realised he had heard of it. "Alexander the Great!" he said.

She laughed, her Adam's Apple bobbing as her eyes twinkled. "Very good! Gandhara was a Greek kingdom in Pakistan, set up by the soldiers of Alexander the Great. It produced beautiful syntheses of Greek and Indian art, Buddhas and Hindu deities who looked like Greek gods. There is a particularly fine collection in the Ashmolean. This exhibition is Gandhara art reimagined for the twenty-first century, a new synthesis of East and West, as I am myself." She closed her eyes and Ben saw how long her eyelashes were. A glance took in the room, the statues of the gods, Buddhas and animals, the architecture on the walls, and he understood and began to appreciate. As she reopened her eyes, she saw it and smiled.

"It's stupendous," he said. "Thank you. It's an honour to meet the artist who can create all this."

Macaulay nodded. "My pleasure, and a pleasure to meet you. Enjoy. And if you really enjoy, buy something."

It was disconcerting to be hit on by a woman, but he was still sorry to leave her. Mahesh led her to some other guests and Ben hurried over to Daisy and Chris. He was just beginning to explain the art, all three gawping at the prices, when a hand landed heavily on his shoulder. It was Harry, grinning wildly. Clearly he had had one too many of the champagne cocktails.

"There you are. Patrick said you were here. I can't believe you see me naked and then disappear for two fucking years. What the hell's been going on? What've you been doing with yourself?"

"Just passing my exams and then trying to get on top of my job."

"Well, come to New Year. We missed you last time. I hope you were thoroughly miserable."

"I was."

"Good. Probably with some ghastly straight people. Serves you right if you don't spend it where you belong. Give me your contacts and I'll send you the details." He kissed Ben on the lips. "I owe you. Your intervention was masterful, and unfortunately quite essential. Now you, still looking so beautiful by the way, I like the residual tan, need someone to return the favour. I'm hosting another singles evening, and you will be the prime meat on the block. I promise you won't see me naked, unless you choose to join me and Bill in a three-way. He still talks about you know."

Ben glanced at Daisy and Chris. Chris was suspicious, but Daisy was agog. Before Ben could do anything, she said, "I didn't realise Ben had done so much good. Please return the favour. He needs a boyfriend. Or at least a good, hard fuck!"

Ben flushed. He had never heard Daisy so crude. "I'm fine," he said. "Married to the job."

"Well, that's a crock of shit," said Harry. "As I said, it's a singles' night, although there's a few less now than before. It's every man for himself, but I'll try to steer someone your way."

He disappeared, although Bill came over a few minutes later and clutched Ben close to him, brushing his lips over Ben's cheek as he air-kissed him. Tight shirt, tight chest, tight waist; Ben experienced a frisson he hadn't felt since Marco. "Harry said you were still looking gorgeous and I can see it's true. Not fat at all. I'll see who I can find for you at New Year's. Hold in there; it's only a month away. You know you were my second choice, don't you?"

Yes, Ben knew. Very nearly happened too. Might happen again if he wasn't careful. And then Bill was gone as well. Ben was tired. He was also slightly drunk and definitely light-headed in the hot, crowded gallery. He found Daisy and Chris. Chris had bought a small statue of the Buddha dressed like Jesus Christ. There was even a small halo. It was very tasteful, and a snip at £3,000.
As they turned to leave, Ben saw Patrick and Mahesh holding hands. It looked fitting, another blending of East and West, old and new. He remembered them two years ago, holding hands as their foreheads touched, readying themselves for that first, tentative, kiss. He'd felt envious then and he felt envious now, but tonight he'd been hit on by three people and that dulled the pain, even if one of the hitters was a woman.
He decided to do something he rarely did. He clutched Patrick by the shoulders and hugged him. Then he turned to Mahesh and crushed the proffered hand into his abdomen, hugging him too. "Good show," he said, holding each of their hands. "Good evening. Great couple. You look beautiful together. Thank you."
Patrick beamed, true pleasure in his gleaming blue eyes. Mahesh looked shaken. "He's back!"
How would Patrick know? He'd only ever seen the damaged version. But tonight Ben was in too good a mood to mind Patrick being a dick. "See you at New Year?" he shot, Parthian-style.
"Wouldn't miss it," said Patrick and raised his hand in salute.

But, five weeks before Christmas, Ben decided he couldn't wait for New Year. The next Friday, surprised how nervous he was and making a conscious effort with his dress, trying to remember to smile, uncomfortable at all the eyes on him, he went to a bar. It was pretty much for the first time. He saw a Bill and decided to go for it. He was curious and it was a good place to start – solve the niggle in his mind, the gap in his repertoire, so to speak. The Bill allowed himself to be bought a drink, listened to Ben talk, appraised him and then offered him a ride home. Ben was excited, but the excitement didn't last long. In bed, this Bill substitute was almost completely non-responsive. Ben had to do all the work, the Bill-substitute clearly thought he was doing Ben a favour even as Ben eventually succeeded in bringing him off a couple of times. But it was when he admired himself in the mirror the second time that Ben gave up. He stopped being nice, satisfied himself and left, disappointed and feeling more fragile and vulnerable than ever.

It was three weeks before he tried again, deliberately lowering his sights almost as far as he could bear, eventually approaching a man in his late-forties with a grey, almost white, goatee who had been staring at him for half an hour. His name was David, but when Ben found he worked in another auction house and knew Patrick, he explained who he was and offered to leave. But David put his hand on Ben's arm, implored him not to, said he was just out of a fifteen-year relationship.

"I haven't got laid in three years. I promise I won't say anything to Patrick. I just want the affirmation."

Ben, dazed at the humble adulation, went back to his art-filled apartment. The sex was better than he'd hoped for, David was out of practise but perfectly experienced and overall it was far better than with the Bill substitute, even though the goatee scratched and the white hair above and below was off-putting. They talked over nice wine afterwards and David recommended Ben keep hooking-up. "Start next January. One a week, fifty in a year. Find out at least what you're looking for, even if you don't actually meet him. You're young; you have time, more than me."
It was good advice and they agreed to meet every few months to compare notes. "Just control that urge to roughness," he said. "When you meet your lover, he won't appreciate it. And the hook-ups talk too."
So, there it was again, the same criticism as Warren and Giovanni. He was still not cured. Ben promised to do so and David kissed him and thanked him. Pulling a twenty-three year-old in his condition was more than he'd ever dared hope. Ben saw it, but didn't mind, happy to see David again another day, and looked forward to New Year with Harry and Bill.

CHAPTER TWELVE

At Christmas that year, Daisy took Chris to meet her parents in Yorkshire and Tom invited them for another convivial year's end in Somerset, and Ben wondered if going to a singles party with Harry and Bill might be a mistake. In the end, he never got to find out. He travelled down to Dorset and, on Christmas Eve, Tony and Estelle announced their engagement. Ben knew he was trapped. He was delighted for them, of course he was, and sincerely, but it was so obvious it was imminent, it was not the surprise to him that it seemed to be to his parents.
He made an attempt to get away, "Do you think you really need me…" but his mother stamped her foot and then actually slapped him, with the power of a wet fish. "You Judas", while his father said, "You're a big disappointment to us sometimes, Ben. You spend much too much time in London." So he spent five days smiling after Estelle's parents caught the next flight from Cape Town, almost completely ignored by everyone.

Everyone toasted the couple and he watched them cuddle into each other, heard again and again the history of their developing love, how they'd split up three times but never managed more than a month apart. He listened to the sighs and 'aahs' as Tony told of that fateful week in Hermanus when he cashed in his life savings to fly to Cape Town and heal their most serious breach and almost got fired from his new job in the process, a story he'd heard before in unexpurgated version from Tony more than once.

Only Tony noticed. He asked what plans Ben had given up and told him to leave. But that just made it impossible. Estelle hugged him and said, "You'll find happiness too one day. I know it." Ben loved Estelle dearly, like the sister she was now to become, but it was the wrong remark and he went to his room.

Opportunities at Harry and Bill's were lost and he turned his mind to the nights he would have to spend in bars instead.

He met David again in early April. They compared notes and then went to bed together. David had shaved off his beard and dyed his hair. He still looked trim and had scored twice, pure casual sex. On top again, Ben made a conscious effort to restrain himself, but David still complained.

"It's not just what you do, it's how you look when you're doing it. You're like ice; it freezes the marrow to see. Please get out there and meet people, but please be gentle."

He heeded David's advice and when they met in early July, they both decided to stay in their clothes, enjoying the wine, the food, the company in a busy but hushed restaurant. David had scored another two times, better but not right. For their final meeting in October, David announced he had found someone, Julian.

"It's early days," he said. "But he's more my age, thirty-nine, and just out of a long-term relationship himself. And he's a bottom, or at least I think so. We haven't actually done anything yet."

Ben smiled and toasted David. "Good luck," he said. But he felt a sense of loss that surprised him. It seemed that even David, almost over the hill, could find someone and rebuild his life, while he was still stuck with the one night stands.

It wasn't that he wasn't getting laid. After their meeting in April, he raised his sights and set a few ground rules. No younger than twenty, no older than thirty. Never at his place. Always gone by three-thirty, whatever was still going on. No giving out of phone numbers or emails. Never mention his employer's name. Never the same man twice. Not too often at the same bars. Always say thank-you afterwards, which usually provoked a reaction, surprise, gratitude, another request for his number. Within that, as much variety as possible. Just chalk up the experience and see what he liked finally.

White, black, brown, yellow and all the combinations, a Black-Vietnamese for whom he expanded the age range slightly, even a Latino or two, although Ben found it hard to relax with them and it showed. Tall, short, big, lacy, once fat, hairy, smooth, butch, a couple of beards. He discovered he liked a light dusting of hairs, the last soft line of resistance before he could take what he wanted. He learnt to stop coming inside people; so much sexual desire but so fastidious, more fastidious than him, and saw how some people just got off on the sight of a man ejaculating. A taxi driver, a supermarket security guard, a hedge fund manager, a freelance journalist, a pizza delivery man, a radio producer, a biochemical engineer, a bond trader, a Tube driver, a foreign exchange dealer, a baker, a policeman, another policeman not nearly as good, an in-house lawyer, an entrepreneur, a construction worker, a computer programmer, a fashion designer, a pilot, a newsagent, a German teacher, a violinist, a synagogue convenor who said 'fuck' more and more as the evening progressed, a married man who lost his wedding ring at some stage during the evening.

He saw rooms from shared bedsits where room-mates pretended not to hear to airy loft apartments to new build riverfront studios to familiar Victorian conversions to Council tower blocks, a few hotels for those like him for whom home was off-limits. He saw collections of antique silver, second-hand books, Hello Kitty dolls, toby jugs, Star Wars figurines, dirty magazines. He discovered cock rings, nipple rings, belly rings, a Prince Albert, tongue studs, liking only the last of them. Neck-chains, chunky and flimsy, a little golden cross that he kissed, twisted material wristbands and silver ankle chains. There were tattoos, so much body art, on the upper arms, the shoulder blades, the nape of the neck, the small of the back, the calf, the big toe, the cheek of a buttock, the crack of an arse, an arrow pointing downwards. Beyond a star on a shoulder-bade, they did little for him.
He was offered coke, E, ice repeatedly, poppers, Special K, but only tried the coke and only once; he felt himself becoming boring. After Marco, he didn't like poppers and the only Special K he would ingest would be at the breakfast table. He upped it to two nights a week, Friday and Saturday, and then once to Thursday as well, but Sophie gave him an odd look on Friday morning and he dropped Thursdays. He dodged herpes, recognising the residual blotches at the last moment for what they were, and caught crabs, from the hedge fund manager who listened to Proust on an audio book as he cycled to work.

He slowed down, dropped Saturdays, became more fastidious and rediscovered Stoppard. There was a revival going on and he saw four plays in a row. He went to the National Portrait Gallery for the first time and then the Courtauld Collection and the Sir John Soane Museum. Once at a leather bar was enough; he didn't really have the gear or want it. He saw As You Like It at the Globe, Measure for Measure in Regent's Park, both with Daisy, and Prick Up Your Ears with Patrick in Sloane Square. He went to London Zoo, the Tate and the Tate Modern. He listened to Vivaldi at Kenwood House and went to Hampton Court Palace and Kew Gardens. And there were men in all these places too, a botanist, a contralto, gallery owners – a younger version of Mahesh who was indeed sweet – a sculptor, tourists whose hotels he filled.

And then there were the foreigners, a Polish electrician, a French investment banker, an Iraqi doctor, a Kenyan fitness instructor, an American management consultant, a Russian mini-garch's preening son, a Mexican beer distributor, a Bangladeshi cricketer, a Burmese refugee who sold car insurance and enunciated beautiful 1950s English, a Korean diplomat, a Thai pasta chef who wanted to open an Italian restaurant in Bangkok, a junior member of the Omani royal family with a yellow Lamborghini. After the Mahesh substitute, he went to Oxford to the Ashmolean to see the Gandhara statues and there was a post-graduate in Anglo-Saxon history writing his thesis on King Aethelstan, the only English king never to marry.

He went sailing on the Norfolk Broads, climbing in the Peak District. He hiked the Ridgeway, a free night courtesy of the hotelier in Wallingford. He went to the Lake District and found a Patrick wandering lonely as a cloud on the shores of Lake Windermere, very good with his tongue. He saw the Burrell Collection in Glasgow and met a red-headed steelworker, twenty-nine and a virgin who cried with relief both during and afterwards. Ben took care to be gentle with him and stayed an extra hour. He went to the Tate Liverpool and the Walker Art Gallery, took a ferry across the Mersey and a twenty year-old draper's assistant who fought him for control and then bit his neck as Ben went in, drawing blood.

There was one threesome, which was hot in its way but too much watching; it was like starring in your own porn movie. There was plenty of bad sex as well, biters, scratchers, premature ejaculators, more self-admirers, many attempts to stretch him unnecessarily, even an attempt to fist him. There was an attempt to do it unprotected, water sports even if delivered by Ben, someone who wanted to be thrashed like a naughty schoolboy, some more abuse of his race or background, although Ben learnt to differentiate between when it was being used as an aphrodisiac and when as genuine contempt.

But he was still alone and by October was tiring of the bed-hopping, even as he did indeed learn things. He read *A Tale of Two Cities, The Picture of Dorian Gray, Swann's Way, Brideshead Revisited* for the second time, *The Immoralist, Like People in History*. He knew a willing man was a privilege, but he felt increasingly like the willing man himself. He never got to kiss as much or for as long as he wanted to, surprisingly seldom in fact. He found someone rifling the business cards in his wallet when he should have been extracting condoms and left, the first time he'd done that. A few people tracked him down and left him voicemails at work, but he never returned them.

He continued to swim, Tuesdays, Wednesdays and Thursdays and even with the extra kilos, he rarely struck out. Pleasantly often, he enjoyed the luxury of choice, even if he made mistakes and even if, this year, he never allowed himself to go on a date with anyone except David. He spent most of his Saturdays alone, unless a chance encounter, and all of his Sundays. Monday nights were for his schoolfriends, usually dinner somewhere, sometimes a drink, or Tony and Estelle, who heard about his trips out of London and the plays, but little else until Tony took him aside.

"Have you met anyone?"

"Not yet."

"Tell me you're at least getting laid."

"A little."

"Good."

Despite trying not to go back to the same bars too often, he found he was acquiring a reputation, and nicknames. 'TBGB' didn't mean 'Tony Blair/Gordon Brown' but 'Thank-you and Good-bye'. 'ILATT' meant 'I leave at three-thirty'.

And then there was 'The Torpedo'. Partly it referred to his swimming, but mostly to that residual and still-unshaken roughness and coldness. When he struck out, he could see it was usually from fear of or distaste towards being sunk in the North Atlantic in winter. He saw it himself and was ashamed and surprised at how it persisted, but it did.

When he was particularly embarrassed with himself, he would choose next time someone who would want him to take the risk instead. Warren had been good and bad in this respect, but he gradually learnt to relax and appreciate it and even to do it for fun on occasion. By the end of that long year, there were fifty-nine notches on other people's bedposts, twenty-one of whom had declined to go all the way. Of the remainder, nine saw him underneath and he picked up some useful tips in the process as well as a few double-takes in the bars as word got around.

He experienced a version of the torpedo himself once and was face-fucked more than that, but learnt to take the good with the bad. He discovered he liked a little consensual bondage enough to try it himself one night, but the guy just used it as an excuse to keep him there all night and he didn't try it again.

Then, at the end of November, he caught the clap, stopped and took stock. He was still in love with Marco, or in love with increasingly selective memories of Marco, but the pain was mostly gone. He hadn't met Mr Right, although the hedge fund manager had stirred something, crabs notwithstanding. He hadn't even really seen him across a crowded room. But he had some better ideas of what he wanted. Someone with Warren's self-respect, experience and physique, race immaterial as long as it was for the other person too. Someone with the confident, relaxed eyes of a Mahesh, a dusting of body hair but no beards, no more than one small tattoo, no piercings even of the tongue, not a bar-hopper. Someone who liked to dance occasionally but not rave, someone with a good mind, a cultural interest. Someone happy to be underneath but no fairies, someone who liked to kiss, no biters. Someone British, one foreign boyfriend was more than enough, urbane but still with a little roughness round the edges for when it mattered, a Londoner preferably, provincials were weird.

It had indeed been a long year and he was tired, pleased it was over, an empty bank account and an agonised dick the main evidence for it, nothing a few months of quieter living couldn't cure. But it had been a year seized, the first since Marco, possibly the first ever, definitely the reason he had wanted to be in London and not Oxbridge. And despite his empty bank account, his student loan was now paid off.

His work had somehow survived as well, got steadily better in fact. All year, he took on as much work as Sophie would give him and, when that wasn't enough, sought out work from others as well. He smiled a lot – a trick he was finding worked well with anybody – was polite, complimentary, grateful, and continued to build up his range of contacts and his knowledge and understanding of his clients. At his annual appraisal that December, as he scratched surreptitiously at his crotch, the department head said, "You've had a good year, in fact you've bloomed. We're all very pleased with how you've developed over the last fifteen months, become quite another person. Sophie can't praise you enough, which is unusual from her. If anything, we're concerned you work too hard. It's good you've been going on those trips out of London at the weekends. Work-life balance isn't just a slogan, you know?"
Ben smiled and nodded. Thank God he was only twenty-four; youthful energy will cover up for a multitude of sins. "I know I'm still learning the ropes. There's much more to this job than I'd realised, if I'm ever going to be half as good as Sophie."
"Yes, and about that. We think you're ready for a bigger challenge. Doing the chores other people don't want isn't enough, we think. So we've decided to promote you to Assistant Account Executive. It's a few months early, but we think you're ready for it. You'll have day-to-day responsibility for your clients, managing their results and anything else they need. We'll start you off with five, all mid-sized FTSE-250 companies. It will get you out from beneath Sophie's benevolent, but lengthy, shadow. See what you can do with them and then we'll see what else we can give you."

For a moment, Ben just stared, resisting the almost overwhelming urge to scratch. Then he grinned, stood up and shook his boss's hand, thanked him and then again as he saw the size of his bonus, his first ever and what seemed like a monstrous sum. The department head laughed and said, "Don't disappoint us."

Ben nodded. He had a new motivation for a new year, a year in which he would grow up, save some money, relax into his career and adulthood, and at the end of which, if everything went well, he would join the property ladder. The year just over had been giddy, necessary, essential even, but ultimately unsatisfying. He wasn't a barfly, a gadfly, he just wanted to be kissed and held. He didn't need any heedless, hedonistic shallowness now. He needed…what? Who exactly? But he told himself he would find him someday and actually half believed it.

He took the time to get to know his clients, travelling to meet senior management and understand them better. One of the companies, a manufacturer of steel cutlery in Bradford, had had a near-death experience a few years' back and was now recovering strongly under its new chief executive. Ben got excited and called the FT. A turnaround story in Britain's battered industrial heartland was surely just what they needed. They turned him down. "Too small. No one cares about a company with a market cap of less than a billion."

But Ben didn't give up, pestering them every few weeks, whenever he was calling up about something else. He was successfully placing stories with efinancialnews, Reuters and Bloomberg, the Telegraph, the Times, the Mail, the Evening Standard, the Sunday Times and the Observer, even The Wall Street Journal, he was getting interviews on Bloomberg TV and CNBC, but the FT was the motherlode; he had to crack it. Together with buying a flat and homing in on exactly what kind of man it was he really wanted, this was his goal for the year.

He reminded the FT that the cutlery company was over a hundred and fifty years old, that its chief executive was a self-made man, a Ugandan Asian refugee who'd turned around two companies already. Then, in the autumn, the company produced record results and its shares rose thirty percent in a week. They just kept going up, five percent a day. The FT finally relented and offered a half-page spread in the Weekend FT, a personal and very favourable interview with the CEO who praised his workforce and announced he was expanding, entirely in Britain. Ben was given three more clients. Just before Christmas, he received his second bonus, even larger than the first.

"You're getting good at this," said his boss.

Ben grinned. "It's easy if the clients are decent," he replied.

His boss grunted. "Nevertheless. What are you going to do with your money?"

"I'm buying a flat," Ben replied. "Just a small one, in Maida Vale. Two bedrooms, nice and cosy. My flatmates are getting a place together, so I think it's time for me to move on too."

"If you want my advice, find someone to share it with," said his boss. "You've been even better this year, more mature, more settled, more confident, less of last year's nervous energy. You're growing up. Let someone help you choose the furniture. Work isn't everything. You don't deserve to be alone."

CHAPTER THIRTEEN

"If you want my advice, find someone to share it with."

Ben had stayed silent at his boss' words, but the man had a point, and it was a point about which Daisy was increasingly hysterical. She was appalled when she heard the number fifty-nine and snapped her lips with righteous satisfaction at the STDs. "What were you thinking! You got off much lighter than you deserved! You could be dead – should be dead!" Even David was taken aback as he called Ben to wish him a Happy Christmas and informed him that he and Julian were now an item. "I know I said fifty, one a week, and I know you're young and pretty, but that's too many. I never seriously expected you to get beyond a couple of dozen at most. The clap's a warning. Stop now, for your own sake."

Now, a third year had begun and he was still alone, still thinking wistfully of Marco in the middle of the night, still nowhere near meeting Mr Right. David had told him to use last year's knowledge to pick someone and try it for a bit longer. He wondered if he should indeed resign himself and settle.

It wasn't that he wasn't trying. He still went to the bars, but more selectively and less often, a few times a month. And he was much more careful about who he left with, often not leaving with anyone, just talking, getting to know a few people, widening the age range and beginning to make friends among the older men, guys between thirty and forty, who he discovered read books, went to the theatre and art galleries and took trips out of London at the weekend. He gave out his personal, although not his work, number and email freely, joined them for events and stayed all night if invited, occasionally even for breakfast.
Two guys he went out with again, actual dates, but nothing was ever quite right. Duncan, a retail stockbroker with his own flat in Fulham, could and would talk about football interminably at the slightest provocation. Their date was in a sports bar, loud and crowded, and David spent as much time gazing at the screens as he did gazing at Ben. They slept together and Ben was invited to watch Fulham play the next weekend. But beyond Tommy's mud-caked rosy young face, Ben had no interest in football. Rugby sometimes, cricket occasionally, but not football. He declined.

Colin was more promising. A meat-packer from Brixton, he was looking to become a foreman at his abattoir and in the meantime used his meagre savings to take himself to a bar once a month and the ballet twice a year, one of them always Swan Lake, his favourite. Ben wasn't much into ballet but he was willing to give it a try. For their second date, he took Colin to Mendelssohn's *A Midsummer Night's Dream* at the Albert Hall, the first time he'd been there since the Last Night of the Proms with Marco and thereby got to exorcise a demon, gazing in rapt attention at Colin's rapt attention at the stage. Colin kissed him so well afterwards, held his hand as they sat in the taxi to Brixton. But then, all hot and bothered, Colin declined to go all the way. "I'm sorry. You're a good guy, but I just remember how it felt the last time."

"Then, do it to me."

"Thank you, but no. I'm sorry, but I think you'd better go now. I'll always remember the Royal Albert Hall, though. Thank you, a wonderful memory; but a reality I'm just not ready for, not strong enough for."

So, apparently, Ben was no longer 'TBGB', he was no longer 'ILATT', but he was still 'The Torpedo'. He took stock as he walked the near-three hours home, his collar turned up against the wind, unable to find a cab south of the river or north of the river either by the time he got there. Colin wasn't ready and nor, it seemed, was he.

Fuck that Marco! Fuck him to Hell! Daisy told him he was in London somewhere, a management consultant, still sleeping around although Ben could no longer judge him for that, still going to raves mid-week, for which Ben thought he could. Ben was relieved he'd never bumped into him the previous year and the knowledge that he was still around made Ben even more circumspect this year. Daisy had heard through the LSE grapevine that he was due to leave for Madrid soon, had begun to hear about Ben and had actually asked after him. Yes, Madrid, the sooner the better. Not even London was big enough to keep them apart indefinitely. Ben offered up a prayer of thanks for the miracle of avoiding him so far; he was well into building a new life, but he still doubted he was strong enough for that.

And Colin was so nearly perfect. Such intelligent rich brown eyes, noticing everything. He was improving himself and wouldn't be a meat-packer much longer, he had too much drive and too much self-respect. The foreman position would soon be followed by manager. If only Ben had met Colin a few years later, later for both of them, it might have worked. His eyes weren't as beautiful as Mahesh's, one of them wandered slightly, but not so you'd notice. Duncan, however, would be a beer-bellied couch potato by the time he was forty, even if still able to get laid for cash. The only similarity between the two of them was their appearance, both the same height as Ben, the same build as him, the same skin-colour as each other, rich café au lait. And therein lay another clue. So many clues now, but never an end to the treasure hunt. Ben wondered as he turned the key in the latch what he would be like at forty. Probably still looking and still being turned down by the ones he really liked.
He made time for his friends, reconnected with Matt and helped him snare his next girlfriend, Jane, not plain at all, at a pub in the World's End. He swam regularly, went to the theatre, read books, travelled out of London, to Edinburgh, Dublin, Bruges, Tom's where he hardly drank at all, to Stonehenge, Warwick Castle and Chatsworth. He discovered live comedy in a pub in Notting Hill one Sunday night, ignoring the occasional eye on him as he drank two pints of London Pride and just laughed. At the end of the year, he had got laid a dozen times and stayed with Harry and Bill for three months between the lease on his old flat expiring after Daisy and Chris moved out and his new place in Maida Vale completing.

"Forget the bars; you won't find anyone there," said Harry, wrapping Ben in a head-lock and punching him in the stomach. "Bill and I are gonna find you someone, we really are. It's a new year now, 2007 – and for you that means two thousand and seventh heaven!"

Ben laughed, but for the first time the party that year was a sit-down dinner. Only four of the twelve guests were single. Harry had Bill, Patrick had Mahesh, even David had Julian – and his goatee, no longer dyed. Ben wished he was with Daisy and Chris at Tom's place as he sipped cocktails and made small talk, taking care to use his professional smile as much as possible and admiring Harry and Bill's growing stock of soft furnishings. But then Tom had Caroline as well.

One of the singles, Rahul, gave him his number and asked him to call, but there was too much to do on his flat. He moved in in mid-January, completely broke again and with a much larger mortgage than he wanted, only got over the line by a useful amount of money left to him in his grandmother's will. He slept on an Ikea futon on the floor.

As he surveyed it in the dark evening of early February, it looked bare, cold and like an expensive mistake. It reminded him dangerously of that denuded flat in Clerkenwell the night he tore the poster of Enrique Iglesias and dumped everything on the landing. He bought some paint, rollers and brushes and taught himself how to use them, sweeping away the old musty atmosphere and replacing it with something warm and inviting. As his bank balance recovered over the next few months, he bought a bed, a king-sized double, a statement of intent. He then added a sofa, long enough to lie down on, some chairs, a couple of side tables, a coffee maker. By June, he even had lamps and had hung a few pictures, eighteenth-century prints of his old school. There was the makings of a book collection and more music on his iPod, which now had a speaker stand.

Yes, this was a home he could be proud of. A pity there was no one to share it with, even if in April he did hold a house-warming party and received admiring comments from a guest count that was gratifyingly high. It was only one evening, but it made a change from getting in late from work, the pool or fruitless nights in bars, with his only real fun two hours on Sunday nights with two pints of London Pride, annoyed when he was occasionally but persistently intruded upon.

He stepped in and picked up the pieces when, a few weeks later and after five years together and with Patrick seemingly about to get his wish to finally move in, Mahesh left for New York and declined to take Patrick.

"'I just don't love you anymore'. What the fuck does that mean?" bawled Patrick as he crumpled a soaking, snot-filled hankie. It seemed pretty clear to Ben, but he also saw the sub-text: that after a while, Patrick's cloying affection and subservient gratitude was just too much. And he knew what it meant to be dumped by someone in whom you had invested everything, someone you had clung to even as they steadily pulled away. It left you emotionally broke as well as spiritually broken. He listened to the stories, heard the mixture of love, hate, anger, confusion, pain, resentment, forlorn hope, for hours, days, weeks. Then he couldn't take it any longer. "I'm going out. Want to come?"
"OK. Can't do any harm."
Ben took him to one of his favourite bars, the first time he'd taken anyone to any of them, receiving surprised raises to the eye-brows as Ben introduced Patrick, but Patrick just got drunk and morose. Without any warning, he threw up violently on the stripped pine bar-room floor to the tune of Maroon 5's Makes Me Wonder, too many whiskies even when mixed with water, and spattered two people's legs. To furious stares, Ben staggered out with Patrick listing against him.

Patrick was better that August as Ben drove them both down to Cambridgeshire for Tom and Caroline's wedding. It was the first wedding Ben had been to since Tony and Estelle's two years before. He'd promised to be on his best behaviour then when, after much humming and hawing about whether it should be in England or the Cape, it was held in Dorset. But then he'd met André, Estelle's twenty-seven year-old cousin and a provincial-level Rugby player, one of his fifty-nine that year, a tourist, quite eager but by July too amateurish and really mainly bi-curious. Even two years on, Ben still dreaded what Estelle would say if and when she finally found out about it. But there was only silence; maybe André had kept his mouth shut; something he hadn't while Ben fucked him.

Patrick looked good in his morning coat, of course he did; to the manner, to the manor, born. He'd brought his grandfather's magnificent top hat, but Ben persuaded him to leave it in the car. And Patrick was jittery so close to Suffolk, wanting to hold Ben's hand for comfort and then afraid one of the guests would notice and recognise him, out with another man who was sharing a room with him. Ben stole a glance as they dressed and saw that the pelt had been radically pared back. He must have known something was wrong between him and Mahesh for some time because he had been bulking up slowly for months and nearly looked quite hot.

"What?"

"Do you manscape below the waist too?"

"Fuck you, Benedict Connelly," he said, throwing a pillow. "What if I do? And dream on, pretty boy."

Ben laughed, but Patrick did indeed know many of the guests and, whenever it looked as if he would drift into forced heterosexuality, Ben grasped his hand firmly.
"Stop it, Ben. My parents are here."
"Really? Introduce me."
"No, idiot; but stop it please. I know these people and they do know my parents."
"Only if you stop being a self-loathing queer."
Patrick was quiet for a while and allowed Ben to hold his hand as he drank a glass of champagne and ate two cheese puffs in succession. "You think I'm self-loathing?"
"No. I know you are. Bluntly, you forced Mahesh away. Stop it."
"You're so much nicer than when I first knew you, but still a real hypocrite sometimes."
Ben was a hypocrite although his life with Marco was becoming only gradually dissipating smoke. He kissed Patrick, even though they were among over a hundred well-dressed guests in the middle of a luxuriant green lawn bounded by a ha-ha with deer beyond, another fifty guests in the long white marquee beside them, a string quartet playing various classical adaptations on the stone terrace behind them, thirty more guests there. Bach's Air on the G-String. Patrick's lips felt good, Ben had forgotten how good. Patrick stared at him through tear-streaked eyes.
"And still very beautiful. Fuck me tonight."
"Buck up and I just might. But it would be better if you found someone else. Now, who do you like?"

Ben wasn't a complete hypocrite. These days, he did at least let people in physically even if he did keep a gradually-narrowing distance emotionally, and he wouldn't mind some action for himself today either. So he scanned the lawn for both of them. It was a perfect English summer's day, low twenties, a few clouds drifting across an aquamarine sky. The quartet played an adaptation of *Morning* from *Peer Gynt*. It was six o'clock, but the music was still entirely appropriate, although like with the Bach it would have sounded better on a larger ensemble. Patrick laughed and leant into him, still holding his hand.

And Ben knew people here too, the parents of his schoolfriends. He introduced himself and met the people they were talking to, not failing to introduce his 'good and old friend, Patrick McLeod, son of Gerald McLeod'. He knew outing Patrick every twenty minutes was immature, but suspected Patrick needed it, and that it wouldn't do Ben any harm either. He was met with approving nods and enjoyed the glances, lingering looks, occasionally envious, even a few out-and-out stares, from both men and women. He kissed Caroline, who hugged him, very strong. "Come down to Somerset often. Patrick's such a nice man and you look so good together."

Ben looked at Patrick, standing two steps back, and thought that, finally he did look good. "It's not what you think."

"Whatever it is, find someone you like and introduce him to us. You've been alone for a long time. You deserve what I've found with Tom." And then she withdrew and squeezed Tom's hand, nuzzling into his side, perfectly content. Tom was a very lucky man and Ben felt his envy as he hugged him close.

Patrick didn't find anyone else that afternoon or evening and nor did Ben. He got into bed alone, but Patrick soon joined him, showing indeed neat manscaping down there as he did so. He was still wearing Mahesh's cross, although Ben declined to kiss it as the button cock transformed itself into something quite impressive. Patrick was indeed extremely good with his tongue and Ben tried to be equally good with his own and then his cock. He made sure to be particularly gentle, even as Patrick egged him on.
"Christ! Where did you learn to do that?" panted Patrick.
"Seventy-one partners in two years teaches you something."
"How many?!"
Ben laughed. "You heard. A year of self-loathing myself, fifty-nine and two STDs. Then a leisurely dozen."
"Fuck me!"
"I just did, thank you for the memory."
"I've only had seven – and I'm three years older than you!"
"Yes, but you manage to keep them. I haven't learnt that skill. A silver tongue, perhaps?"
"Don't be flippant. What do you want?"
And so Ben told him. They talked for half an hour before Patrick made a move on him, thought better of it and quietly returned to his own bed.

He was reserved at breakfast, even though he let Ben see him naked after his shower. "I won't deny it," he said eventually. "That was quite some fuck, better even than Mahesh most nights if that were possible, but you are never getting near my body again. It's not that you can't do it, you can, but there's something missing. You need to respect the man you're with and you clearly don't respect me."

It was a different criticism, but criticism nonetheless. He hadn't sunk Patrick in a North Atlantic winter, but evidently something of his old problems had survived. And it was true anyway; he didn't respect Patrick and never really had. He might be smart and good company when he wasn't talking about Mahesh, but he was too easy and, whatever Ben did, he always ended up lecturing him. Ben kissed him as he dropped him off back in London.

Work continued to be intense but satisfying. After his success with the Bradford cutlery maker, Ben had set himself a target of getting at least one decent article into the FT each quarter. Bloomberg and Reuters he had long since cracked, as well as the Telegraph and Evening Standard, while even The Wall Street Journal seemed to be amenable to his approaches and efinancialnews lapped his stuff up. But the FT was still playing coy. He made a point of offering them at least one story a week, often on Tuesday because it was usually a slow news day. But the first quarter they took nothing. In the second quarter, he managed a one-paragraph 'news in brief' about one of his clients' plans to move manufacturing from the UK to Malaysia to cut costs. It was good copy, but not what Ben had in mind.

Then, finally, in late September and early October and as he was becoming dispirited, the paper took two in a row, the first four hundred words on a client's acquisition of Poland's largest manufacturer of energy-efficient light bulbs and the second a thousand words to accompany the flotation of a green energy fuel cell systems manufacturer, a mandate he had helped to bring in himself. Neither was quite the splash he'd made with the boss of the cutlery manufacturer, but it was progress.

And it was noticed. Shortly after the successful listing of the fuel cells manufacturer, he got a call from one of the head-hunters he had got to know when looking for a hire for one of his clients. "Come in and see us," said the headhunter. "I think it'll be worth your while."

"Who is it?"

"Starter for Ten Public Relations. You know them?"

Ben did. The firm was small, but growing rapidly. It focused on young, fast-growing companies, often just as they started out on the stock market, hence the company's slightly jokey name.

"Great," said the head-hunter. "I'll set you up to meet Gary."

Gary, Ben knew, was Gary Evans, one of the two founding partners, industry stars who had left to set up on their own. The meeting went well and over the next few days Ben met the rest of the team before Evans sat down opposite him, palms on the table top. "You've impressed us," he said. "But we knew you would. You've spent three years quite rightly with your head down earning your spurs. Now's your chance to put it work. How would you like to be a full Account Executive?"

For a moment, Ben was struck dumb. Then, he grinned and Evans grinned back. It was a two-rung promotion, directly responsible for all aspect of his clients' PR, financial and commercial.

"You can build your own client list," Evans added. "In fact, we'll insist on it. You did very well with that fuel cell company. Now, use your connections with the investment banks to bring in mandates for all the new companies coming to market."

Ben knew he had to join. This was what he'd been waiting for, his break and his reward for the long hours and clean nose, or public appearance of one. He punched his knees beneath the desk and remembered to smile politely. Then, he nodded, thanked Evans and said, "I'd like that. It will be an exciting challenge."

"The bonuses will be better as well," Evans said. "We're a lean operation with low overheads. In fact, if you sign on with us, we'll buy you out from your upcoming bonus where you are now, so you won't lose out. We're a bit worried about the outlook for the market, there might be some choppy waters ahead, very choppy, but we've thought through the impact of hiring you and still want to do it."

They shook hands and a week later, Ben signed on the dotted line. When he handed in his notice, his boss said, "Stay. Next year's going to be terrible, but I'll find a way to promote you."

But Ben was committed, and now he wanted it. The idea of building his own client list attracted him. It was like arriving at the LSE, freedom once more, an opportunity to spread his wings and try new things. It was another step forward, away from his old life. There would be less casual sex, more dates and less time on his own. He turned twenty-six in October, resigned in November, banked his sign-on bonus cheque in December, spent New Year with Tom and the gang in Somerset, a more civilised affair with Caroline there and more fun, and joined Starter for Ten in January.

CHAPTER FOURTEEN

"Just stop being such a fucking loser," Daisy told Ben as she kissed him on New Year's Eve. "You've got no excuse now. Jesus, one indifferent shag from a two-timing motherfucker and you turn into a monk. Well, hardly a monk, but a martyred saint. And come to our wedding in July. Bring your new boyfriend."

Yes, it wasn't just Patrick that lectured him; Daisy did too. But she had a point, everyone was moving on, especially the straight ones. He was already an uncle and Tony said Estelle was pregnant again. He smiled, kissed Daisy and promised he would even as he suspected he wouldn't bring anyone. Starter for Ten was too important and would be different; it needed his attention, he would invest in it. He was no longer a PR virgin, but an experienced and capable Account Executive, although the thought of that title and the responsibility it bore was intimidating at first.

Six months of concentrated attention wasn't too long and he went to bars a couple of times a month, just to talk, and met more new people. One of them collected stamps, none worth less than £2,000, another was an amateur archaeologist who had just returned from a dig in Turkey, enthusing about the Hittites. A third, Winston, was the host of the early-evening show for Smooth Radio, soon to move to the prime-time afternoon slot when it was relaunched as Jazz FM. Ben liked him and Winston liked live comedy, but Sunday nights remained Ben's alone time.

So, instead of scoring in bed once a month, he set himself the task of winning at least one new client a month and in February won a mandate for a small company that was going to list on the stock market that May. It was through an old contact of his, an investment banker named Edward Makins, who had also switched from a large bank to a specialist boutique. It was 2008 and the world was indeed becoming difficult, although in the first six months the markets were still open for business. Just. Ben applied himself harder than ever, developing a PR strategy and implementing it through a string of interviews and puff pieces leading towards the IPO. Makins noticed the effort - and the good results – and steered a further two clients Ben's way.

The IPO was a success. Even in a difficult market, all the shares were sold and the share price rose on the first day of trading and stayed higher for the next few weeks. Other advisers took note and Ben won more business, even as he successfully helped with other IPOs in June and early July. But it was clear to Ben as early as May that 2008 was going to be the most difficult year of his career: just when you thought it was all over, things got worse again. He decided to do something different.

He cold-called the features editor of the Gay Times and Attitude magazine and arranged lunches. Over the next few months, as markets deteriorated and share prices collapsed, Ben placed a series of stories with them, emphasising his clients' diversity and inclusiveness, which he recycled for the mainstream media, how his clients were tapping the 'Pink Pound' and promoting progressive thought and behaviour of all kinds in their businesses. As he did so, he plucked up the courage, bought a small rainbow flag and posted it on the wall of his cubicle.

The news articles tided him over those dark days after the collapse of Lehman Brothers and then almost everything else. A couple of his gay colleagues copied him, as well as one straight one, and Ben won kudos for developing a new angle to garner coverage at a time when everything seemed to be going to hell. "Well done," said Evans in December as he handed Ben his bonus. "Your quick thinking has helped a dozen of our clients and your in-tray is full for whenever the markets recover. Good job."

Ben glanced at the bonus figure and gasped, twice what he'd made the year before. It would make a major dent in his mortgage. "Seriously?" he said.

"Seriously," said Evans. "You brought in four new clients on retainer and have seven companies more to list next year, one of them incidentally after reading some of your work in the Gay Times and Attitude. I don't care what you do with your free time, you're not a boy, and I recommend you take more time off by the way, but in the office your results speak for themselves. I don't know what happened to you in July, it's none of my business. Still waters run deep, but you seem to be fighting your way through it. And it never affected your work, took it to a new level actually."
Ben nodded. He'd found a way to keep the newshounds interested and his boss happy and that was a consolation. Because what had happened in July was Marco. Daisy had warned him that he was coming to her wedding as a guest of Sebastian, but that hardly made it much easier. For all she was getting married, Daisy could be a real fag-hag sometimes, far closer to the LSE gay network than he was. "I tried to persuade Sebastian to come alone, but he insisted and Chris said it might be good for you."
"It'll be fine," said Ben, knowing it wouldn't.
He told Winston the next time they met in a bar.
"Chris is probably right," said Winston. "Want me to come with you, Caspar?"
"Caspar?"
"I've never seen anyone looked so spooked."
"Yes, please."

Winston was thirty-one, six foot two and nicely muscled. He was also HIV-positive and made sure everyone knew it. As a result, he was mainly, although not always, a wallflower. In addition, to Jazz, he enjoyed Dylan Thomas, Ted Hughes and Sylvia Plath. When Ben said he thought Sylvia Plath was a little morbid, Winston said Ben knew better than to stereotype.
"I' have no intention of dying until I'm at least fifty."
He had the blackest skin Ben had ever seen, the fineness and smoothness of polished ebony.
He also looked good in a suit. For the wedding, he wore one in midnight blue with a soft yellow and blue tie. Ben also wore a suit. Throughout, Winston was suave, polite and attentive. As he smiled, remembered people's names and details Ben had told him and made small talk, Ben felt the admiring, envious eyes on him again and again and they felt good. And then he started. Winston noticed and took his hand, turning to see where Ben was staring.
How could he have loved that man? He must weigh well over a hundred kilos. And those tits. And that artificial arse, after so long sculpted into an obscene travesty of the real thing. And what was he wearing? A florid patterned green and red waistcoat under a tailored morning coat that didn't really fit, a knotted white silk tie, a top hat in his hand. His English fetish had returned, Anthony Blanche to the cloth-banging Flyte beside him, with the same flamboyance but without any of the same powers of insight.
And then he noticed Ben. He smiled that smile and walked over, his hips swaying. Ben had forgotten the hips, but he had also forgotten the power in that smile. He skittered and shied; Winston reined him in with a vice-like grip. "Nice smile, nothing else," he muttered.

"He's brilliant, so successful, effortless."
"He's a fat, entitled wanker and he hasn't even opened his mouth. For someone so intelligent, you've really been remarkably thick. You're better than him every day of the week. And you know it."
Entitled; they'd called him that at the LSE too. And then Marco was there, asking him how he was, telling him about Madrid, saying he'd heard how well Ben was doing at work, that management consulting bored him and took away from his partying, that he'd been head-hunted and would be moving back to London.
That Spanish-American lilt was like a lullaby, but there was much to dislike in his words. He was casual, thoughtless, needlessly cruel, arrogant and shallow. All the time, as Ben struggled to get out real replies to the torrent of conversation, struggling to move away from his early grunts and monosyllables, Marco smiled that smile and then, finally, Ben saw it for what it was – it was a smile of possession, entitled ownership, as if everyone and everything existed to do his bidding, bow down willingly before his power and right. Marco assumed, even now, that if he chose him, he only had to put out his hand and Ben would come running.
He had completely ignored Winston, not even shaking his hand. Ben shuddered with violent anger. But Marco was almost finished, suggesting they meet up in London, go to a rave. "I heard you like to party," he leered. Ben couldn't wait for him to leave, aghast that he had thrown away his heart, flayed his soul, for this man. Yes, he had indeed been remarkably stupid.
And then Marco said, "You still look like perfection, my English rose. That yellow pansy Rio was a real mistake." And there was perhaps a hint of regret at the back of his eyes. "Look me up sometime."

Ben nodded and Marco was gone. Winston was boiling, but for Ben, who got the references, five years of growing peace vanished instantly. Why did he have to say that? Why couldn't he have just left? Pain seared his soul, a hand around his heart, crushing it, squeezing the life out of it. He staggered into the marquee and put his hand against the tent-pole, bent over, his breath ragged.
"Throw it up," said Winston. "Throw it all up, once and for all, and then be done with it."
The bile came out, green, yellow, bitter, stinging, just the second time since Leicester Square. It loosened stinging tears and as he saw the mess, the mess within him so clearly revealed, he just knelt and stared down at it. Winston knelt beside him and then helped him to his feet and held him, found him a glass, made him drink it and then kissed him.
Ben flinched. "Don't touch me," he said. "No one is to touch me, ever again."

Winston took Ben's chin and forced his head up, eye contact. "Stop being so fucking stupid, Ben. But I see now how we need to do this. So I'm going to touch you, I'm going to kiss you, I'm going to stroke your naked body and then we're going to fuck. I see what this is, puppy love, nothing more, but grown malignant and cancerous through ill-attention. I'm going to cut it out, cure you once and for all, even if I have to use a blunt rusty knife. He's intelligent, not brilliant, just intelligent, and he's clearly successful although he doesn't deserve to be with that attitude. He is effortless only because he makes none. He is a fat, entitled wanker and you're better than him every day of the week. And I'm not letting go of your body tonight until you acknowledge that to me in your responses, open up and let me in. You can fuck me as hard as you like, I enjoy a bit of roughness from the right man, but we are disarming this damn torpedo of yours once and for all. I'm going to be the last stop you make in this Pilgrim's Progress, finally out of the Slough of Despond and up to the gates of the Celestial City, where your true love is waiting for you."
He was glaring, but Ben heard the words. "Sorry," he said. "And thank you. Thank you for being here today."

Winston sighed. "There's a lot to like about you, Ben, really a lot, despite an extraordinary and very dangerous flaw, however well-hidden. Your body, your smile, your broad and cultured mind, your generosity to others, your lack of pride, I like them all. But to me, the nicest thing is still your willingness to thank people and look like you mean it. So, thank you in return. Now, to business." He kissed Ben again and this time Ben didn't flinch. Winston took his hand and led Ben to congratulate Daisy and Chris again; then, they left. As he turned at the car, Ben saw Marco, his head thrown back in that raucous, twittering laugh of his. He curled his lip and got into the car.

But he was nervous with Winston, gun-shy; this was the first man he'd slept with in years whose good opinion he cared about. Winston, however, was gently persistent. It took an hour before Ben was allowed to come for the first time. Then Winston, after assiduously checking him for cuts, allowed Ben to bring him off in his hand, under a condom. It was still incomprehensible to Ben that Winston had let himself get positive.

"A dirty needle when I was sixteen, experimenting for the first and last time with drugs, a little peer pressure and a lot of youthful stupidity. My dad saw the marks on my arm the next day and forced me to get tested. I've never knowingly infected anyone and I won't do it tonight. Am I your first?"

"To my knowledge."

"And that's part of the problem. Get yourself tested next week, just for peace of mind. We want you virginally pure, renewed, reborn like Aphrodite washed in the waters of Paphos, for when you meet Christiana."

The breadth of Winston's erudition always surprised Ben and he laughed.
"That's better. We're half-way there."
Ben initiated the next kiss and, for the first time, felt Winston genuinely enjoy it. That enjoyment, the knowledge that Winston was no longer just doing Ben a favour, was a spice, a jolt to the senses, and Ben came back to life. He looked at Winston's fine body, naked and open beneath him, and began to play with it properly, the taut skin, the hard nipples, the flat stomach, the broad back, the hard cock Winston would not let him touch until sheathed. He was in one too and then Winston relaxed. Tantalised by Winston's lips and fingers, Ben was truly aroused and pushed Winston beneath him and went down on the condom, Winston gently pressing him down with his hand. "Start with the mouth but finish with the hand. I'll pinch you."
Ben did and, afterwards, Winston was actually sweating, contented. But he wouldn't kiss Ben until he had cleaned away even the perspiration. He drew Ben down over him. "If you're not afraid, we're going to fuck now. The condoms are steel-reinforced, but if you feel anything is wrong, stop immediately. Otherwise, release it all into me, all that stupid hate, that sublimated rage, that hurt, loneliness and despair and then be rid of it. Let it out, all out, once and for all and be done with it."

Ben moaned at the truth revealed, but it was cathartic, all of this was. Winston stroked his chest and slowly coaxed him down and in. Ben wasn't afraid of infection, but he was afraid of finally letting go, being rudderless even if free. He took Winston slowly at first, then fast and very hard and then, seeing the discomfort on the man's face, seeing a living, breathing, warm, gentle, kind, sympathetic, generous, intelligent, thoughtful man beneath him, he finally slowed down and truly relaxed, lengthening his stride as he approached the finish line.
"Come in me if you want to."
No, Winston deserved better and Ben wanted him to see his release, his ecstasy at discovery of his new-found freedom, for Winston was right: it would be freedom. He withdrew, slid off the condom, and in a few short strokes came, Winston raising his head to watch and stoke himself as Ben stopped. He shot translucent strands across Winston's hard belly that shimmered white against Winston's blackness. The sight brought Winston off again and it seemed like an omen, a barrier removed. They rose and washed together in silence before returning to the bed, where Ben lay side on to Winston and allowed himself to be cradled.
"I saw it," Winston said. "I felt the hate and the rage and the hurt and then I saw it go. I think you might be cured, Ben. Love yourself; I do. You're a very special man, even if you've been behaving like a moron. And you're not bad in the sack." He laughed. "I'd forgotten how nice it is to get a real animal fucking sometimes. I'm glad I got to see and feel The Torpedo, but it was much more erotic to watch it be disarmed in front of my eyes, decommissioned for the last time."

Ben was about to apologise when Winston put his fingers to his lips and kissed him. They lay together, looking into each other's eyes, stroking each other's sides and backs. "You must be tired," Winston said. "It's been a long day. Ready to sleep?"
It had been a long day; it had been a long five years. He nodded. "Thank you." Winston kissed his forehead and then held him until he fell asleep.
But Gary Evans was right. July had been a trauma, a profound Earth-shaking dislocation that shifted Ben's tectonic plates. Despite Winston's excellent work that night, and he provided an after-care service as well for which he was rewarded with a first edition of Under Milk Wood at Christmas, the aftershocks continued with slowly decreasing intensity for the rest of the year. Ben felt completely drained, emptied physically and emotionally, exhausted as if from the simultaneous combination of the most intense orgasm and the final breaking of a life-draining fever.
He still swam regularly, drank little, ate properly, slept well, had no headaches, saw his friends and Tony and Estelle, went to a pub in Notting Hill every Sunday night for two pints of London Pride, but he felt exhausted, tired, listless. He wasn't even particularly horny, once a fortnight with Winston was enough. No more torpedoes, just gentle and increasingly intense, open love-making. Winston took him to jazz bars, always scouting for new talent, and then to bed.

One night in November, after a dinner with Winston's brother Desmond, an architect with two children, just back from Brazil where he was designing the new headquarters for a bank, Ben wondered if Winston was good enough, if he should just settle. But Winston, even as he said he was enjoying Ben's company and showed it in bed, knew he was just a way-station, an interlude, and said he liked it that way. And Ben, try as he might, just couldn't really get into jazz, even if he could begin to understand and appreciate it. Winston knew that too and, in December, took him to The Magic Flute instead. "My favourite opera," he said. "Good choice," said Ben. "I loved it. Thank you."
So he fought through, increasingly strong, still hollow inside but with a comfortable hollowness, purged and cleansed. He had been tested and was negative. With Winston as a support, he turned his focus to his most important new client, an entrepreneur looking to list his men's designer clothing company on the stock market. The man was gay, the first time Ben had worked for one and as 2008 became 2009 and the market slowly improved, Ben hoped it would be one to remember, the one that would finally make Ben's name. He promoted the client heavily through both the mainstream and gay media and the flotation, in early March, was one of the first of the year. The share price rose steadily afterwards. It was good, but not quite as satisfying as Ben had hoped. Winston told him to be patient.

Patrick had also slowly pulled himself together the previous year after hooking-up a dozen times himself, a new experience for him. When Ben thought he was ready, he had introduced him at drinks over Christmas to Nick who worked with Winston at Jazz FM and whom he had met at those jazz bar evenings. White, public-school educated, twenty-nine, single, negative, recently but not too recently out of a relationship, B3n knew he was perfect for Patrick and that what Patrick really needed in his life was some jazz. He was right and they quickly became inseparable, two peas in a pod, although this time Patrick was no longer insufferable as, to Patrick's awe, Nick fell rapidly and deeply in love with him. And at work, in the months that followed the listing of the clothing company, Ben began to receive more and more approaches from LGBT business owners.

Ben had the flag in his cubicle and he never tried to conceal he was gay, but no one asked and he said nothing. In his office, only Brian who did the desktop publishing, was truly out, talking loudly to his boyfriend and arranging events for AIDS Concern, but he was nearly fifteen years older than Ben and not really Ben's style, so he kept his distance.

It was one of the secretaries, Lucy, a kind, bubbly girl his own age from Witham in Essex with long blond hair and huge tits, who was the first to raise it with him directly. It was late March 2009 and the team were having drinks in a bar near the office to celebrate Gary's engagement to his long-time girlfriend, Helen, diaphanously beautiful. Ben's in-tray was nicely full, the afterglow of the clothing IPO not fading but gearing up for a second round and then a third. He had also won mandates from another three companies that were already listed. After two hours of drinking, Lucy put her arm round Ben's shoulders, kissed him on the cheek and waved her wedding ring at him. "When are we going to see you hitched?" she said. "You're not getting any younger, you know."

Ben laughed and kissed her back. Gary was hosting bottle after bottle of champagne. Ben had drunk more than his share, and more than he usually did as well. "Thanks, darling," he said. "I feel old. I'll be twenty-eight this year!"

Lucy went for it. "So, where is he then, this boyfriend of yours? Is he hidden somewhere, a sweaty bricklayer you can't bring out in polite society but the best lay you've ever had? Or are you playing the field? I bet the blokes just can't keep their hands off you."

Ben noticed a couple of people eavesdropping. He was still seeing Winston sporadically, although even his patience was starting to crack at his failure to move on. "Find a real date," he'd said more than once.

Ben had been out with a couple of guys, but the dates hadn't really gone anywhere and he hadn't slept with either of them. For the other, he eventually showed some tongue when the guy stamped his foot in frustration but the guy saw Ben's heart wasn't in it, said so and, with a flick of the wrist, left. Ben knew he was being too critical, but now he was looking to finally fall in love and was looking for perfection.
"No sweaty bricklayer. I'm married to my work."
"I know a guy," she said, curling her fingers around the stem of her wineglass. "He's in my Pilates class. Straight-acting, non-scene like you. White, public schoolboy, late twenties, very flexible, works in publishing, always looks a bit lost. I think you'd like him. I can set you up."
He sounded too much like Patrick. It would be settling. Ben wasn't yet thirty, he still had time. He took a sip of champagne and said, "Thanks, Lucy. But no thanks."
She tutted. "Nice eyes, cute smile, rocking body – don't waste it, Ben; you won't have it forever."
He smiled and thought, Oh, fuck it! What the hell? Why not? Surely the new Ben was about being more open, letting people in. "His name's Winston and he's a radio DJ. But it's almost over, just coming to a gentle stop."
He thought Lucy might actually have an orgasm on the spot.

CHAPTER FIFTEEN

Ben was surprised to open his email that Monday morning after two desultory weeks in Phuket with Fred, the guy he'd been seeing each weekend for the past three and a bit months, and find an invitation from Peter Weller. He'd met Fred at a City fundraiser for AIDS awareness. He was a derivatives trader, white, thirty-three, originally from County Cork, married to a job that was slowly killing him but desperate for love, urgently submissive in bed as he temporarily put aside the cares of the office, only occasionally pulling himself together enough to take Ben and finally show him some spunk.

Phuket had been make-or-break for them and Ben knew which it was. Fred was neurotic, jangled his knee constantly, spent all his time on his BlackBerry or phone, and took coke, not too much but still quite a lot, mainly but not always when Ben wasn't there. Ben had known he would be settling when he'd taken him on; but Fred had been keen and Ben had done it, mainly to please Winston, testing himself again before his first night with Fred, but he was still negative.

Lucy had googled Winston relentlessly until she found out who he was, of course she had, and was very disappointed to hear about Fred. "Winston sounds so much more exciting!" Now Ben thoroughly agreed, but he put thoughts of Fred aside and looked at the email again. He was even more surprised when he noticed that it was from Peter's personal email, which came up with the name 'Peter&Graham'. He had to read it twice to be sure that it was indeed from Peter Weller and that it was the Peter Weller he thought it was.

> To celebrate the end of the quiet season, to welcome in the Autumn and before any of us get too busy, Peter and Graham would like to invite you to drinks this Friday. It is just an informal event, for friends, so please don't dress up. Rum punch and summer pudding will be served.

At the bottom was the address and the time, together with a small picture of Peter with an Asian man draped over his shoulders that Ben couldn't quite see. He was very flattered to be asked. He had only met Peter Weller four times. The first three were events to launch new companies, young companies in which Peter was an angel investor and where Ben's firm was handling the public relations, as they moved to the next stage and launched flotations on the Alternative Investment Market. The fourth was when Ben had been asked to arrange an open day forum for new businesses to network with potential investors and he needed a keynote speaker. Ben had asked Peter, never expecting him to agree, and had made a point of being very polite and even a little obsequious as he guided Peter around the forum afterwards to a few of the more promising start-ups.

But none of these things, to Ben, quite justified an invitation to Peter Weller's house or to meet his boyfriend. True, both Peter and Ben knew the other was gay and Peter had even made a point of highlighting the fact at the open day when he said, "You know, I'm glad you're promoting so many LGBT businesses, but I do invest in straight people as well." Ben was crushed and then saw that Peter was laughing at him. He laughed too, partly from politeness, but mainly from relief.

So, he accepted the invitation immediately and, on the day, made sure to go home, shower, shave and change before he set out. He wore a blue flannel jacket over a pink office shirt over neatly-pressed cream cotton trousers and smartly polished brown loafers, with plenty of business cards in his jacket pocket. He bought a bottle of Krug and hoped that Peter, well known for his good taste as well as his financial success, would approve. He looked up at the magnificent white Georgian house and felt small as it towered above him, its long sash windows and black balconies. Tom's house was much more magnificent, of course, but Tom didn't count; he hadn't had to earn the money to buy it himself. Peter had. And, despite continued small victories, several medium-sized, real success still eluded Ben. He had deliberately arrived half an hour late and nervously ran the top of his shoe down the back of his leg while he waited for the door to open.

"Ah! Ben! Welcome! Come in, come in."

Peter's smile seemed genuine, warm. Ben felt better.

"Thank you for the invitation. You're too kind to think of me."

"Nonsense, man," said Peter, shaking his hand. "Oh, you shouldn't have – and Krug, too. How lovely!" He took the box, pausing to admire it, obviously checking the vintage which Ben knew he hadn't done himself, grunted and then introduced the room with his arm. It was already crowded and, much to his relief, Ben recognised a scattering of the guests, other business and professional people, just like him. "Go and find Graham and get a glass of punch," said Peter, closing the door. "I'm going to put this in the back where no one can find it. Graham and I will enjoy it later."

Ben walked through a knot of people, saw an Asian man leaning over a large steaming tureen, stopped and stared – Peter Weller's boyfriend was Graham Tsang, the famous society photographer. He hadn't had any idea. He moved himself carefully to the front and waited for Graham to raise his eyes. "Good evening," he said, nervous but excited. Starter for Ten had tried to get Graham to do shoots for them before, but Graham had always turned them down. "I'm a…business contact of Peter's. Ben Connelly. Starter for Ten Public Relations," he added, pulling out his card.
"Oh, yes; I've heard of you," Graham drawled, unenthused, although he took the card even if he didn't really look at it. Ben had been afraid he wouldn't take it all and decided not to push it. He took a sip of the punch. It was hot and strong, but also warming and tasty. "This is really excellent, delicious," he said, meaning it, and was relieved to see a more genuine smile on Graham's face.
"Have some more," Graham said. "And then, please mingle. I'm sure there are lots of people you know."

Ben took a top-up and then went off to mix. In addition to the people he knew, several of them early-stage entrepreneurs as well as advisers and other consultants, and Ben made sure to say hello to them all, there were also much more enticing people, successful established businessmen who had raised the money they needed and were on their way to success and recognition. These were exactly the people Ben needed to bring to his firm. He wormed his way into conversation with one of them, until they were interrupted by a scream of joy from Graham Tsang. Both of them turned in surprise as Graham threw up his hands and squealed, "Oh, darling; you're here! My dear Aunt Mary! So lovely to see you and looking so beautiful! It's been too long!"
Ben blinked and then stared for a moment at the woman Graham was kissing so loudly and effusively. In her late fifties, she was dressed in a neat, but clearly very cheap, blue dress that extended down to her ankles. She was somewhat overweight with large breasts and her flesh protruded at her side and front, distending the dress. She carried her small handbag in front of her like some kind of modern-day reticule. She was black, but that wasn't the issue. There were well over a dozen black, brown or others in the room. The issue was that she so obviously didn't fit in, even if Graham was lionising her. She was completely out of place and uncomfortably aware of the fact. Ben narrowed his eyes and tried to understand, but couldn't; something was missing. Who was this woman, however modest and quietly dignified, that Graham was so genuinely delighted to be with when he would barely take Ben's card? What made her Krug and him vinegar?

"Anyway, as I was saying," said his companion and Ben hastily recollected himself and focused back on their conversation. But his curiosity was piqued. He looked out for the strange woman and saw her sitting on a stiff-backed gilt chair by the fire. She looked part-bored and part-scared, lost in a sea of people with no anchor now that Graham was busy refilling punch glasses.
And then she looked up and beamed. It didn't make her look any less dumpy, but it did make her look kind, gentle, loving. Ben turned to see where she was staring and started as electricity finally jolted through him, a violent, physical reaction that made the punch swill in his glass. Walking towards this Aunt Mary was a man, coffee-coloured, tall, straight-backed, well-muscled, lithe, naturally athletic. His hair was cut very short, almost to the scalp, and he had a twinkle in his chestnut eyes that animated his features. Everything about him was animated, alive, flowing, graceful and yet intensely masculine. Ben just stared.
The man was young, Ben couldn't tell how old, anything from a mature seventeen to a youngish twenty-two, but definitely a man. Self-confident, relaxed, his shoulders back, his taut skin shining with youth and health, he was in complete contrast to his Aunt Mary, because he was obviously the nephew, the missing piece of the jigsaw, the key that unlocked her presence here. He leant over and kissed his aunt, squeezed her hand, she kissing him back, looking so happy. As he walked towards her, he looked like he owned the room, but he had eyes only for her and that seemed right, she deserved it, braving this evening for him. Ben smiled at their silent shared happiness.

This man was nicely dressed too, much better than his aunt, in a roll-necked green pullover above brown corduroys. It made him look straight, but he was obviously gay. It also made him look older, but older was good; Ben didn't want a boy. It made him look mature, seasoned wood, tempered steel, strong yet flexible. Perfection, so long a dirty word after Marco used it on him, now finally he had found perfection. The room had hushed as he watched the man, boy, approach his aunt and kiss her, but in the time it took for him to do so, Ben fell in love. Finally. Head first, headlong, head-over-heels, he dived into his suppressed emotions and let them suck him under, let them bubble up around him as he released them. How could Peter and Graham possibly know this man and yet how wonderful that they did!

He had to meet him, tonight, here, now. He wouldn't make the same mistake he'd made at the LSE freshers' drinks, let the opportunity slip away. There would be no changing rooms second chance with this man; this was a once in a lifetime opportunity. He wanted, needed, to know him, but he also wanted to understand. He was obviously special, but why was he so special to Peter and Graham, here tonight at a business drinks, much the youngest in the room, even as his aunt was among the oldest, as out of place as her, if in a different way. Unlike Ben and the rest of the room, these two were friends of Peter and Graham. Why were they here? Tell me, look at me, and smile at me as you do so, the way you smile at Aunt Mary. In his breathless excitement and tingling anticipation, his heart pounded even as his soul sang. He stepped forward.

And then noise crashed in. The whole room shifted, someone bumped him and he stumbled. He tried to see the nephew again, but two people were in front of him, pointing and craning their necks. Ben turned. There was a commotion at the door, well-bred pushing and shoving, craning and muttering, a genteel but increasingly urgent riot breaking out. Ben saw Peter standing on his tip-toes, leaning over the crowd, shouting, trying to be heard over the hubbub of excited conversations. "Graham! Honey bun! Darling! Come here please. There's someone you need to meet. He's here."

The crowd parted just enough to let Graham through, precariously holding a small glass of punch. Who was it? Prince Charles? Ben craned in turn.

"Lovely to meet you," Graham said. "You must be Jamie."

"Yes. And you must be Graham. Thank you for the invitation."

"You're very welcome, Jamie. Come in and have some punch."

Ben caught a glimpse of this Jamie as Graham steered him through the crowd and understood finally what the fuss was about. It was another form of royalty and probably less accessible. James Sassoon, a serial internet entrepreneur who had started and sold four businesses, whispered to be worth over £400 million, the founder of Solveit!.com, a business that had reputedly saved DHL almost £1 million a week in logistics costs, and Pinkevenings.com, by far the most popular high-end gay introductions service, as well as several more, was allowing himself to be man-handled away from the door by Graham, his punch slopping messily in its cup and all the time threatening to pour onto Sassoon's immaculately white linen jacket and trousers. Jamie? Just Jamie? Expected but unknown and already Jamie? For Sassoon? James Sassoon? It didn't seem possible. For a moment, but just one, Ben was torn. He, like everyone else, wanted to meet Sassoon; the man was a legend and had made countless people, including many financiers, lawyers and indeed PR consultants, very rich. Ben couldn't pass up this opportunity, he'd never be able to look at Gary afterwards. But then there were other, more pressing, personal concerns: Ben just wanted to meet the young man with the unprepossessing aunt. Mr Right, because that was who he was. He let his heart decide and squeezed through the throng crowding past him, away from James Sassoon and his millions, towards the boy that Ben hoped would one day make him very happy.

He was almost there. He was gazing at him, drinking him in, even as everyone else ignored him. And then he looked up, noticed Ben and smiled. The light that flooded into Ben's world temporarily blinded him. He was sure he'd smiled back, how could he not, but he would never find out. Aunt Mary also glanced towards him and there was a violent jolt to his arm. Peter pushed past, ignoring him, almost sending him flying, running like the Red Queen, flustered like the White, in another world as indeed was Ben until now. Ben paused to stabilise his wobbling glass, punch slopping into the saucer. Peter rushed up to the young man and grabbed his arm. Ben was close enough now to hear what he said as Peter spat in a staccato whisper, "James Sassoon! That's your 'Jamie'? James fucking Sassoon! You're fucking James fucking Sassoon!"

Aunt Mary squeaked, but everyone ignored her, including Ben, for whom hope had been replaced by horror, dread building in his gut. Say no! Please say no! It's another Jamie!

"Stop it, you're hurting me," said the young man, squirming in Peter's grasp. His South London accent was a melodious tenor that made Ben's guts quiver. He was Warren, Colin and Winston all rolled into one. The boy looked up at Peter with those eyes, clever and searching, so like Mahesh's, and saw the growing understanding there. "He did say he was a 'big fish' but I didn't know what he meant. Is he famous?"

Peter laughed, yanked him to his feet and hugged him. "Famous? He's not just famous, you dolt; he's gay royalty."

Ben's world crashed around him. He gazed at the young man, the one who had so recently looked at him and smiled, and saw him fade away. All that was all gone now. The boy's eyes were focused only on Peter as they talked in hushed whispers that Ben no longer wanted to hear. He took a step backwards and then another. He couldn't take his eyes away, but he couldn't stay; tears were forming. James Sassoon! How could he ever compete with that, a man who let the object of both their desires call Jamie and live in blissful ignorance that he could blight his life forever with a click of his fingers?

Oh, God no! Do You really hate me that much? Is there to be no justice, no salvation, no happiness for me ever? Perfection in human form, of course James Sassoon had him; James Sassoon had everything. Some words goateed David had used their first night together as Ben started his year of fifty-nine one-night stands came to him; 'And then you'll see someone and they'll be unattainable and your heart will melt and your reserve will drop away.' Oh, David, you were so right! Perfection – and completely unattainable.

He shrank away, put down his cup on an ornate side-table; he wanted to leave. But that would be the final defeat. There were people in this room that he needed to talk to, that Gary would kill him for if he found out he hadn't tried to meet, not least Sassoon of course. And still, despite everything, he didn't want to leave that other man, the one who had smiled at him, if only so briefly. He needed one more smile; he would settle just for a glimpse of eye contact and recognition, however slight.

Peter was leaving and Ben, moth to the flame, began another slow advance. But then Graham sat down next to the man and his aunt and glared at Ben so sternly that Ben knew it was hopeless. The young man noticed him, but didn't smile and Ben knew he couldn't either. He swallowed and turned away. It would be marching into the Valley of Death, but he had to do it, he had to introduce himself to Sassoon. Gary deserved no less and if Ben was a martyred saint, he might as well take those fucking arrows.

There was still a crowd, but he noticed Peter pull Sassoon away surprisingly forcefully. Peter might be rich and powerful but he stood to Sassoon the way Ben stood to Peter. The two men sat down on uncomfortable stiff-backed chairs in front of the curtained windows, billowing in the breeze, and talked in an earnest undertone, their heads forward, some important deal no doubt. Ben thought of using his in with Peter to interrupt and then thought better of it; the conversation was getting heated. He wasn't sure what to do. He turned back to see the young man, but he was on the wrong side of the room.

"You should try the summer pudding." Ben jumped. "The cream is full of brandy. Delicious." It was Edward Makins, the investment banker whose firm handled a lot of Ben's flotations. Ben sagged with relief at a friendly face and settled in to talk. But Makins could not attract all of Ben's attention; he kept trying to glimpse either the young man or Sassoon and, to his surprise, saw that they never seemed to be together. On the contrary, Sassoon seemed comfortably ensconced with a coterie of eager advisers and entrepreneurs, several of them known to Ben, while the young man continued to talk to Graham Tsang.

Eventually, Ben could stand it no longer, helpful as Makins was, this was not the evening for it. Makins had got him another punch and then a second and Dutch courage was rising within him. He apologised and left, threading his way through the crowds, bumping one man who spilled his drink and pushed in turn as he made his way remorselessly to Sassoon. The man was talking to Peter again, both leaning against a wall. Ben approached. God, the man was handsome, so relaxed, so self-confident, so fit and slim, so elegant in his expensive but casual clothes. No wonder the unattainable had been attained without any need to flaunt Sassoon's wealth.

"Nevertheless, I think it's wrong," Peter said and then glanced towards Ben. He smiled and added, "This is Ben Connelly. He works for Starter for Ten Public Relations. Ben, James Sassoon. Jamie."

Ben pulled himself together. Thank you, Peter. You don't know what's in my heart, what I need. You barely know me, but given what little you do know, an introduction to this man is more than I deserve. "Mr Sassoon, I just wanted to introduce myself before I leave. May I give you my card?"

Sassoon sized him up slowly and he cringed, died a little more. It was business and he was vinegar again, he was sure of it. It was a golden opportunity, but he was so intimidated, and ashamed he felt so inadequate. He extracted a card from his pocket and offered it. He could see his hand shaking.

But Sassoon took it. "Thank you. I've heard of your firm," he said. His voice was also melodic, also a tenor, and surprisingly soft in delivery. "It's helped a lot of LGBT firms come to market. Was that you?"

Ben nodded and dared a glance. Sassoon seemed to want to know the answer. "Yes, sir," he stammered.
"Well, let me see if I can steer a few more your way," Sassoon said, flicking Ben's card in his fingers and sliding it into his jacket pocket. Ben knew the interview was over, nodded and stretched out his hand. Perhaps he wasn't vinegar after all, just an indifferent table wine, even if he was dying of jealousy and hurt. Sassoon shook it. So firm, a man in complete control. Ben imagined that grasped around the young man's quivering erection and stammered out, "Thank you."
Sassoon nodded and Ben knew he'd been dismissed. He slid back into the crowd, losing himself, allowing the noise of the room to drown him in anonymity. It was time to leave, Gary couldn't criticise him now, he had done his duty for God and Country, sacrificed himself on the altar of propriety. He looked for Peter and saw him talking to the young man again. His hopes rising for a second introduction, Ben slithered through the crowd, quickening his step. But then Peter and Graham both stood up. Peter saw Ben, smiled at him and walked towards him, away from the young man.
"Did you get what you wanted?" he asked.
Ben nodded. The final disappointment. "Yes, thank you for introducing me and thank you for inviting me tonight. He took my card."
Peter shook his hand and clasped his shoulder.
"Good," he said. "Your firm's one of the better ones. I'm glad I was able to help."

He had been dismissed again, and now it really was time to go. He glanced after the young man, but he was focused on his aunt. Peter noticed and said, "A good friend and a dear one, but his purpose here tonight was different to yours. I hope I have helped him as much as I have helped you." The remark was cryptic, but Ben knew it was all he would get. He wished he knew his name! He turned to Graham and said, "Thank you so much for tonight. The punch and summer pudding were wonderful."
Graham smiled something that looked half-real and actually air-kissed him. Gary would be delighted. "You're most welcome," he said. "Come back anytime."
Ben nodded and left. He stole a last glance at the boy and saw him in profile. He was laughing at something his aunt had said and it made him look so happy, so care-free, so young, so beautiful, that Ben felt physically sick. He tripped over his feet and then hurried down the stairs, flinging open the front door, quickly letting himself out and into the square.
He wondered what to do. The thought of that young man, his perfect physique, the promise of the gentle spikiness of his almost-smooth head, the lightness of his face as he smiled, made him breathless. He was due to see Fred, but Fred would be two, possibly three, lines down by now, cloying and clawing. But nor could he just go back to Maida Vale; not like this. He didn't want the night to end. He needed time to savour perfection, to dwell on what might have been, to wallow, if only for one night, on the thought of how things could have been. He hurried through the streets to a quiet pub he knew.

CHAPTER SIXTEEN

Ben pushed open the heavy wooden door of the pub and scanned the room. The solidity of the wood, permanence in a changing, fleeting world, was reassuring. It was ten-thirty on a Saturday night, but the place was mostly empty; he was too early. Still, he saw what he was looking for: a companion, someone to unburden on, to bore until tears came to his eyes and he begged Ben to stop, someone Ben would never see again. He was Ben's age, same height and build, Indian or Pakistani, and he had glanced up from his cushioned wooden seat at the bar and was smiling at him.

Ben sat down. "Pride, please," he said to the barman – and the other man. No smart drinks needed now, no one to impress, look for action. The barman nodded and started to pull the pint.

"Hi," said the man. "I'm Ibrahim."

Ben appraised Ibrahim's smile, noted how the skin colour was wrong, how the teeth were yellower and less even. His hair was too long and his clothes were cheap, rough jeans and a tight collarless blue cotton top.

"What are you drinking?" he asked.

"Rum and Coke."

Ben laughed inwardly. No delicious steaming rum punch, just a hustler's drink. The young man in Peter's comfortable apartment didn't drink rum and Coke, not with James Sassoon. And the laugh died inside him.

"And a rum and Coke, please." The barman nodded and served them.

"Thanks, man," said Ibrahim and toasted Ben, before taking a long draught. "So," he added as he put his drink down, "You gonna tell us your name?"
Ben thought about excusing himself and then reminded himself he'd made a decision. This man would take his misery as surely as Winston had. "Ben," he said.
Ibrahim smiled. There was a gap in his front teeth. "Cheers, Ben," and, with a second draught, half the drink was gone. "So, what's a nice-looking bloke doing all alone on a Saturday night?"
Ibrahim's accent was almost cockney, and Ben had a thought. Second best, third best; it hardly mattered now. "Where are you from?" he asked.
Now Ibrahim appraised Ben. "Watford," he said. "Why, where are you from?"
Ben pursed his lips – not black, not sophisticated, not at home in a Bloomsbury saloon, not from South London. Just a hustler, but a hustler that might be paid to listen, even in rums with Coke. "Sorry," he said. "I didn't mean that. I just hoped you might be from South London."
"Ah!" said Ibrahim, running a hand over Ben's thigh and making sure to catch his eye. "You prefer black to brown, do you? Don't you know the best things come in brown packages?" Then he started to sing, "Brown paper packages, tied up with string…"
It was absurd. Ben laughed and Ibrahim stopped and smiled. He did that quite well, a trade skill perhaps. "That's better," he said. "Now, why don't you buy me another drink and tell me all about this black dude of yours? Then we'll see what we can do about your favourite thing."

Ben laughed again and Ibrahim leant over and kissed him. Ben made no attempt to stop him and felt the soft, pleasant warmth of Ibrahim's mouth, a whiff of alcohol. Then, Ibrahim pulled away and Ben motioned the barman for a second round. Ibrahim downed his when Ben had barely taken a sip of his own.
"Want to get out of here?" Ibrahim asked, leaning into Ben's side and nuzzling the nape of his neck. It reminded Ben uncomfortably of Marco, but then Ibrahim slid his hand into Ben's and it was all right. "Usually, I'm on the clock, but tonight I've made my stash." He slid Ben's hand into the back pocket of his jeans and Ben felt the crumple of many banknotes. "And you're a rare looker. Want to show me a good time?"
Ibrahim wanted Ben to take him home, but Ben wasn't going to do that, he never had with anyone, not even Winston. He didn't shit where he ate. But he didn't want to leave. "I just want to talk. Know anywhere quiet?"
"Oh, Ben," said Ibrahim with a toss of his head. "A tete-a-tete and not at your place? Most disappointing! And I'm not looking for a tete-a-tete, not with you, maybe a lip-a-lip. Take me dancing. Then I'll think about giving you what you really want."
Ben liked dancing and hadn't done it for too long. He allowed Ibrahim to lead him into a taxi and then to a club in an old brick and stone warehouse in Wapping Ben had never known existed.

It was not yet midnight, but the place was heaving, two floors, the second open in the centre, crammed with pulsating male bodies. There was a stage of dancers in front of the DJ, most topless and the dampness of the sweat-drenched air was intoxicating. Ibrahim pulled Ben into the middle of the throng, melt into the heavy, thunderously booming beat as the lights strobed above. Ibrahim wriggled closer, putting his arms over Ben's shoulders, pulling him into a kiss. Ben never got tired of kissing, never got enough of it, and kept the man's mouth on his as Ibrahim rubbed his crotch against his own, cupping Ben's arse. He slid his lips across Ben's cheek to his ear, tantalising him as he tickled the soft hairs. "I know what you need, even if you don't. Black Beauty has eluded you and you need to shake away that tension or you'll never gambol in those fields again." Black Beauty. A nineteenth century children's book about a horse; the name had an absurdly truthful ring to it. Ben had never read the book, but the purity of the concept, the innocence of the idea, appealed to him. He sought out Ibrahim's mouth, willingly provided, leant in as Ibrahim frotted both of them with an expertise Ben had never felt before. He gasped and almost withdrew his mouth as he shuddered and released, the first time anyone had done that to him. Ibrahim just laughed in his mouth and then slid his parted lips across Ben's cheek, before whispering in his ear, "Good boy. Now you return the favour," before grinding harder with his crotch and heaving and panting into Ben's ear. Not that long after, although it felt longer to Ben, came a rush of breath in his ear as Ibrahim yelled, "Yeah," and put his lips back on Ben's.

Ben's crotch was soaked, his trousers would be ruined, and he wondered how much Ibrahim still had in him after a day at work, but he let Ibrahim keep kissing him. He was intoxicated, by the heat of the pulsating room, the unexpected enthusiasm of Ibrahim's contact, his silly erudition. He pulled back from Ibrahim's face and grinned. Ibrahim, after a brief look of dismay, grinned too and then both of them shot their hands into the air as Katy Perry's Waking Up in Vegas came overhead, 'Shut up and put your money where your mouth is'. They did and then punched their hand into the air, shouting, "Yeah! Yeah!" That's what you get for waking up in Vegas.

But his crotch itched and scratched. He leant in to Ibrahim and said, "I need to go; I want a shower."

"Golden?" laughed Ibrahim.

Ben signalled the door with his arm. Ibrahim pouted. "Hot n Cold," he whispered as he leant in, "No wonder you're single." That hurt and Ben let it show as Ibrahim took his hand. Outside, rain was falling steadily, it took time to find a cab and Ben was soon soaked all over. Ibrahim too, his top clinging to a very muscled front. "Want to see something I'll bet you've never seen before?" said Ibrahim, sticking his tongue in Ben's ear. Ben flinched. "I think I'd better be off."

Ibrahim slid his hand over Ben's crotch, squeezing and making Ben feel all the dampness there. "Come on, Ben, old man," he teased. "No you don't. You haven't unburdened your soul yet. And you haven't fucked me either."

"Haven't you been fucked enough for one day?"

Ibrahim chuckled and gave the driver directions for somewhere in Bayswater. "You'll like it," he said. "Very salubrious. A private members' club. I'm privileged to have a key."
"Where are we?" asked Ben, nervous as he looked at the white stuccoed nineteenth century terraced building close to Paddington Station.
Ibrahim noticed and stroked his shoulder and upper arm, grasping the latter. "Don't worry; you're perfectly safe. You don't need to tell me where you live, you don't need to give me your phone number, you don't even need to tell me your last name. But you do need to come inside. Go on, Ben. You're among friends, which I suspect doesn't happen enough. Do it for me. You won't regret it. And there are showers."
He pulled a key from his pocket and led Ben inside. Downstairs was a bare room with dirty white walls where several men of various ages and in various stages of undress where lounging about, watching TV, playing pool or just reading magazines. There were beer cans and several pizza boxes on the floor.
"What's this?" Ben asked, hardly believing his eyes. "A hustlers' club?"
Ibrahim chuckled. "Give the man a medal. I told you I'd show you something different. It's a place where we can come to rest, wash and brush up. There aren't many rules and fewer questions, but we have one overriding rule: no paying guests." He kissed Ben again, lingering for a moment. God, he was good at it, a lot of practice, no doubt. "But friends are exempted, so as I say, you're quite safe."
"Why? Do you do this often?"

"Wouldn't you just love to know? You know a girl never reveals all her secrets. Now, come on." He led Ben to an empty room with a toilet and shower at the back. "Wash up," he said. "I'll just go and find us something to drink."
Ben did as he was told, even brushing his teeth. There was a small towel and he self-consciously pulled it around his waist as the bedroom door opened.
Ibrahim came in, with a bottle of white wine and two glasses. He saw Ben and grinned. "Take it off please. What it's hiding is going to be hard and in me before this night's much older, so let me see if I want to change my mind."
Ben dropped the towel and stood while Ibrahim, pausing to look a few times, put down the bottle and glasses.
"Meet your approval?" asked Ben.
Ibrahim cocked his head. "Did I say I'd changed my mind? But we haven't put it through its paces yet. I still might."
"I don't understand," said Ben.
Ibrahim stripped, revealing a nicely-muscled chest with good stomach definition and a beautiful dark cock, slightly aroused, amid neatly cropped pubic hair.
"Don't understand what?" said Ibrahim, taking the towel, throwing it over his shoulder and stroking Ben as he passed. "Nice," he added as he walked to the shower.
"How can you let men fuck you all day and then look for more in your time off? How old are you anyway?"

Ibrahim laughed and washed. As he came back into the bedroom, towelling himself dry, he said, "I like cock. By my calculations, since my Dad chucked me out fifteen years ago for blowing the Imam on the carpet of the mosque, I've got off over five thousand blokes, one way or another, seventeen to seventy, race religion background politics no obstacle although sexual health is. That bearded Iranian cunt was as bad as any Catholic priest and I haven't been in a mosque since, or seen my Dad for that matter. It was rough to start with sometimes, in all senses, but I quickly worked out what to do and learnt to take the rough with the smooth, again in all senses. Now, I'm packing away the cash. And tonight, you walked into the pub not two hours after I passed my latest savings milestone, looking much better than a late-night movie. So, to answer your question, I'm kicking back. No, I don't make a habit of giving it away, but seventeen year-olds come too fast, as do seventy year-olds, while those in the middle often leave a lot to be desired. You were nice in the pub and got nicer afterwards. Cute too," he added and slid his fingers down Ben's cheek and then over his chest. "Call yourself my way of sticking it to Ramadan, which is on at the minute. But don't worry, you do what I say in this room or you're out on your ear before you can say 'Lesser Eid'."

Ben nodded and Ibrahim grinned. "Good man, Ben. Now, you get over here so you can stick it to me." He picked up the wine, unscrewed the top and took a swig. Then, he poured a large slop down his chest and into his crotch. Ben wasn't sure, even as he caught the condom. Ibrahim winked, took his hand and brought Ben down over him as he said, "I'm looking forward to a good time from you, Ben. Don't let me down, please. It might sound an odd thing to say, but I don't do this very often. Now, work my body until I tell you to stop."

Ben sucked him with his mouth full of wine; the squelching sounds made Ibrahim giggle until his breathing became laboured, his flat stomach heaving and twisting under Ben's caresses, and he said, ragged, "Fuck me, deep, hard and fast."

Ben worked his way in, not difficult, and looked him in the eyes. They were sparkling with desire but as Ben started, he saw age in the face. As he worked, it was erotic to see someone so experienced get into it so completely. A thought flitted in, wondering how it was between James Sassoon and Black Beauty, whether 'Jamie' ever consented and looked like this. But he knew the answer. Ben was angry for the young man, he would consent for that boy if that was what it took, consent again and again. He deserved it, he was a man too after all, and what a man! With him, young as he was, he would be always reaching, never settling.

"What the fuck's wrong with you? You want to be out on your ear? Fuck me, you pussy! I felt it. Now, give it to me like you fucking mean it!"

Ben returned to the task in hand, a Mark II New Ben version of The Torpedo, a one-night invitation-only performance. He looked down, everything rock hard down below, glinting eyes, parted lips and distended limbs up above. Yet, for all Ben provided the strength and speed, it was Ibrahim who determined the direction and depth and he continued to work on Ben until he was satisfied with the result, gasping and grasping Ben's hands in his, over his head, voluntarily restraining himself as he released and the hardness of his body and the softness of his surrender sent Ben over the edge. Ben worked them both down until Ibrahim paused to recover his breath and pushed himself upright, face-to-face, he could have done it at any time, and kissed him. "Good man," he said, barely a whisper. "Nicely done, my friend." He patted Ben's chest and then slid his palm over it. "Very nicely, even if there was one little wobble which may prove an insight into your character. Now, we wash and then I get some more wine. I've told you mine, now you tell me yours. I want my bedtime story."
Ben was amazed the condom wasn't ripped to shreds. He smiled, sure it wasn't just his fantasy that had come true that last half hour. And now, in the shower, this man who'd wanted to be fucked into surrender was soaping himself down as if he'd just come off the sports field having scored the winning goal, whistling. It was a different sort of perfection, but a little perfection nonetheless. Whatever he did with his body for a living, Ibrahim was a good man too, and one in full control of what happened to him. And then Ben realised Ibrahim was whistling the theme tune to the 1970s TV series of The Adventures of Black Beauty and laughed.

Ibrahim grinned and smacked him. Then, still naked and wet, he ran downstairs and came back with another bottle of wine. He filled the glasses, handed one to Ben, lay on the bed and patted the space next to him. Ben lay down and told his story, about Marco and Rio, about Patrick and Warren and David and Bill and Harry and fifty-nine partners and two STDs and Tom and Caroline and Daisy and Chris and Marco again and Winston and Fred and the young man he'd met the party, unattainable.

Ibrahim nodded, listened, asked the occasional question and paused him while he got a third bottle from downstairs. He drank his wine steadily but not hastily.

"I'm twenty-nine," he said after Ben had finished. "I'm saving up for a flat."

"A flat!" said Ben.

"Don't sound so surprised, Mr Good-with-his-body-and-not-much-else. I can't get a mortgage, but I still want the security of a roof over my head. When I've got it, I'm going to buy cars and go into mini-cabs."

Ben nodded. "Sorry," he said. "I understand. How much do you have?"

"Three hundred thou'. Another fifty and I'm there. In fact, I crossed the three hundred mark today. That's why I'm in such a generous mood."

Ben was impressed. "How much do you make a week?"

"Depends, of course, but more each year. People know me, I have regulars and can charge the one-offs more for the privilege, even the regulars sometimes. Say, two grand, a bit more, and I try to save two-thirds if I can."

Ben whistled. With bonuses, he made considerably more, but after taxes and the mortgage saved a lot less.

"I work hard," said Ibrahim and emptied his glass before refilling it.

"I can see that," said Ben. "And I felt it too; five thousand shows." Then, he looked at the window; light was shining through the brown canvas curtain. "Jesus! What's the time?"
Ibrahim rolled over to pick up his phone. "Seven-thirty," he said.
"I've got to go. I have a boyfriend to dump."
Ibrahim nodded and stood up as Ben dressed. Quite unexpectedly, he pulled a business card from a black roll-wallet and handed it to Ben along with a kiss.
"You're a good man, Ben. I hope you find what you're looking for, get what you so obviously deserve. But if you don't and you get lonely sometime, give us a call. It's highly unlikely I'll be off the clock, but either way, I'll let you know before I come over and you come over me."
Ben pocketed the card and kissed Ibrahim in turn who reciprocated. So nice. "Thanks. And good luck with the flat. It's been a privilege to be your bonus tonight. And thank you for this, all of this. You were right; you did know exactly what I needed."
"Aw, you big softie. Get away with you! And don't come back until you've got a new tale to tell, preferably night-time to bedtime. Now, piss off. I'm going to sleep."

Ben smiled as he descended the stairs. Yes, there would be some explaining to do to Fred, and probably a lot of tears, but Fred was history, even if meant being alone again. Ibrahim had been unexpected, but had been the right end to the evening. He had got to unburden his soul and onto someone surprisingly sympathetic. As he walked past the dirty living room on the ground floor, there were whistles, catcalls and a shout of 'walk of shame!' Ben just laughed, opened the front door and hailed a cab home; no way was he going on the Bakerloo Line looking like this.

CHAPTER SEVENTEEN

Ben had a lonely Christmas. He was in the bosom of his family, at his parents' home in Dorset along with Tony, Estelle and their three small but loud children, but he felt bereft. Christmas itself was fine, busy and bustling, with stockings and church and presents and drinks and lunch and visitors and tea and TV, but on Boxing Day, as he sat in the detritus of the previous day's maelstrom, he sighed. Yet again, he was alone. Since Peter Weller's drinks party in early September had reset the clocks and then immediately stopped them, he had drifted through two relationships and turned twenty-eight. Time was running out and even though he knew now where his opportunity for happiness lay, he also knew that road was closed. As he sat on the Bakerloo Line on the way home one night in mid-October, he saw a photo of him with James Sassoon in the Evening Standard. It was the final confirmation. They looked so good together, so happy, both so assured, the age difference hardly noticeable. And still no name. Despite this, asking the neatly-dressed man sitting eyeing him up from the opposite side of the swaying train carriage whether he could see the paper was the source of the second relationship.
"They look beautiful together don't they?"
"Yes. Perfection in human form."
"I don't think you're too far from that yourself."

Now, Ben could barely remember his name, Charles, although the real reason was that Ben had been busy in the run-up to Christmas. Finally back in his cosy little flat in Maida Vale, having been told by Charles the previous day to step up or step out, he received a long, maudlin, rambling email from Fred, illiterate and almost incomprehensible. He thought nothing of it and then woke up at four in the morning and called the police, who broke the lock to get in. He arrived at Fred's flat just as they were wheeling him into an ambulance. He had overdosed on crack with vodka chasers. As soon as his bank realised he wasn't going to die, they fired him. Ben picked up the pieces, dealing with the police, the hospital, Fred's parents whom he had never met and who didn't know their son was gay, the ex-employer, Fred's mountain of unpaid bills and bigger mountain of unwashed clothes. He had the front door repaired. Yes, it was partly Ben's fault, dumping him the final straw, but it had been coming for a long time and it was Fred's decision to steepen the decline afterwards with crack, whose ugly-looking dealers came round twice during the period looking for their money, and three teenage rent-boys who also came round looking for the same. It was a mercy that Fred's mother saw none of them, although his father did and insisted on reimbursing Ben after he had forced the full story out of him. All of them tired, Ben checked a broken, shuffling Fred, still in a dressing gown, into rehab on Christmas Eve and then drove down to Dorset, having turned down a quite unexpected invitation to spend Christmas with his parents in Cork.

He thought of his night with Ibrahim. Of the three men he had been with since Peter's party, only Ibrahim understood. In Dorset, he found a broken-spined paperback of Black Beauty on a white shelf in the little sitting room, his mother's room. He decided not to read it. Yes, that evening with Ibrahim had been very satisfying in many different way, but it was no substitute for the one relationship he truly craved.
He looked at Bethany, Tony's eldest. She had been born when Tony was younger than Ben was now. And, by then, Tony had been married almost two years already and been living with his future wife for four years before that. Sure, Tony was an early starter by modern standards, married at twenty-six and a father within a year, but for the first time Ben felt life slipping away. Children were a realistic possibility for gay couples these days, but how could Ben start a family if he couldn't even find a boyfriend he could commit to? The only consolation was that he was finally in love and, to his surprise, it felt good, a little candle burning warm and steady inside him, a night-light to keep the demons away. He admired the good taste of any man who would choose James Sassoon and was consoled that James Sassoon wouldn't waste his time on someone unworthy of it, a kitemark rating of quality.

Usually, he enjoyed New Year, an urban antidote to a quiet Christmas in the country with its long walks in damp woods and damper fields. But this year, Daisy was pregnant, as was Caroline. Devoid of alternatives, Ben accepted yet another invitation to Harry and Bill's, dinner at their new house in Islington. They were now very settled, indeed almost boring, even Harry smoothed off and polished. They were all but married, in a civil partnership, and looking to adopt at least one child. Ben knew, just knew, he would be the only single left.

He waved good-bye to his family with both relief and dismay. Bethany, approaching four, hugged his legs tight and said "Don't go, Uncle Ben", and this just made it worse. His heart fell at the sight of Harry wearing a navy blue lambswool cardigan as he opened the door and hugged him. A cardigan!

"We're mostly going to be couples, of course," Harry whispered as he kissed him. "But we haven't forgotten you. There's someone coming, Samuel, Sam, that we think you're going to like. He's a banker, starting to get pretty rich – and more than pretty studly already to boot."

Great, thought Ben. Harry always kept trying and always kept failing.

His spirits rose as he saw a big, smoothed-skinned if slightly over-weight black man introduced to him as Sam, but it fell again as he heard the man's voice, all Eton and Oxford, probably the Guards as well, a brittle high-pitched bray. He was like some ghastly amalgam of the worst of Warren's body, Fred's career and Patrick's character, lacking any of their authenticity, a socially-ambitious wannabe James Sassoon who was anything but. No Black Beauty, he fell at the first fence. Nevertheless, Sam manoeuvred himself next to Ben, standing alone by the fireplace. "Do you like wine?" he asked, his voice already grating.
Ben shook his head. He really didn't.
"How about golf?"
Ben loathed golf, walking around in the rain, searching for balls in the trees that were invariably lost, pretending it was exercise, a real sport. It was the only business networking he consistently refused to do. "I'm sorry," he managed.
Sam pulled down the sides of his lips. Yes, too fat; those cheeks made him look like Droopy. "Looks like you left your heart in San Francisco," he said.
Ben smiled. Sam would undoubtedly prefer the Frank Sinatra version to the Tony Bennett, if he had indeed heard either. Maybe the Westlife version. Sadly gay, Ben didn't like any of them. "Yes. I'm sorry. Is it that obvious?"
Sam looked as if he'd been punched. Crest-fallen, he looked even more like Droopy. Yes, he was entitled as well. The man had been trying to make a joke.
"You know the irony of it? I don't even know his name."

Sam walked off and didn't speak to Ben again that evening. Ben looked across at him a few times during dinner, Sam was regaling the table with some moderately amusing, if needlessly cruel, anecdotes about some people in his office and about the gay liaison of one of his clients, but Ben knew he was right. Sam was a braying donkey. He wondered where the beautiful couple were spending their New Year, probably drinking gluhwein from each other's cups in front of a log fire in Gstaad after a hard day on the slopes. The thought made him happy, but also lonely, alone and isolated as he sat in silence. He got steadily drunker as the conversations grew louder and more boisterous as the evening progressed. He tripped over his feet and poured champagne down his leg as Sam tried to sing Auld Lang Syne, but of course didn't know the words. He should have known better. Ben stumbled over to Harry, "Get me a minicab, please."
He was so hung-over the next morning, he caught his leg in his duvet and fell over as he tried to get out of bed. "Fuck!" he shouted as he righted himself.
He stretched out his arm to steady himself against his chest of drawers, missed and banged his side into its lip, just below the armpit. "Shit!" he shouted even louder. "Fucking, shitting hell!"

He stumbled into the bathroom and reeled as he stood uncertainly over the toilet. He splashed widely and wildly and then a wave of nausea came over him and he knelt down and threw up into the bowl of dirty water. It helped a little, as did the water he downed with the headache pills from the cabinet. He hadn't been this drunk in a long time and, as he flopped back onto the bed and closed his eyes, he felt a wave of self-loathing. He had glimpsed perfection and then ended up with a Pakistani hustler. He had swapped Charles' Warwick Avenue apartment, so similar to his own, for Fred, choking on his own vomit. He moaned and turned on his side.

New Year's resolutions: find a real boyfriend, and no more fucking booze. Great, now he was turning into Bridget Jones.

But after sleep, eggs and bacon, more sleep, a shower, a run and then another shower, he felt no better. Maybe he should have gone skiing as well instead of wasting his time with Harry and Bill. As he bought some salad for his dinner from the local corner-shop, he also pulled down a bottle of Chablis, which he drank in less than an hour before passing out on the sofa. He woke the next day with less of a head and feeling surprisingly rested. What he really wanted to do, though, was to call Peter Weller and ask him the name of the one who had stolen his heart. But he knew Peter wouldn't tell him. He almost welcomed the approach of the new work week and the return to routine, humdrum as it might be.

Then, life took a turn for the better. His first client meeting, just days into the new year, was an introduction from Edward Makins, his most reliable investment banking contact.

"He's looking to IPO," Edward said. "It's a bit of a rush, to be done before Easter. We've been working hard for the last couple of months to get everything ready. But when I raised PR, he mentioned you by name and was anxious to have you on board. Just meet him; I think you'll like him, I know I do. He was pleased I knew you actually."

And Ben did like Robert Wilkinson, immediately. He was a serious-looking, straight-acting gay man in his mid-thirties in a sober business suit that fitted his neatly-maintained body perfectly. His only affectation was his shock of thick, lustrous blond hair. He had set up a company, Green Fields, in 2004 that had chalked up a few moderate successes before hitting it big with the arrival of the smart phone. It had started designing and developing apps for companies unable to do it themselves before then branching out into a range of other things with rapidly increasing success. Apps were still the largest part of its business, but now only made up about a third of revenues. Overall, the company was growing at a prodigious rate and had turned down an offer six months before from Yahoo! for almost a billion dollars. "I want to show the Brits can do it, too," he said as he ran through one of the best-prepared presentations Ben could remember seeing. The bane of working with smaller, younger companies was their general ignorance of proper public positioning, even if they knew how to market their products.

"We're valuing it at a billion pounds, hoping for more," Edward had whispered down the phone. Ben could see why. He had to secure this deal and, from a slightly sullen indifference before the meeting, he pulled himself together, blooming into an oratorical flourish as he ran through his ideas that took even him by surprise.

"So, you buy into our premise?" Wilkinson asked.
Ben was taken aback by the man's modesty. "Yes, I do. Frankly, it would be an honour to work with you. You could go anywhere with this deal and I'm very grateful you've come to see us."
Well, you were recommended by one of the best." When Ben looked confused, Wilkinson added, "Jamie Sassoon. He said he knew you and rated you."
Ben gripped the side of the table with both hands. A kitemark from Sassoon for him too? Better than indifferent table wine? For all he had taken his card, Ben had no thought that the man would even remember his name. And to recommend him to the owner of what would obviously be one of the year's hottest new stock market listings. Wilkinson noticed Ben's loss of cool and laughed and, with it, his whole demeanour changed. His smile was boyish, both innocent and with the hint of mischief, and Ben noticed that shock of blond hair again. It shook and waved and Ben had visions of cornfields and women in long dresses running hands through rippling stalks, looking back and laughing as they did so. He smiled and knew it was sincere.
"I like you, and you've convinced me," said Wilkinson. "You shouldn't look so surprised; you're becoming one of the go-to people for the new overlap Pink/mainstream economy. And Jamie is a sound judge of character." He stood and put out his hand across the table. "Call me Bobby. Everybody does."

So Ben called him Bobby, took him on personally as a client – something Bobby had insisted on anyway – and spent the next three months preparing the marketing story for the IPO. As part of his work, he saw the shareholder list one day; James Sassoon owned 4.99 percent, one of five who did, each the largest shareholder after Bobby. He looked in the prospectus and matched it to a 24.99% consortium investment three years ago for £25 million. Christ, did that man just get everything? And there was Peter Weller's name too, with a 0.75 percent stake, along with nine others, an even earlier investment, but Ben couldn't see how much he had paid for it.

The work was tiring, but exhilarating. He stopped looking for dates or even going to any bars, although he still swam and jogged, his sexual energy transferred into his work. He got excellent coverage in all the online and print media, the Financial Times even doing a full-page 'Lunch With' interview in the Weekend edition, the newswires, and on Bloomberg, CNBC, the BBC and Sky News, not to mention the Gay Times and Attitude. Finally, this was going to be the transformational deal that Ben had been waiting for.

"You've done a good job," said Bobby a few days before the share sale went live.

"Your story sells itself," Ben said.

Bobby nodded, stared at Ben and then grinned, his boyish good humour bubbling out. "That's partly true, I'm sure," he said. "But I know skill when I see it. I appreciate the way you keep me informed and briefed. You and Edward are doing a very good job."

Ben was flattered and more so when Bobby hugged him. But he only felt satisfied when the IPO was put to bed, with the offer size increased and the price raised substantially. Despite this, the shares still soared twenty per cent on their first day of trading, a Thursday, and Ben arrived late at the celebration party Edward's firm had arranged that night as he tried to assure news editors both that the shares hadn't been sold too cheaply and that they weren't too expensive after the first day's rally.

CHAPTER EIGHTEEN

By the time Ben arrived at nine-thirty, the party was three hours old and in full swing. Edward's firm had hired the ballroom of the Grosvenor House Hotel. Already hot and sweaty despite its size, it was filled with upwards of four hundred people, many of them employees now rendered paper millionaires by the flotation. The remains of a long buffet table stood forlornly to one side of the room and the round dining tables were all full of dirty plates, half-drunk wine glasses, crushed beer cans and clusters of people leaning on the stained tablecloths talking, a few sitting alone looking dazed but content. The DJ was playing 90s dance music, Finally by Ce Ce Peniston replaced by Vogue by Madonna as Ben descended the curving staircase. Perhaps fifty people were crammed onto the hard wooden dance floor, with the residual of the room, almost ninety people, crowded around the bar. Although Bobby was gay, most of his staff weren't and almost half the people in the room were women, some the wives and girlfriends of the employees, many employees themselves and the rest advisers and consultants to the IPO.

Ben was hungry and made his way to the ransacked buffet table. He located a clean plate and some tepid beef goulash and boiled potatoes. He served himself and then found an empty table and sat down to eat. After he had shovelled in half a dozen mouthfuls, a shadow fell across him. He looked up, saw the handsome angular face leaning forward and jumped to attention. "Mr Sassoon!" he said and put out his hand. Sassoon shook it and smiled, bending to catch Ben's nervous, flickering eyes.
"Call me Jamie," he said and placed his other hand on top of Ben's. Oh God, with a voice like that, a smile like that, an easy graceful power in those hands and throughout his lean body, so assured and with such real presence, saying 'call me Jamie', how would the unattainable ever want to leave? "I just wanted to say, nice job. Bobby has been singing your praises."
Ben realised he was going to stammer and got a grip on himself. He needed to make a good impression. He was on parade. "Thank you for recommending us to him. It's been both an honour and a pleasure working with him. I'm extremely grateful to you for suggesting our firm. It's a big deal for us to work on something like this."
Jamie smiled, released Ben's hand and slapped him on the back. Ben swayed but luckily didn't stagger. "Oh, Ben, you're too modest," he said. "I didn't recommend your firm, good as it is. I recommended you. I also had a word with Gary Evans just now and said I thought you were someone who would go far."
Ben went crimson. "I don't know what to say, Mr Sassoon, Jamie. Er…thank you, thank you very much." They shook hands, Ben trying not to be too vigorous, afraid his own was clammy.

"Gratitude, when sincere as I see yours is, is pleasure enough. And your politeness is something of a legend, I understand. I'm glad I was able to help and that you didn't let me down. Now, have a drink, kick back, enjoy yourself. Just make sure to support the shares in the after-market. I've got a stake in Bobby's success as well, as I'm sure you know."

Ben stammered a 'yes', but Jamie Sassoon was gone as quickly as he'd arrived. Nevertheless, the compliments from a man like that went straight to Ben's head. He felt briefly like a god, a grand cru. But then, what was that about politeness and a legend? Had there been a twinkle in the man's eyes then? What did he know? Probably everything. Oh, fuck!

Then, finally he let in the thought that had been there all through that interview, knocking at the back of his mind, demanding entry. If Sassoon was here, perhaps perfection was too. He looked around, but although he saw Sassoon briefly, talking to Bobby's number two at the bar, he couldn't see Jamie's boyfriend anywhere. Slowly, a little despondent, he set off for the bar, just in case the man was there too, close to Jamie but hidden from view in the crush. He wasn't at the tables, he wasn't on the balcony and Ben couldn't see him on the dance-floor. He walked to the bar.

Bobby noticed him and beckoned him over. His serious work face was gone, replaced with that boyish smile, suffused with raffish good humour and happiness.

"Ben! There you are!" Bobby yanked him powerfully in by the small of his back, almost a bear-hug, completely genuine. "I've been looking for you. So has Jamie Sassoon."

"Yes, I saw Jamie."

"Great," said Bobby, his smile increasing even further. "Now, time to get sloshed. This is my other half, Greg, and Edward you know, of course."
Greg was a slim, handsome man somewhere over forty with mousey brown hair that was greying at the temples. Effeminate but dignified, his handshake was firm. "Well done, Ben," he said. "You've done Bobby proud. Thank you." Then, to Ben's surprise, Greg hugged him and whispered in his ear, "I haven't seen Bobby this happy in a long time. Thank you for your part in it." Ben struggled to hide his astonishment, but Greg looked him in the eyes and raised his eyebrows.
"Ben, go and get a drink with Edward and then come and dance. I want to see you strut your stuff. Come on, darling, dance with me." And then, making strutting movements, he pulled Greg along to the dance floor and they began to dance, very well it seemed to Ben.
Ben scanned the dancers and then turned to look around the bar area, but there was no sign of the young man. Nor, Ben realised, could he see Jamie Sassoon either. He resigned himself to the probability that they had both left.
"Is it all done?" asked Edward Makins, handing Ben a glass of champagne.
Ben looked back at Edward, puzzled as he tried to reconnect his thoughts. Then, he nodded. "Yes, I've spoken to everyone, even the Gay Times."

Edward laughed and downed his champagne in two quick gulps. "That was inspired, you know?" he said. "That and the full-pager in the FT. This deal's made both our firms; you wouldn't believe what I had to do to keep those lazy bulge-bracket bastards out. Sure, a cow could have sold the shares, but with a little hard work on my side and the buzz you created – it was electric!" He downed a second glass of champagne and Ben smiled and copied him. "Time to get shit-faced, my friend," he said, laying his hand messily round Ben's shoulder. "This deal hasn't just made our firms; it's made you and me too. I could kiss you."

"Don't," said Ben, laughing. He knew very well that Edward was engaged to a fiancée who was pregnant with their second child and didn't have a gay bone in his body. He also knew that Edward had done a lot more than a little hard work.

"Well, I'm going to anyway," said Edward and landed a very sloppy one on Ben's cheek, handed him another glass of champagne and said, "Better find the old ball and chain. Maybe I can persuade her to take a quick turn on the dance-floor before she turns me in for the night."

Ben nodded and Edward wandered off, weaving unsteadily. Ben smiled as he saw the banker go and then turned his eyes back to the room, scanning it carefully, but there was no young man in it. It was past eleven now and the DJ had slowed it down and changed the mood. He was playing Shania Twain, You're Still the One. He watched as Bobby and Greg cradled each other slowly. After that came Brandy's The Boy is Mine. Then, he speeded it up with Shania Twain again, this time That Don't Impress Me Much. Ben smiled, downed his glass and weaved his way onto the dance-floor. He hadn't danced since Ibrahim and he was in the mood.

Bobby and Greg saw him and smiled. They drew apart and the three men danced, their arms twirling above their heads. A group of women joined in and the six sang along to the song. Then, the DJ changed the pace completely, putting on ABBA, Money, Money, Money, to a roar of approval from the whole room. The number of dancers rose to over a hundred and fifty. The DJ played Dancing Queen next, the crowd demanded it, but then he changed the pace again, Halo by Beyoncé.

Bobby, his face flushed and sweat streaming down his temples, clasped Ben into his side as he held Greg with his other hand. "So, Ben," he said. "Who have you shut out tonight?"

Ben thought. How he would have liked to have danced with perfection, just once, even if Jamie was watching. Then, afraid his wistfulness might show, he rallied and said, "Just me, Bobby. Young, free and single; the way it's meant to be."

But Bobby had noticed. He patted Ben on the chest. "Not to worry," he said. "A looker like you won't be on the shelf for long. Need any help?"

Ben shook his head. Part of him wouldn't mind, Bobby would do it much better than Harry ever could, but the presence of Sassoon tonight and, with it, the breeze of his boyfriend put him off. "Thanks," he said. "Let me find my destiny by myself."

"Destiny?" Bobby said. "Few of us find that, myself excepted." He planted a big kiss on Greg's lips. "At least get yourself laid, Ben; you deserve that. There're a few cute guys here tonight, some that I know are available. Or are you saving yourself?"

Then he grinned. "Maybe just too drunk to fuck."

Greg made a face. "No, darling. Please."

"Oh, but I think so." He winked at Ben. "A relic of my mis-spent youth. Too drunk to fuck! Too drunk to fuck!" He pushed his way over to the DJ, punching the air in time to the words as he did so. Greg smiled at Ben and then followed Bobby.

Ben found himself alone again. He was tipsy and light-headed, but he wasn't really drunk and certainly not too drunk to fuck. He pulled out his phone and scrolled through the names, looking for someone to call. There were so many names now, even excluding business contacts and schoolfriends. Hook-ups, exes, just friends, stamp collectors and archaeologists. He saw Winston's name. Winston would come and make him look good too. But Winston wouldn't enjoy it; Ben would be imposing and he had imposed on Winston long enough. He shook his head, shook it at all of them. None of them felt right and he put his phone away.

He pulled out his wallet. Ibrahim's card was one of several, but Ben found it easily. It was calling to him. It was dangerous, probably very stupid, but it was right. He wanted to read Ibrahim the second chapter of his failure to meet Black Beauty. "Ben here," he texted. "Want to go to a party?"
A minute later, Ibrahim called. "Hey man, what's up? Wow! Is that Too Drunk To Fuck?"
Ben laughed. "You like it?"
"I like any party where they play music like that!"
"They also play Dancing Queen."
"Hell, and I'm not there!" squealed Ibrahim. "The original, the one and only?"
Caution crept into Ben's befuddled brain. Why risk all the success, the approbation that he had finally, but so recently, received? But he also knew that Ibrahim was the only one who would really understand what he needed tonight, to be taken away from reality and back into his dreams. "Can you make yourself look decent? It's a business do."
"Afraid I'll embarrass you?"
"Frankly, yes."
"Well, don't worry that pretty little head of yours. I'll be all you could want, cut-off jeans and a skimpy tanktop. Three hundred."
"There's free food and booze."
"Two fifty and I cover my own travelling expenses, even if I've got to take a taxi."

Ben agreed, gave him the address and suggested he hurry. But when he saw Ibrahim standing on the balcony and scanning the room, he was astonished at how demure he was, cotton trousers beneath a yellow-striped cotton shirt over which he had a put a buff suede jacket. He had made a huge effort and that made him more desirable. Ben nodded and waved. Ibrahim saw him, flashed a brilliant smile and walked down the long, curved staircase, took Ben's hands and kissed him. Still so nice.

"Classy," he said. "Are these your friends?"

Ben looked around. It was twelve-thirty and the party still had two hours to go, but most of the people he knew had already left. Now, it was the serious party animals and they were downing the wine and munching on cold apple pie as they danced and chatted, almost shouting now over the music.

"Looks like I missed the best of it," said Ibrahim.

"Have a drink."

"Don't mind if I do." He had four in quick succession, while Ben had two.

The room was blessedly empty of work colleagues, although Bobby and Greg were still there, dancing slowly to the Backstreet Boys. But then Ben noticed Peter Weller standing to one side of the bar and watching the dancing. Ben was surprised not to have seen him earlier and shocked to see him here so late.

"I see him," said Ibrahim, whispering in Ben's ear. The hairs there tingled.

"No," said Ben, putting out his arm to grab Ibrahim, but as he did so, Peter turned and saw him, them, together. Ben stood appalled at the start of recognition on Peter's face and hurried over, Ibrahim following close behind.

"Ben!" said Peter. "I hadn't seen you and didn't want to leave without saying hello. You did very well, I heard."

"Thank you so much for inviting me to your party," said Ben, sobering up as quickly as he could. "It was all down to Jamie Sassoon and I would have never met him if you hadn't introduced us."

Peter nodded. "No problem. You've earned everything you've received."

Beside him, Ibrahim was quivering. Peter glanced at him, his distaste poorly hidden. Ibrahim put out his hand. "Ibrahim Muhktiar," he said. "A friend of Ben's."

Peter shook it with the minimum possible politeness. Ben wanted to slap him; Peter usually showed more grace. But he also realised how he had slipped up, and heard it in the hardness of Peter's disapproval. "A friend by the hour?"

Ibrahim smiled, showing his bright teeth, but replied, deeply offended, "No, for Ben it's by the evening, my very best rate. But I see you are familiar enough with us to recognise a man of the flesh."

Peter stiffened. Ben put up his hand. "Okay, enough. I'm sorry, Peter," he said. "I really am. I just wanted someone to talk to and what Ibrahim does best is listen."

Peter unbent slightly, but only very slightly, and nodded. "I understand," he replied. "It's not a problem. Just keep Ibrahim away from Bobby, please."

"Ooh," said Ibrahim. "Who's Bobby?"

Peter wrinkled his nose.

"You said you wouldn't embarrass me," said Ben.

"Sorry," said Ibrahim modestly. "So, this is a big day for you?"

"Huge," snapped Peter. "This is the day Ben arrived."

"And you invited me," said Ibrahim, serious. "I'm flattered. Thank you."
"Yes, that's a lesson for all of us," said Peter, frigid, regarding each of Ben and then Ibrahim slowly in turn. "I suspect the two of you should leave now."
And Peter did, much to Ben's relief. Ben put his hand in Ibrahim's and tugged it gently to follow Peter into the night, but something had caught Ibrahim's attention and he resisted. Ben turned to see. Ibrahim was staring at Bobby. And then it happened a second time. Bobby turned slightly and saw them both, hand in hand. Another start of recognition and then, to Ben's horror, Bobby walked over, sweating wildly and smiling, with Greg following. Ben blushed, but Bobby chuckled and slapped his shoulder. "Well, Ben. There's more to you than meets the eye. I see you took my advice literally. While I am indeed too drunk to fuck, I hope you aren't and I hope you have a good evening."
Ibrahim grabbed Bobby's hand and shook it vigorously. "It is you!" he said. You're that guy! Robert Wilkinson! The Internet millionaire. You're a real inspiration, you know? I read about you in Attitude. I'm Ibrahim Muhktiar, your biggest fan."
Bobby laughed. Ben just wanted the ground to eat him up.
"I am indeed that guy, Mr Muhktiar," said Bobby. "And treat my friend nicely. You only read that article because Ben put it there, as he did many, many others for me over the last few months. He's on to good things and for him to invite you to this bash is a great honour for you."
"No, I get that," said Ibrahim. "But I see you're the big cheese here tonight. Thank you for not kicking me out."

Ben looked at Greg, who seemed dubious although less obviously hostile than Peter, but Bobby was laughing, tears forming at the rims of his lower eyelids, mingling with the sweat on his flushed cheeks.
"I told him to get laid," he said, shaking. "But I didn't expect him to be able to organise someone so experienced quite so quickly."
Ibrahim grinned.
"Well, when Ben clicks his finger, I come; or something like that."
Bobby put back his head and just roared, Ben wanted to die, Greg smiled politely and Ibrahim shook Bobby's hand again and then took Ben's. "It's been an honour, Mr Wilkinson, a real honour. Now come on, Ben. One more champagne and then I need you to bore the bejesus out of me."
Ben knew Ibrahim meant listen to him talk, but it didn't come out that way. He tried to keep his face straight but the sound of Bobby's renewed laughter filled his ears.

CHAPTER NINETEEN

Ben sat up in his bed as sharply as he had when he realised Fred was killing himself. He clapped his hands to the top of his head. It was Friday morning and sunlight was shining through the slats of his blinds. He looked at his clock. Seven-thirty. He wasn't late. Somehow, he also didn't have a hangover, didn't even feel tired; the wine must have been good last night, sticking to champagne probably helped. But he remembered, remembered Peter's outrage, Greg's studied politeness, Bobby's shameless amusement.
"Fuck!" he shouted.
The bedclothes rustled, revealing Ibrahim's naked back, his head turned towards Ben, a dark burr of fuzz on his cheeks and chin. And now there was a man in his bed, the first time in six years that had happened. Never Winston, never Fred, never even Charles. The last rule had been broken, don't shit where you eat. And with a gap-toothed Pakistani tart.
"What?" mumbled Ibrahim and slid his hand over Ben's thigh, cupping his cock.
Ben jumped out of bed, ignored the fact he was naked, and said, "You've got to go. I've got to go. I don't know what got into me. I must be losing my mind."

Ibrahim rolled over onto his side and looked up.
"Actually, you have rarely sounded saner. Black Beauty is coming into focus, thanks to this Jamie person. And I sure as hell know what got into me, very nice it was too. If you lose your job today, consider taking it up professionally."
"Fuck off, Ibrahim. I'm a total idiot. I never should have called you, never have brought you here. I don't shit where I eat."
"Oh, well that's nice," said Ibrahim. "And you haven't paid me yet, either."
"Sorry, yes. Two hundred and…seventy-five," said Ben pulling all the notes from his wallet and counting them out on the bed. "It's all I have."
Ibrahim picked them up. "And more than we agreed on. Thank you." He got out of bed, kissed Ben and slapped his arse. "Don't worry. You'll get some innocent ribbing and then you'll find a real boyfriend, whoever it may be, and it will all be forgotten. Now, I'm going for a shower and then I'm going to use that extra twenty-five to treat you to brunch."
"I don't want brunch. I have to go to work and you have to leave!"
"And I will after I've had my shower and something to eat. If you don't want to eat, you can sit and watch me. And you don't have to go to work; after a night like that one, no one will be at their desks before noon. Just buy the papers and make a few calls to say sorry."
Ben looked at him, saw Ibrahim's smile and managed a weak one himself. "Thanks," he said. "You're a good guy."

Ibrahim beamed and kissed him. "There he is, that good man from the pub, at home in both Wapping and Park Lane. And I get you, Ben, how at the end of the day you called me to get it off your chest and out of your balls at the same time. Yes, there will be some very humiliating comments, but your friends will forgive and forget sooner or later. Now, are you coming in the shower? I want to."

Ben shook his head. "You go. I'll make some coffee."

Ibrahim ran his fingers along Ben's jawline. "Don't be long. I want to be made weak at the knees. And you, my dirty little friend, needs a good soaping down."

He disappeared into the bathroom and Ben pulled out the coffee percolator. Coffee brewing, he checked his phone, saw nothing, pissed, brushed and shaved, and then joined Ibrahim in the shower. The man was a professional with over £300,000 of evidence he was good at it, while Ben needed a clear head today. Ibrahim lathered him up and soaped him down.

He was also insistent about brunch and Ben took him to a café he had seen but never used half way between his flat and his office, vowing he would never go there again. Ibrahim guessed as much and laughed when Ben blushed at the accusation. It was nine-thirty and Ben was late for work for the first time in his professional career. But the sun was shining, birds were singing, a plane high above left white streaks in the blue sky. The little white wrought iron table and chairs looked inviting and he needed time to think before he met anyone he knew. Ibrahim ordered while Ben went to the bank to buy the newspapers and to repay Ibrahim for the cab fares. A glance across the business sections didn't throw up any horrors, but he wanted to read them carefully.

"You don't have to eat," said Ibrahim as Ben stared at his Eggs Benedict and orange juice. "But call Peter and Bobby and make your peace with them. Now, please."
"I thought I might just email them. They might not want to talk."
"No," said Ibrahim. "If these people are important, can screw up your career, your life, you talk to them and you do it now and it better be sincere. I don't mind what you say about me."
Ben hesitated and then sighed. He pulled out his phone and found Peter Weller's number. With the sun shining and Ibrahim saying the right thing, it suddenly didn't seem so bad. Peter answered almost immediately.
"Peter, it's Ben Connelly. I just wanted to say how very sorry I am about last night. I really let the side down, spoilt other people's evening, insulted you after you've helped me so much. I can only promise it was a momentary lapse that will never happen again and I do hope that one day you will forgive me."
After a short silence, Peter said, "It could have been worse. Have you seen the papers today?"
"Only glanced," he said, fear replacing his stress. "Did I miss something?"
"Not at all. In fact, quite the contrary. The coverage is uniformly positive. Keep up the good work and in time I'm sure we'll all forget, or at least forgive."
"Yes, thank you," gushed Ben, his fear dissipating through his clenched teeth. "I promise this won't happen again."
"I can hear food being eaten. Is he still with you?"
"He's just leaving; he wanted me to call you first."

Peter grunted. "Well, I'll admit he's not as bad as he could have been, he wasn't as bad last night and it sounds like he isn't this morning either. And I am reliably informed I'm a bit of an old woman sometimes. Do you love him?"

Ben couldn't believe the question. "God, no!"

"Why don't you find yourself a real boyfriend?"

And Ben knew he just had to ask. He wouldn't get a second chance. "I'm looking, believe me. But Peter, if I can try your patience, there was something I've been meaning to ask you. Who was that man at your party, Jamie Sassoon's boyfriend?"

Silence. Ben wondered if Peter had hung up and almost did himself. But Peter came back quite quietly, almost gently. "Interesting you noticed him when everybody else was obsessing over Jamie. And I remember that you did notice him. He's a protégé of mine, still work in progress although coming along nicely. His name's Trevor Stephens. But while we're on the subject of Jamie Sassoon, have you called Bobby yet?"

The moment had passed, Peter's tone had picked up, but Ben had a name, an astounding victory from the ashes of the past twelve hours. "He's next on my list."

"Well, get yourself up to speed on the papers and then get on to him as quickly as you can. I'm not important, but he is – in his own right and because he leads back to Jamie who has made you and can break you just as fast."

"Yes, yes I know," he said. "And thank you, Peter."

"Good. Thank you for the call. I appreciate it. You're absolved. Now call Bobby."

Ben rechecked the papers and then the newsfeeds on his email and the news sites on his phone while Ibrahim ate. The coverage was indeed good, very good. A few neutrals, which he could work on, but no negatives. He called his junior in the office. "What's the share price?"
"210p, up another five percent," she said. "Are you coming in today? Esquire called; they want an interview. 'Thoroughly Modern Ben', they want to call it."
"Interview me? Not Bobby?" he said, sitting back sharply in his seat.
His junior laughed. "Yup."
"I'll see them at two." He hung up.
"Who wants to interview you?" asked Ibrahim.
"Esquire magazine."
Ibrahim laughed. "Bobby's right. There is more to you than meets the eye."
Ben pursed his lips. "Why did you never get a real job. You're obviously smart enough."
Ibrahim patted Ben on the leg. "And so I will – once I've got a bit extra in the bank. I need more than three-fifty; I've seen the place I want and it's nearly four. And for all I say, I actually enjoy my job, you know? Meet a lot of new people; stay in touch with quite a few. Now, call Bobby or I will."
Ben did, but it went to voicemail, the first time it ever had. Either Bobby was furiously tearing down Ben's career brick by brick or he was dead in a gutter somewhere; either was possible. He left a fulsome apology together with a few comments about the news coverage, the share price performance and a reminder of Bobby's appointments with BBC News on Saturday and Sky News on Sunday, recommending he brush up on the bullet points Ben had sent him the night before.

"Very nice," said Ibrahim and kissed him. "Now, it's time for us both to go to work. Go and find Black Beauty and break the young stallion in. Take it from someone who knows; you've got the moves. Believe in yourself and it'll happen." He gave a cheery wave and left. Ben paid, surprised that none of the other diners had taken any real notice of them.

He caught a taxi to the office, arriving at his desk at eleven fifteen. He called Bobby again, but again got voicemail so he hung up. He needed to talk to him. But apparently he hadn't been fired yet. Gary actually hugged him and called him 'the man'. He had a cup of coffee and made a few quiet calls about those neutral stories.

By two o'clock when the reporter and photographer from Esquire arrived, he had spoken to everyone in the office, the PR team at Green Fields, and half the editors in the City. No one had so much as curled the side of their lip. "Why do you want to interview me?" he asked the reporter, a grizzled man of about forty in a grey woollen sweater whom Ben hadn't met before.

"Recommendation from James Sassoon," the reporter replied. "He called us this morning and reminded us that all this hype about Green Fields is down to you. He said no one understands better than you how to integrate pink businesses into the wider community, promote diversity and acceptance."

Oh, Christ! Now what was happening? What a day for Sassoon to make such an incredibly unnecessary and generous gesture. Ben felt filthy and couldn't wait for the reporter to leave. He dreaded the call he had to make now, but knew he had to do it.

"Sassoon."

"Mr Sassoon, it's Ben Connelly. I just wanted to say Esquire have just left. Thank you for suggesting me to them. After your compliments last night, I really didn't expect or deserve anything more. Thank you." It all came out in a rush and Ben wondered if he should go on, whether he should fill the long black silence that followed, wondered what Sassoon knew and why he'd done it.
But he told him. "Good. I'm glad it worked out. I thought after last night's wobble, you might need a helping hand to steady your feet."
Ben wanted to throw up. He lost all his cool, hunkering over the phone. "Oh, God. So you do know? You're the last person I would want to hear. I'm so sorry. You've been the making of me and I know it. I've apologised to Peter Weller and Bobby Wilkinson, although I couldn't get to Bobby in person. It…it was a mistake and one I won't make again. To receive a helping hand from you; I will be forever in your debt."
Then, to Ben's surprise, Sassoon laughed, clear and sonorous. "It's my impression that Peter's a bit of a prude, and I've told him as much on several occasions, but Bobby thought it was the funniest thing he'd ever seen. He called me at six this morning, off his face, roaring about it. He said it was so out of character, he couldn't stop laughing, you so buttoned up that it was almost a relief to see you relax. And apparently, with someone very handsome, and surprisingly well-turned out, knowledgeable and polite."
Not as handsome as your boyfriend, though. "Thank you, Mr Sassoon," he said.
"Oh, call me Jamie, Ben."
"Not today, I think, sir."

"Alright, not today. But from Monday, after the weekend coverage is good. If you called me Jamie more often, things like this might not happen. And don't worry about Bobby. He's been a little bit in love with your professionalism for months. And he likes nothing better than a laugh and now you've given him that too. We all have our little slip-ups. My own personal behaviour is far from perfect. I've done things I'm thoroughly ashamed of, far worse than bringing a professional to an office party. Just find yourself someone to love. You're a very good-looking man, and a very good man."
Ben was drained, but the candour was disarming. What had Sassoon done, and to whom? Ben knew he'd never find out, but it was intriguing, and intoxicating to be let even this far into the great man's life. "Yes, Peter Weller said the same thing." And then it just came out, Sassoon's words a laxative. "And I think I've found the person I'm meant to love. I'm just hoping he'll become available one day."
"Well, Peter may be an old woman, but he's not thick; take his advice. I wish you luck with your friend, sincerely, but if it doesn't work out, I recommend pinkevenings.com. Its success rate is surprisingly high."

With that, Sassoon hung up. Exhausted, Ben sighed, closed his eyes and put his head on his desk. Sassoon would never know who he meant, but it was still a stupid thing to say. But his emotions were everywhere today. And he was still worried that he hadn't heard from Bobby. He reached along the desk for his phone, grabbed it and checked the time. Four-thirty. He slowly raised his heavy head and was just about to call when an email landed in his in-box. "Got your VM," it said. "Too hung over to talk. Didn't get in 'til seven and only just woken up. No apology necessary. All forgiven – if not forgotten! Won't forget the TV. Come to my birthday in July."

Ben sagged with relief, his head back onto the desk top. Gary laughed and then said, "Don't stop now. You're nearly there, but you've got the weekend press to sort out. Then you can rest. In fact, I'll insist on it."

He did and then slept all weekend. It was still April and he wondered if Bobby would remember about the invitation by July, but at least it seemed he was forgiven. He took Sassoon's advice and signed up for Pinkevenings.com. The algorithm wanted a great deal of information about both him and what he was looking for. He was detailed on the first, but sparse on the second, just mixed-race Londoners, 25-29, his height and build, no specific educational requirements, regular exercisers but no gym freaks, no sports fans, cultural interests, specifically music, literature and the arts, sexually 'flexible'. The algorithm spat out three possible matches, all professionals living in South London, Putney, Clapham and the Oval, although the 'loveometer' reading was grading at 50-60% and he was advised to refine his search criteria.

The problem was, he didn't really know and three names weren't many anyway. He extended the age range to include 30-34, adding four names, but from their profiles they all looked too much like Sam the donkey. He extended it to 19-24, but there were no hits at all. You needed a certain income to subscribe for Pinkevenings.com, £750 to join and £750 per connection made. The three photos all looked OK, and they were going to cost him £3,000 if they all agreed to see him so he left it at that. None of them was his mystery man, unfortunately, the one he now knew was called Trevor Stephens and whom a bit of selective cyberstalking had shown him worked for a children's TV company. But what he learnt there didn't really help him refine the criteria either.
The company, Little Devils Productions, had an excellent website and there was even a photo of Trevor with his name and title, 'Deputy Compositions Director'. He was wearing a suit in the photo and looked very dapper and proud. Ben opened his heart a little further. The suit was neat and smart but, in the high resolution image on the website, it was clear that Trevor hadn't got it from Jamie's private tailor, a mark of independence perhaps that made Ben happier to see.

'Mr Stephens is responsible for compositions in programming for our core four-to-six-year-old market, with a particular focus on The Three Bears, Matilda and Muffin and Aliens to the Rescue. He joined LDP in May 2009 after a successful three-year career managing an independent music retailer.' No indication of age, unfortunately, but clearly no university education either. And a deep love of music. He reminded Ben of Colin, the ballet-loving meatpacker from Brixton, and the thought made Ben smile. He found a series of videos on Youtube with Trevor's byline and sat forward as he clicked on them in turn. So much variation. A lot of classical, especially takes on Schubert and Mozart, orchestral introductions even into pop songs, one particularly powerful variation on Tremble not, my dear son in an episode of Aliens to the Rescue when monsters from the planet Giganta were turning all the children to jelly and the purple aliens were preparing for their ultimately successful last-stand. It sent shivers down Ben's spine to hear.

So, Trevor was a romantic who liked opera! Ben was too. And not just opera, there was Elton John, Kylie Minogue, Robbie Williams, George Michael, David Bowie, James Blunt. And there was a recent one, Magic, about a snake-charmer's snake that had lost the will to emerge from his basket because he was bored of the charmer's tunes, who finally rose to 'true magic', a melodious take on Beyoncé's *Smash into You.* No wonder the snake just floated into the sky, singing 'you're magic, I love you. I'm magic, you love me. We're magic, we love each other' until he arrived in Paradise, soon joined by the charmer, the edge of his turban trailing like another snake from behind his head, to make true magic together for the rest of time.

It might be cyberstalking, but it was one of the happiest, most peaceful, most calming three hours Ben could remember. Unfortunately, there was no Facebook page, so no indication of current relationship status, but there was a LinkedIn profile and Ben so wanted to connect. But, even so, the music wasn't all great, and Ben would have preferred more insight into what Trevor would write for himself, rather than for four-to-six year-olds. Nevertheless, it was finally a window onto a life, a life he wanted to know, and he contentedly leant on the frame and gazed through, the candle inside him burning higher and brighter than ever.

His dates on pinkevenings.com now had some competition, but Ben got acceptances from each, two immediately and one almost a week later. He set up evenings with all three, on Fridays two weeks apart across May and the start of June. He told himself he wasn't settling yet, even as he yearned to reach for the unattainable. With Trevor Stephens, he would always be reaching.

The first two were both decent people, mostly what they'd said on their resumes, polite, friendly, a little bit funny, fairly relaxed, not bad looking, and he slept with each in turn. But they both turned out to be tops, not the flexible they had promised. One eventually consented reluctantly and then complained the whole way through; the other steadfastly refused and demanding that Ben turn over himself. Ben did, but from the gleam in the other man's eye knew that it would always be that way. He said, "Thank-you, but good-bye," and left before three-thirty for the first time in years. He thought of calling Jamie to complain about misrepresentation of product and then remembered the reading on the 'loveometer' and the exhortation to refine his search.

And then he met Carl.

CHAPTER TWENTY

Carl was the most interesting and the most problematic of Ben's dates. He was twenty-eight and did on-line advertising sales for *the Guardian*. He had his own place in the Oval, a tiny but immaculate one-bedroom flat on the fourth floor of a 1930s mansion block close to the cricket ground. Ben had suggested they go out for dinner and had offered to pay, but Carl had written, "No, I know how expensive it is to use this site and I don't want to burden you further in case we don't hit it off."

With that in mind, Ben bought a cheaper bottle of wine and found himself actually bounding up the four floors, two steps at a time. When Carl opened the door, he had the makings of Mahesh's eyes but without his easy self-confidence. His pale blue short-sleeved cotton shirt showed firm upper arms and chest and his cotton trousers promised a narrow waist. He was wearing brown lace-up office shoes.

But it was his eyes that wouldn't let Ben go; they just widened at the sight of him and then stayed wide as he served a simple but delicious chicken and melon salad at the small Ikea white table with two matching white chairs. There was an Ikea two-seater sofa as well and a TV, but no DVD or CD player. Rather, along every available wall-space were Ikea bookshelves, stuffed with novels, all clearly bought second-hand and all subsequently read again.

There was Smollett, Fielding and Austen, Dickens, Thackeray and Mrs Gaskell, all the Brontes, Robert Louis Stevenson, Sir Walter Scott, EM Forster, Virginia Wolff, Evelyn Waugh, George Orwell, Graham Greene, John Fowles, AS Byatt, VS Naipaul, Kingsley and Martin Amis, Ian McEwan, Julian Barnes, Salman Rushdie, Zadie Smith. It was hard to criticise. Even though Ben knew the authors, he hadn't read most of the books. There were no Americans or anyone else and so little fun. No Ian Fleming, no Conan-Doyle, no Agatha Christie, no Terry Pratchett, not even any PG Wodehouse. And no Shakespeare. Just an unfocused hunger for self-improvement with no definable goal. As they sat on the sofa after dinner, Ben listen as, slowly, the story came out backwards. Carl had bought the flat two years ago when prices crashed in the financial crisis and he could finally afford something, but the mortgage still took every penny he had. He never went out beyond the gym at the leisure centre three times a week and had never eaten in a restaurant, although he'd worked in one as a cook and before that a cleaner. He had got the job at the Guardian six years ago after he finished a degree in English and journalism from the Open University. Before that, he lived with his Nigerian grandmother in Stockwell, on welfare supplemented by cooking and cleaning while he studied for his GCSEs and A Levels at night school after dropping out of regular school at 15. He was from a broken home and his father, blind drunk, had smashed the door down on his fourteenth birthday and tried to rape him. He had fought him off and gone to the gym three times a week ever since. His unmarried parents had split up when he was nine.

"So, you see, Pinkevenings.com was a big investment, but sometimes you just have to try, you know? When I saw your invitation, I wasn't really sure, that's why I took so long to reply. But it's hard being alone all the time."
Then, after two hours, Carl stopped talking and looked at Ben. His sad serious eyes seemed in wonder that Ben was even there, without hope or expectation of anything, just grateful for having been listened to. Ben wasn't sure what to do. He had long since put down his glass of wine on the kitchen table. Carl had looked terrified when he put it on the pine floor by the sofa, but here was no other table. No corkscrew in the kitchen either; he'd had to ram in the cork with a knife. He had his arm along the top of the sofa, over but not really touching Carl's shoulders, and his hand on Carl's thigh, which Carl was gently touching.
"Thank you for telling me your story. I'm glad that things are better for you now than before. You have a beautiful flat and a really good collection of books."
Carl squeezed Ben's hand. "I read a lot, on the bus, in my lunch hour, at home."
"Have you ever had a boyfriend?"
"Not really. There were a few guys at the gym, a couple I've saw more than once, but no one regular. There was an advertising guy I met through work but he was a bit scary, especially when he wanted to tie me up. After my dad, I don't think I want that."
"No, I sympathise."

Carl had dignity, he had made an effort to cook, Ben had never had a home-cooked meal for a first date before. Carl deserved his money's worth. But Ben wasn't quite sure what that meant tonight. He lowered his arm from the sofa top and stroked Carl's shoulder and neck, ran his fingers over the frizzy steel curls of his head and then down his smooth, carefully-shaved brown cheek. He cupped the side of his head and drew it towards him. He glanced at his lips, reddish-black and slightly parted, and looked him in the eye. "Would it be all right if I kissed you?"
A slight nod. "I'd like that."
Ben clasped the thigh-hand and then drew them both in. Soft and wet, he took his time, not sure when Carl might baulk and not wanting him to. And slowly, tentatively, Carl started to respond. Ben waited until the eagerness exceeded his own and then matched it as it built. The grip on his hand intensified and then Carl's hand brushed the back of Ben's head, withdrew and then returned. Ben started to enjoy it. Carl was strong, but yielded suddenly and then came back, increasingly hungry, urgent and, not demanding, but desiring. Ben restrained himself from giving in to it, even as he felt Carl do so. But it was a good kiss, even a great kiss, a first kiss, and Ben was in no hurry for it to end. He liked kissing and hadn't had a good one since Winston, who did everything well. Charles had been cold while Fred had tried to eat his mouth every time in his desperation. But then it had to end, Carl's breathing was becoming ragged. Ben slowly disengaged and made sure to make eye contact again. He smiled. "Beautiful. Thank you."

And Ben saw Carl start to fall in love with him. There was an almost physical jolt as Carl bumped down half a flight of stairs. His head went back, his pupils dilated, his lips parted, a sigh slithered out. "Yes, Beautiful. Really, really nice."
Yes, dignity. No messy rush of 'the best I've ever had'. Still some quiet restraint.
"What would you like to do next?"
Carl looked stunned. "Would you hold me for a bit?"
Ben stood and took off his shoes and socks. Carl mutely copied and Ben caught a glimpse of a massive erection distending his trousers. As they held each other, Carl slowly relaxed and copied Ben as he slowly moved his hands across Carl's back, side, buttocks and head. Finally, he pulled him in the last inches, raised a hand behind Carl's neck and kissed him again. Carl's head went back, no urgency now, just pure steady-state enjoyment. Ben let the kiss linger and then withdrew. Whither now? He was getting horny now, but knew tonight was not about him. He undid the buttons of Carl's shirt, one by one, as Carl stood, paralysed in his happiness, only his very firm abdomen heaving as Ben parted the curtain on a beautiful chest, a string of curled black steel balls rising up the midriff and spreading over the firm pecs. He kissed each brown hard nipple in turn and Carl finally reacted, gently tightening the grip he still had on the back of Ben's head. Ben withdrew and caught those shocked, disbelieving, eyes filled with gratitude and growing adoration. He slid his fingertips across Carl's chest and shoulders until the shirt fell away.
"Take mine off."

Carl convulsed with a rack of choked, silent misery, pain and sorrow in the eyes. "But that's just it," he whispered. "I want to, I really do. But I also don't. This is the first date, the first real date, I've ever been on and I don't want to spoil it. And I've met somebody totally wonderful. It's been so romantic. I don't want to sully it. I'm sorry. I've really messed up, wasted your time. You must really hate me."

"I don't hate you, Carl and you haven't wasted my time. You're the third date I've been on at Pinkevenings and the best so far."

Carl straightened his back, bit back tears, stilled his lip. He so obviously wanted to give in, but what he'd said was also the truth, tonight he wanted the romance. A very dignified suffering.

Ben suspected it would be worth the wait. "Can I see you again? I'm free next Friday. You decide and email me. I genuinely want to hear from you."

Carl gave a nervous nod, his eyes flickering. Ben got ready to leave.

"Ben?" That magnificent chest, a chest designed for self-defence that had gone far beyond that. The distended torture of the erection, dampness visible on the cotton. Not an orgasm, just genuine excitement. "Thank you for not pushing me. Nobody's ever restrained themselves with me before. You probably could have pushed me, but then everything would have been ruined. Thank you for not doing it."

And that was all so obviously true. And it was indeed nice when people said thank you and so clearly meant it. Ben nodded and Carl leapt forward and took a kiss, quick, just a parting of the lips, but so expressive. "I'm sorry."

"No apology required. A perfect end to a perfect evening."
"Oh, God!"
Ben left, wondering if he would ever hear from Carl again, hoping he might.
The email took six days to arrive. Carl, in the same shirt, served a home-made Quiche Lorraine. At work, he was getting accounts to manage. They made it to a belly rub before Carl lost his nerve.
"Join a book club," said Ben as he left. "It doesn't cost anything beyond the price of a cup of coffee or an orange juice. You can borrow most of them from the library."
The next email arrived on Monday morning, half an hour after Carl arrived at work. Ben didn't mind that he'd been asked to leave. The romance of the dignified resistance, the slow measured steps of gradual surrender, was starting to affect him too. It was highly erotic, such a beautiful body, charged kisses. Ben had never had two dates without an orgasm, seldom one, but it felt surprisingly good.
The third evening, he brought over Chinese takeaway, along with second-hand copies of *Live and Let Die, The Hound of the Baskervilles, 4:50 from Paddington, The Colour of Magic* and *The Code of the Woosters.*
"You shouldn't buy me presents."
"The books cost £11 together."
"Still. You paid for dinner."

Then hand-jobs. But this, fun as it was and it was fun, very intimate, watching Edward Bear slowly bump down stair after stair, was taking too long. Ben wanted to get busy on one of the best bodies he'd seen in a while and stayed the night. He didn't ask, he just never got out of bed and Carl never asked him to. Tentative fingers and lips touch him in the night, more release in the morning and another insight into Carl's sad life: a body previously only for the pleasure of others, a blower who'd never been blown, the only hand on his cock his own. No, allowing himself to be tied up and then fucked by an advertising agent would have been very wrong.

They took the bus to Clapham Common, hand in hand. In a very simple café by the Tube station, he had Eggs Benedict while Carl had wholemeal toast and strawberry jam. Ben had never seen him look so pleased. They went to the black and white gabled Starbuck's. "Try something," said Ben. "Maybe a latte, tall size only."

"Stop buying me things. But thank-you for the coffee. I've never had a latte before, not even a bar of chocolate, and I've heard they're really good."

Oh, for God's sake. Why did the world do this to people sometimes? Ben bought him a 50g bar of Fruit & Nut and Carl insisted on giving Ben exactly half. They drank their lattes lying on the warm, springy grass of the Common. The sun shone in a blue sky, aeroplanes left vapour trails, there was a light breeze, birds twittered, joggers ran past, a child on a scooter, couples who noticed them and smiled, red double-deckers roared in the distance.

"I think I want to go home now,' said Carl. "I need to rest. But thank you so much for the books and thank you for the latte."
Carl took the bus and Ben took the Tube. The next Friday, all the books had been read and there were two additional Pratchetts, two additional Wodehouses, and *Like Water for Chocolate* on the floor. "It's for my book club. It's an LGBT one."
Better blow-jobs, pretty good actually while the curry got cold in the kitchen, and then Ben demanded to be let into Carl's finances, to find a way to locate £10 a day for a little fun, a latte, a bar of chocolate, small luxuries, or possibly instead £50 a week for some new clothes, £200 a month for a phone, a laptop, an iPod. It turned out Carl wasn't poor at all; it was all in his head, scarred by his childhood. He made over £30,000 a year and had a £100,000 mortgage which he had already reduced to £80,000 and no other debts. Apart from his flat, the most expensive thing he had ever bought was a pink evening with Ben, all the Ikea furniture costing barely half as much.
Ben tried to persuade him to relax a little and enjoy life more, but Ben saw the terror in Carl's eyes, his horror of squalor and destitution, and stopped. "You need a few new clothes at least, a couple more shirts, a pair of shorts, some casual shoes."
For four nights in a row, Carl had worn the same clothes. Ben had brought over two polo shirts from his mother that he hated and an old pair of combat shorts, but saw it was all unnecessary if he could just persuade Carl to believe in himself, that he wouldn't be fired tomorrow and left with a mortgage he couldn't pay. "Life is for living, Carl. It's only short."

"I know. I'm being silly. I will buy some new clothes, I do need a few. Thank you for these; there's really nice. I'm sorry."

Ben kissed him and was kissed in return. "Shall we take it to the next level?"

And then Carl finally had the courage to ask for something, to be given something he really wanted instead of always gazing through the shop window and sadly walking away. It was hesitant, but at last there was a breath of life in him. "Would you do something for me, please? Only if you don't mind. It's just I've never made love to a man before. And your profile did say you might be willing to be flexible?"

He saw the hope, the burning desire. In the surrender of Carl's love, he would settle for less, but he yearned for more. "I'd be honoured."

"I want you to go first, though. After all, I promised to be flexible as well. But before I share everything with you, please answer one question. Why are you here? You could have anyone, why are you here with me?"

Still dignity and grace as he ran up the white flag and prepared to open the doors of his conquered city. There could be no lying or equivocation.

"I'm in love with someone else. But he's with a much better man and I can't compete. I too have to live my short life sometimes."

Carl's face flashed pain and then immense gratitude.

"Do you want me to leave?" Ben asked.

"No. I'm so glad you told me, so I can understand. You let me see you properly and I'm ready for you now. Take possession of my body, please. It's what I want."

And finally Ben got to fuck him and by the end Carl's eyes were thrilled. Afterwards, he tried to restrain himself but couldn't wait and Ben let him take him, hard and fast, very hard, very big, very out of control, after so long and so much denial intent only on itself. Ben made sure not to complain, but he finally understood what the torpedo felt like, undammed hunger for relief and oblivion, years of suppressed wants and hurt and injustice released. It was very unpleasant. Carl came in him with a violent whoosh and then sagged, looking contrite. "Did you want to watch me come?"
"No, it's fine. It's actually how I like to do it myself sometimes."
"Thank you so much. I feel so wonderful, reborn." He stroked Ben's chest. And then, "I know you're in love with someone else, but there's something I need to say. Something I want you to hear and want to hear myself say. I love you, Ben. I love you with all my heart. You're the best thing that's ever happened to me. I can't believe I hesitated before replying to your contact. I've been so stupid, hiding in my books."
Ben smiled, pulled down Carl's head and kissed him as Carl shuddered. They showered in turn, there wasn't the space to do it together, and shared everything again in the morning, Carl much more gentle and with more than a hint he would become good at it. They took the bus to Clapham and this time Carl did have Eggs Benedict.
"Benedict is actually my full name."
"I'll remember that forever. They're delicious, so tasty and rich. I'll eat them once a month, I promise, and think of you. Will I ever see you again?"

Ben raised his eyebrows. "That's up to you. All this is up to you; you know that."
"It's just that it's my book club next weekend, the first meeting."
Ben laughed for the first time in this relationship.
"Well, you decide and let me know. But I think it would be a good idea if you didn't miss your first book club."

Made in the USA
San Bernardino, CA
30 March 2017